PENGUIN ⏺ CLASSICS

THE DOUBLE

FYODOR MIKHAYLOVICH DOSTOYEVSKY was born in Moscow in 1821, the second of a physician's seven children. When he left his private boarding school in Moscow he studied from 1838 to 1843 at the School of Military Engineering in St Petersburg, graduating with officer's rank. His first novel to be published, *Poor Folk* (1846), was a great success and was immediately followed by *The Double*. In 1849 he was arrested and sentenced to death for participating in the Petrashevsky Circle; he was reprieved at the last moment but sentenced to penal servitude, and until 1854 he lived in a convict prison at Omsk, Siberia. Out of this experience he wrote *The House of the Dead* (1860). In 1860 he began the journal *Vremya* (*Time*) with his brother; in 1862 and 1863 he went abroad, where he strengthened his anti-European outlook, met Apollinaria Suslova, who was the model for many of his heroines, and gave way to his passion for gambling. In the following years he fell deeply in debt, but in 1867 he married Anna Grigoryevna Snitkina (his second wife), who helped to rescue him from his financial morass. They lived abroad for four years, then in 1873 he was invited to edit *Grazhdanin* (*Citizen*), to which he contributed his *Diary of a Writer*. In 1880 he delivered his famous address at the unveiling of Pushkin's memorial in Moscow; he died six months later in 1881. Most of his important works were written after 1864: *Notes from Underground* (1864), *Crime and Punishment* (1865–6), *The Gambler* (1866), *The Idiot* (1868), *The Devils* (1871–2) and *The Brothers Karamazov* (1880).

RONALD WILKS studied Russian language and literature at Trinity College, Cambridge, after training as a Naval interpreter, and later Russian literature at London University, where he received his Ph.D. in 1972. Among his translations for Penguin Classics are *My Childhood*, *My Apprenticeship* and *My Universities* by Gorky, *Diary of a Madman* by Gogol, *The Golovlyov Family* by Saltykov-Shchedrin, *How Much Land Does a Man Need?* by Tolstoy, *Tales of Belkin and Other Prose Writings* by Pushkin, and seven volumes of stories by Chekhov: *The Party and Other Stories*,

The Kiss and Other Stories, The Fiancée and Other Stories, The Duel and Other Stories, The Steppe and Other Stories and *Ward No. 6 and Other Stories*. In addition, he has translated *The Shooting Party*, Chekhov's only full-length novel, as well as *The Little Demon* by Sologub.

FYODOR DOSTOYEVSKY

The Double

Translated by RONALD WILKS

PENGUIN BOOKS

In memory of Margaret – R. W.

PENGUIN CLASSICS

Published by the Penguin Group
Penguin Books Ltd, 80 Strand, London WC2R ORL, England
Penguin Group (USA) Inc., 375 Hudson Street, New York, New York 10014, USA
Penguin Group (Canada), 90 Eglinton Avenue East, Suite 700, Toronto, Ontario, Canada M4P 2Y3
(a division of Pearson Penguin Canada Inc.)
Penguin Ireland, 25 St Stephen's Green, Dublin 2, Ireland (a division of Penguin Books Ltd)
Penguin Group (Australia), 707 Collins Street, Melbourne, Victoria 3008, Australia
(a division of Pearson Australia Group Pty Ltd)
Penguin Books India Pvt Ltd, 11 Community Centre, Panchsheel Park, New Delhi – 110 017, India
Penguin Group (NZ), 67 Apollo Drive, Rosedale, Auckland 0632, New Zealand
(a division of Pearson New Zealand Ltd)
Penguin Books (South Africa) (Pty) Ltd, Block D, Rosebank Office Park,
181 Jan Smuts Avenue, Parktown North, Gauteng 2193, South Africa

Penguin Books Ltd, Registered Offices: 80 Strand, London WC2R ORL, England

www.penguin.com

The Double first published 1846
This translation first published in Penguin Classics 2009
This edition published in Penguin Classics 2014
002

Translation and Notes copyright © Ronald Wilks, 2009
All rights reserved

The moral right of the translator has been asserted

Set in 10.21/12.27 pt PostScript Adobe Sabon
Typeset by Rowland Phototypesetting Ltd, Bury St Edmunds, Suffolk
Printed in England by Clays Ltd, St Ives plc

ISBN: 978–0–141–39618–7

www.greenpenguin.co.uk

Contents

THE DOUBLE

A Petersburg Poem

CHAPTER I

It was a little before eight o'clock in the morning when Titular Counsellor[1] Yakov Petrovich Golyadkin awoke after a long sleep, yawned, stretched and finally opened his eyes wide. However, for about two minutes he lay motionless on his bed like a man not yet entirely certain if he has woken up or is still asleep, if everything around him was now actually happening or was simply a continuation of his chaotic daydreaming. But soon Mr Golyadkin's senses began to take in more clearly and distinctly their normal, everyday impressions. The dirty-green, grimy, dusty walls of his little room, his mahogany chest of drawers, his imitation mahogany chairs, his red-painted table, his sofa upholstered with reddish oilskin patterned with tiny green flowers, and finally the clothing he had hastily discarded the night before and thrown in a heap on the sofa glanced familiarly at him. And finally that foul, murky, dreary autumn day, peeping into his room through the dim windows with such an angry, sour look that Mr Golyadkin no longer had any doubts whatsoever that he was lying in bed, in his own fourth-floor flat, in a huge tenement block in Shestilavochnaya Street,[2] in the capital city of St Petersburg and not in some distant fairy realm. After making such a momentous discovery, Mr Golyadkin convulsively closed his eyes as if feeling regret for his recent slumbers and wishing to recall them if only for one brief moment. But a minute later, he leapt out of bed in one bound, having in all probability finally hit upon the idea around which his scattered and thoroughly disorganized thoughts had so far been revolving. Once out of bed he immediately ran over to a small round mirror that stood on the chest of drawers.

Although the sleepy, weak-sighted countenance and somewhat balding head reflected there were so insignificant as to command no attention at first glance, its owner was obviously perfectly satisfied with all he saw in the mirror. 'A fine thing it would be,' said Mr Golyadkin under his breath, 'a fine thing it would be if there were something not quite right with me today – if, for example, some kind of unwanted pimple had popped out up, or something else just as unpleasant. However, it's not too bad. So far so good.' Positively delighted that all was well, Mr Golyadkin replaced the mirror and, although he was barefoot and still wearing the same apparel in which he usually retired for the night, ran to the window and started anxiously searching for something in the courtyard that was overlooked by the windows of his flat. Evidently what he discovered in the courtyard was also to his entire satisfaction; his face lit up with a complacent smile. After first taking a peep behind the partition into his servant Petrushka's cubby-hole and convincing himself that he wasn't there, he tiptoed over to the table, unlocked one of the drawers, rummaged around in a far corner and finally extracted from beneath some old, yellowing papers and various rubbish, a worn, green wallet, cautiously opened it and carefully and delightedly peered into its furthest, most secret compartment. Probably the bundle of nice green, grey, blue, red and other brightly coloured banknotes[3] looked at Mr Golyadkin approvingly and cordially as his face was radiant as he placed the open wallet before him on the table and vigorously rubbed his hands in a manner that indicated the greatest satisfaction. At length he drew out his comforting bundle of banknotes and, what's more, for the hundredth time since the previous day started counting them, carefully smoothing out each note between thumb and index finger. 'Seven hundred and fifty roubles in notes!' he finally murmured in a half-whisper, 'seven hundred and fifty roubles . . . a tidy sum! A most agreeable sum!' he continued in a voice that was trembling and somewhat weakened by pleasure, squeezing the wad of notes and smiling significantly. 'A most agreeable sum! An agreeable sum for anyone! I'd like to see the man for whom that might be a trifling sum! A man could go far with a sum like that . . .'

'But what's going on here?' wondered Mr Golyadkin. 'Where's that Petrushka got to?' Still in the same apparel, he took another look behind the partition: again there was no sign of Petrushka, only the samovar that had been set on the floor, and was quite beside itself, fuming, working itself into a frenzy, constantly threatening to boil over, lisping and burring in its own mysterious language something that sounded like: 'Come and take me, good people, I've boiled now and I'm quite ready!'

'To hell with him!' thought Mr Golyadkin. 'That lazy devil could drive a man to distraction! Where's he loafing around now?' In righteous indignation he went out into the hall that consisted of a small passage with the entrance door at the end, opened it a little and caught sight of his servant surrounded by a sizeable crowd of footmen, sundry menials and chance riff-raff. Petrushka was busily regaling them with some story and they were all ears. Evidently neither the topic of conversation nor the conversation itself were to Mr Golyadkin's liking, for he immediately summoned Petrushka and returned to his room looking thoroughly dissatisfied and even upset. 'That wretch would sell anyone for a song – and particularly his master!' he mused. 'And he's sold me, no doubt about that – and for a few lousy copecks, I'm prepared to bet. Well, what is it?'

'They've brought the livery, sir.'

'Put it on and come over here.'

After donning the livery, Petrushka went into his master's room, grinning stupidly. His costume was bizarre in the extreme: he was attired in the green, second-hand livery of a footman, trimmed with gold braid, very worn and clearly fashioned to fit someone a good two feet taller than Petrushka. He was holding a hat that was also trimmed with gold braid and adorned with feathers, and at his side he wore a footman's sword in a leather scabbard.

Finally, to complete the picture – and faithful to his favourite practice of always going around in a state of domestic undress – Petrushka had nothing on his feet. Mr Golyadkin inspected Petrushka from all angles and was apparently well satisfied. The livery had obviously been hired for some ceremonial occasion. What was more, throughout the inspection one could clearly see that Petrushka was eying his master with a strange air of expectancy and following his every movement with marked curiosity, which embarrassed Mr Golyadkin no end.

'Well, what about the carriage?'

'That's arrived too.'

'Do we have it for the whole day?'

'The whole day. For twenty-five roubles.'

'And have they brought the boots?'

'Yes, they've brought the boots.'

'Nitwit! Can't you say, . . . "Yes, they've brought them, *sir*"? Now, give them to me.'

Having expressed his satisfaction that the boots were a good fit, Mr Golyadkin ordered his tea and his things for washing and shaving. He both shaved and washed with extreme care, hurriedly sipping his tea in between and embarking on the principal and definitive enrobing. Then he donned an almost completely new pair of trousers, a shirt-front with little brass buttons, a waistcoat with a nice, extremely bright little floral pattern; around his neck he tied a multicoloured silk cravat and finally pulled on his uniform jacket, also quite new and carefully brushed. As he dressed he glanced lovingly at his boots several times, first raising one foot and then the other to admire their style, constantly whispering something under his breath and occasionally winking with an expressive grimace at every thought that came to him.

However, that morning Mr Golyadkin appeared to be extremely preoccupied, since he hardly noticed the little grins and grimaces directed at him by Petrushka as he helped him dress. At last, when he had checked that all was as it should be and was completely dressed, Mr Golyadkin slipped his wallet into his pocket and cast a final, admiring glance at Petrushka, who by now had put on his boots and was thus in complete readiness. Observing that everything was duly completed, he scurried busily down the stairs, his heart throbbing with trepidation. A light-blue, hired carriage, embellished with a coat of arms of sorts, came rolling up to the door with a loud clatter. After exchanging winks with the driver and some idle bystanders, Petrushka saw that his master was seated; in a

peculiar voice and barely able to suppress his idiotic laughter,
he shouted: 'Drive off!', leapt up on to the footboard and with
much jingling and creaking the entire equipage thundered off
towards Nevsky Prospekt.[4] No sooner had the light-blue carriage passed through the gates than Mr Golyadkin rubbed his
hands feverishly and broke into a soft, barely audible chuckle,
like some bright spark who has brought off a splendid joke and
is tickled pink about it. Immediately after this fit of merriment,
however, the laughter gave place to a strange, apprehensive
expression on Mr Golyadkin's face. In spite of the damp
weather he lowered both windows and started scrutinizing
passers-by to left and right, immediately adopting a decorous
and dignified air the moment he noticed someone looking at
him. At the junction of Liteynaya Street and Nevsky Prospekt,
a most disagreeable sensation made Mr Golyadkin shudder
and, frowning like some poor devil whose corn has been acci-
dentally trodden on, he shrank back hurriedly and even fearfully into the darkest corner of his carriage. The fact was, he
had encountered two of his colleagues, two young clerks from
the same department where he himself worked. For their part
the clerks, so it seemed to Mr Golyadkin, were utterly bewildered at meeting their colleague in these circumstances; one of
them even pointed his finger at him. The other, so it appeared
to Mr Golyadkin, even shouted his name out loud, which was
of course most improper in the street. Our hero hid himself and
didn't respond. 'Those urchins!' he reflected. 'So, what's so
strange about it? If a man needs a carriage he simply goes and
hires one! But all they are is riff-raff! I know them – just little
brats who could do with a good thrashing! All they can think
of after they're paid their wages is playing pitch-and-toss, or
roaming around the streets. That's all they're concerned with!
I'd like to give them a piece of my mind, only . . .' Mr Golyadkin
didn't finish and he froze. A pair of lively Kazan horses, very
well known to Mr Golyadkin and hitched to a fancy droshky,
were rapidly overhauling his carriage on the right. The gentleman seated in the droshky, happening to catch sight of the face
of Mr Golyadkin, who had rather rashly poked his head out
of the window, also appeared absolutely amazed at such an

unexpected encounter. Leaning out as far as he could, he started peering with the greatest curiosity and interest into that corner of the carriage where our hero had made haste to conceal himself. The gentleman in the droshky was none other than Andrey Filippovich, head of the same department where Mr Golyadkin was employed as assistant to his chief clerk. When he realized that hiding was impossible, since Andrey Filippovich had fully recognized him and was staring at him wide-eyed, Mr Golyadkin blushed to his ears. 'Should I bow or not? Should I respond or not? Should I acknowledge it's me or not?' wondered our hero in indescribable anguish. 'Or should I pretend it's not me, but someone else remarkably like me, and look as if nothing were the matter? Really, it's not me, it's not me at all – and that's the end of it!' exclaimed Mr Golyadkin, doffing his hat to Andrey Filippovich and without taking his eyes off him. 'I'm . . . I'm all right,' he barely managed to whisper, 'I'm all right, quite all right, it's not me at all, not me at all, Andrey Filippovich – oh no! And that's all there is to it.' However, the droshky soon overtook the carriage and no longer was he subjected to the magnetic power of the head of department's gaze. But he was still blushing, smiling and muttering to himself: 'I was a fool not to respond!' he thought at length. 'I should simply have taken a bolder approach and, with an outspokenness not lacking in nobility, I should have told him: 'So that's how it is, Andrey Filippovich. I've been invited to dinner as well – so there you are!' And then, suddenly remembering that he had made a hash of things, our hero reddened like fire, scowled and cast a terrible and defiant look at the front corner of the carriage – a look positively calculated to reduce all his enemies to ashes in one instant. Finally, in a sudden fit of inspiration, he tugged the cord attached to the driver's elbow, stopped the carriage and gave instructions to turn back to Liteynaya Street. The truth was, Mr Golyadkin had an urgent need – probably for his own peace of mind – to tell his doctor, Krestyan Ivanovich Rutenspitz, something of the greatest interest. And although he hadn't known the doctor for very long at all – he'd called on him only once for something he needed the previous week – but, as they say, a doctor is like a confessor and it would have been stupid to hide himself away since, after all, it is a doctor's responsibility to know his patients. 'Will it be all right?' our hero continued, alighting from his carriage at the entrance to a five-storey building in Liteynaya Street where he had ordered the driver to stop. 'Will it be all right? Will it be proper to call on him? Will it be convenient? Ah well, what of it!' he added, pausing to catch his breath as he mounted the stairs to stop his heart pounding, as it was wont to do on the staircases of others. 'Well, what of it? After all, I've come about what concerns me personally and there's nothing reprehensible about that. It would have been stupid to hide myself away. So, I'll just pretend I'm all right, that I came for no special reason but simply happened to be passing. He'll see that I'm in fact doing the right thing.'

Reasoning thus, Mr Golyadkin went up to the second floor and stopped outside flat number five, whose door bore a handsome brass plate with the inscription:

KRESTYAN IVANOVICH RUTENSPITZ
DOCTOR OF MEDICINE AND SURGERY

As he stood there our hero lost no time in giving his countenance a relaxed, seemly expression that was not lacking in a certain degree of affability and prepared to pull the bell. But just as he was about to ring he immediately and quite appropriately concluded that might it not be better to return to tomorrow as for the time being there was nothing he really needed. However, when Mr Golyadkin suddenly heard footsteps on the stairs he hastily reversed his decision and at the same time rang Dr Rutenspitz's bell with the most determined air.

CHAPTER II

Krestyan Ivanovich Rutenspitz, Doctor of Medicine and Surgery, an extremely healthy, although rather elderly gentleman, endowed with thick, greying eyebrows and side-whiskers, with

an expressive twinkle in his eyes, which alone appeared sufficient to banish all ailments and wearing an important decoration on his chest, was sitting that morning in his consulting
room, in his comfortable armchair, smoking a cigar, drinking
coffee that his wife herself had brought him and writing out
prescriptions for his patients from time to time. After prescrib-
ing a draught for his last patient, an old gentlemen with piles,
and seeing him out through a side door, Krestyan Ivanovich was
sitting down awaiting the next caller. In came Mr Golyadkin.

Evidently Krestyan Ivanovich wasn't in the least expecting
Mr Golyadkin, nor did he want to see him, since all of a sudden
he was taken aback and involuntarily assumed a strange –
some might say even disgruntled – expression. For his part, Mr
Golyadkin would almost invariably, and at precisely the wrong
moment, falter and become flustered just when he was about
to approach someone about his personal affairs – and so it was
now: having failed to prepare the opening sentence, which was
always a real stumbling block for him on such occasions, he
became dreadfully embarrassed, muttered something – apparently an apology – and, at a loss what to do next, took a
chair and sat down. However, realizing that he had sat down
uninvited, he immediately acknowledged the impropriety of his
action and made haste to rectify his mistake and ignorance of
etiquette and good form by immediately rising from the seat he
had occupied so discourteously. Then, collecting himself and
dimly perceiving that he had committed two blunders simultaneously, he decided, without a moment's delay, to commit a
third, that is, he tried to make excuses, muttered something
with a smile, became flushed and embarrassed, lapsed into
eloquent silence, finally sat down for good and, to safeguard
himself against all eventualities, protected himself with that
defiant look which had the extraordinary power of allowing
him to crush all his enemies and reduce them to ashes, without
saying one word. Besides, it was a look that fully expressed Mr
Golyadkin's independence, that is, it showed quite clearly that
'all was well' with Mr Golyadkin, that he was his own master,
like anyone else, and that in any case what other people did
was no concern of his. Krestyan Ivanovich coughed to clear

his throat, apparently as a sign that he approved and agreed to all this, and directed an inquisitorial, searching look at Mr Golyadkin.

'Krestyan Ivanovich,' Mr Golyadkin began, smiling. 'I've come to trouble you a second time and for a second time I venture to crave your indulgence.' Mr Golyadkin clearly had difficulty in choosing the right words.

'Hm . . . yes!' said Krestyan Ivanovich, emitting a stream of smoke and placing his cigar on the table. 'But you *must* take what I prescribed. I did explain that your treatment should consist of a change of routine. Yes, I mean diversions. And . . . we . . . you should visit friends and acquaintances – and at the same time don't be an enemy of the bottle! And regularly keep only cheerful company.'

Still smiling, Mr Golyadkin hastened to observe that he considered himself to be just like anyone else, that he was his own master, that he had his diversions like anyone else . . . and that of course he could go to the theatre since, like anyone else, he too had the means; that he was busy at the office during the day, but was at home in the evening; that he was quite 'all right'; he even mentioned in passing that, as far as he knew, he too was as well off as the next man, that he was living in his own flat and that, finally, he had his servant Petrushka. At this point Mr Golyadkin hesitated.

'Hm . . . no, that kind of routine is not what I meant . . . that wasn't what I wanted to ask you about. What I'm really interested in is whether you are a great lover of cheerful company, whether you spend your time cheerfully. Now, do you lead a melancholy kind of life or a cheerful one?'

'Krestyan Ivanovich . . . I . . .'

'Hm,' interrupted the doctor, 'what I'm telling you is that you need to radically change your whole lifestyle and in a sense you must completely transform your character.' (Krestyan Ivanovich particularly emphasized the word 'transform' and paused for a moment with an extremely significant look.)

'Don't shun the gay life, go to theatres and clubs, and in any case don't be an enemy of the bottle. Staying at home is out of the question for someone like you.'

'I love peace and quiet, Krestyan Ivanovich,' Mr Golyadkin said, casting a meaningful glance at the doctor and obviously seeking the words that would most successfully convey his thoughts. 'In the flat there's no one but myself and Petrushka . . . I mean, my manservant, Krestyan Ivanovich. What I want to say is that I go my own way, my own independent way, Krestyan Ivanovich. I keep to myself and as far as I can see I don't depend on anyone. I also go for walks, Krestyan Ivanovich.'

'What? . . . Oh yes! But it can't be much fun going for walks at the moment, the weather's simply awful.'

'Yes, Krestyan Ivanovich, as I've already had the honour of explaining to you, I'm a peace-loving man, but my path lies in a different direction from other people's. The road of life is broad . . . what . . . what I mean to say is, Krestyan Ivanovich . . . Oh do forgive me, I'm no expert at fine phrases . . .'

'Hm . . . you were saying?'

'I was saying that you must excuse me, Krestyan Ivanovich, for not having, as far as I can judge, a gift for fine phrases,' Mr Golyadkin said in a half-offended tone, growing a little muddled and confused, 'in this respect, Krestyan Ivanovich, I'm not like other people,' he added with a peculiar kind of smile. 'I'm not a good talker and I never learned to embellish my style with fancy expressions. On the other hand I – act, Krestyan Ivanovich. I *act*, Krestyan Ivanovich.'

'Hm . . . what's that . . . you . . . *act*?' replied Krestyan Ivanovich. There was a minute's silence. The doctor glanced somewhat strangely and incredulously at Mr Golyadkin, who in turn squinted rather incredulously at the doctor.

'I, Krestyan Ivanovich,' continued Mr Golyadkin in the same tone as before, rather irritated and puzzled by Krestyan Ivanovich's extreme stubbornness, 'I love peace and quiet and not the hurly-burly of society. With that class of people – I mean, people in high society – you must know how to polish parquet floors with your boots . . .' (Here Mr Golyadkin gently scraped one foot on the floor.) 'That's what they expect of you – they also ask you to make clever puns and you must know how to pay scented compliments – yes, that's what they expect of you. But I've never learned to do that kind of thing, Krestyan

Ivanovich, I've never learned all those cunning tricks – never had time for them. I'm a simple, straightforward sort of person, there's no surface brilliance about me. On this point, Krestyan Ivanovich, I lay down my arms – in that sense of the words I lay them down!'

Of course, Mr Golyadkin said all this in a way that made it quite clear that our hero had no regrets whatsoever about laying down his arms *in that sense*, that he had never learned cunning tricks – the exact reverse, in fact. As Krestyan Ivanovich listened he gazed at the floor with a very unpleasant grimace, as if he had somehow been expecting something like this. Mr Golyadkin's tirade was followed by a long and significant silence.

'I think you've rather strayed from the subject,' Krestyan Ivanovich said at length, in a low voice. 'I do confess, I couldn't quite get your drift.'

'I'm not skilled in eloquence, Krestyan Ivanovich, I . . . I've already had the honour of informing you of this,' said Mr Golyadkin, this time in a sharp, determined voice.

'Hm . . .'

'Krestyan Ivanovich!' Mr Golyadkin began again in a low but significant and to a certain extent solemn voice, dwelling on every point. 'Krestyan Ivanovich, when I arrived I began by apologizing. Now I repeat what I said before and again I crave your indulgence for a while. I, Krestyan Ivanovich, have nothing to hide from you. I'm a little man, you know that yourself. But fortunately I don't regret being a little man. Even the contrary, Krestyan Ivanovich. And to be perfectly frank, I'm even proud of being a little man and not a big one. And I'm proud that I'm not an intriguer either. I don't act furtively, but openly, without deception, and although I in turn could harm people – and do it very well – although I even know whom to harm and how to do it, I don't want to sully myself and in this sense I wash my hands. Yes, in this sense I wash my hands of it, Krestyan Ivanovich!' For a moment Mr Golyadkin lapsed into an expressive silence again. He had been speaking with mild enthusiasm.

'I go about my business openly and honestly,' our hero continued, 'I don't act deviously because that's what I despise and leave to others . . . I don't like double-talk, I abhor slander and gossip, I've no time for wretched duplicity. Only when I go to masquerades do I wear a mask, but I don't parade one in front of people every day. All I'm asking is this: how would *you* go about taking revenge on your enemy, your deadliest enemy, or on whom you considered such?' concluded Mr Golyadkin with a defiant glance at Krestyan Ivanovich.

Although Mr Golyadkin had expounded all this with the utmost clarity, distinctness and self-assurance, weighing his words and counting on their maximum impact, he was now looking at Krestyan Ivanovich with ever-increasing alarm. Now he was all eyes, timidly awaiting Krestyan Ivanovich's reply with morbid, vexed feelings of impatience. But to Mr Golyadkin's amazement and utter dismay, all the doctor did was mutter something under his breath; then he pulled his chair up to the table and announced – rather coolly but nonetheless politely – something to the effect that his time was precious, that somehow he didn't quite follow and that he was prepared, as far as he could, to be of service, but beyond that he would not delve into matters that did not concern him. Here he picked up his pen, drew a sheet of paper towards him, cut off a piece the size of a prescription and announced that he would prescribe what was appropriate right away.

'No, Krestyan Ivanovich, that's not appropriate, not appropriate at all,' said Mr Golyadkin, half-rising from his seat and grabbing the doctor's right arm. 'There's no need for that at all in my case.'

While Mr Golyadkin was saying this, a weird transformation came over him. His grey eyes shone with a strange fire, his lips quivered and every muscle, every feature of his face twitched and shifted. He was shaking all over. Following his first movement, holding Krestyan Ivanovich by the arm, Mr Golyadkin now stood motionless, as if he had lost all confidence and was awaiting inspiration for further action. And then a rather bizarre scene followed.

Somewhat puzzled, Krestyan Ivanovich momentarily stayed glued to his chair, quite taken aback and gazing wide-eyed at Mr Golyadkin, who gazed back in similar fashion. Finally the doctor stood up, supporting himself to some degree by one of Mr Golyadkin's coat lapels. For a few seconds they both stood there like that, without budging or taking their eyes off each other. Then followed Mr Golyadkin's second impulsive movement, moreover in a most peculiar manner. His lips trembled, his chin twitched and quite unexpectedly our hero burst into tears. Sobbing and nodding, beating his breast with his right hand whilst grasping the lapel of Krestyan Ivanovich's domestic attire with the other, he tried to speak, to offer some immediate explanation, but he was unable to utter one word. At last Krestyan Ivanovich recovered from his amazement.

'Come, come! Please calm yourself! Sit down,' he said, trying to seat Mr Golyadkin in the armchair.

'I have enemies, Krestyan Ivanovich, I have vicious enemies who have vowed to ruin me . . .' Mr Golyadkin replied in a frightened whisper.

'Now, that's enough of enemies! No need to bring enemies into it – absolutely no need to. Now sit down, please do sit down,' continued Krestyan Ivanovich, finally getting Mr Golyadkin into the armchair.

Mr Golyadkin settled down, without taking his eyes off the doctor, who began pacing his consulting room from one end to the other with an extremely disgruntled look. A long silence ensued.

'I'm grateful to you, Krestyan Ivanovich, extremely grateful and I deeply appreciate all you've done for me. I shall not forget your kindness until my dying day, Krestyan Ivanovich' Mr Golyadkin finally said, rising from the chair with a hurt look.

'Now that's enough, enough! I'm telling you that's enough!' exclaimed Krestyan Ivanovich, reacting rather severely to Mr Golyadkin's outburst as he once again made him sit down. 'What's the matter with you? Tell me what's bothering you now?' Krestyan Ivanovich continued, 'and who are these enemies you keep mentioning? What's it all about?'

'No, Krestyan Ivanovich, we'd better leave that for now,' replied Mr Golyadkin, looking down at the floor. 'We'd better put that aside for the time being . . . for another time, when it's

more convenient, when all will be revealed, when masks will
fall from certain faces and various facts will come to light. But
in the meantime, after what's happened between us, of course
. . . you yourself will agree, Krestyan Ivanovich . . . Please allow
me to wish you good day,' said Mr Golyadkin, this time solemnly and determinedly rising from his chair and reaching for
his hat.

'Ah well, as you like . . . hmmm . . .'

(A minute's silence followed.)

'If, for my part . . . well, you know, if there's anything I can
do . . . and I sincerely wish you well . . .'

'I understand you, Krestyan Ivanovich, I understand you
perfectly now. At all events please forgive me for disturbing
you.'

'Hm . . . no, that's not what I meant. However, as you wish.
Carry on with the same medication as before.'

'I shall carry on with the same medication as you say, Krestyan Ivanovich, I shall carry on with it and get it at the same
chemist's. It's quite a big thing, Krestyan Ivanovich, being a
chemist these days.'

'How so? In what sense?'

'In a very ordinary sense, Krestyan Ivanovich. I mean, that's
what the world has come to these days . . .'

'Hm . . .'

'And any little urchin – and not only in chemists' shops–
sticks his nose up at respectable citizens nowadays.'

'Hm . . . what do you mean by that?'

'I'm talking about someone we both know, a mutual acquaintance, Krestyan Ivanovich – Vladimir Semyonovich, for
example.'

'Ah!'

'Yes, Krestyan Ivanovich. And I know several people who
aren't so enslaved by public opinion that they can't occasionally
speak the truth.'

'Ah! And how is that?'

'Well, that's how things are. But this is a totally different
matter. Sometimes people know how to serve an egg with sauce.'

'Serve *what*?'

'Serve an egg with sauce, Krestyan Ivanovich. It's a Russian proverb.⁵ Sometimes they know how to congratulate someone at the appropriate time, for example. There are people like that, Krestyan Ivanovich.'

'Congratulate?'

'Yes, congratulate, Krestyan Ivanovich, as a close acquaintance of mine did the other day.'

'A close acquaintance ... ah! And how was that?' said Krestyan Ivanovich, looking intently at Mr Golyadkin.

'One of my close acquaintances congratulated another close acquaintance – what's more, a comrade, a bosom pal as they say, on his promotion to assessor's rank.⁶ He put it like this: "I'm genuinely delighted, Vladimir Semyonich," he said, "at this opportunity of offering you my congratulations, my *sincere* congratulations on your promotion. All the more so, as now-adays, as the whole world knows, those in high places who give others a leg up have become virtually extinct!"' Here Mr Golyadkin gave a roguish nod and screwed up his eyes as he looked at Krestyan Ivanovich.

'Hm ... he said that, did he?'

'Yes he did, Krestyan Ivanovich, that's what he said – and then he looked at Andrey Filippovich, our little treasure Vladimir Semyonovich's uncle. But what do I care, Krestyan Ivanovich, if he's been promoted to assessor? Is it any concern of mine? What's more, he's wanting to get married, when he's still wet behind the ears, if you'll pardon the expression. That's just what he said. Now, I've told you everything, so please allow me to be on my way.'

'Hm ...'

'Yes, Krestyan Ivanovich, please allow me to take my leave. But to kill two birds with one stone, after I'd cut that young whippersnapper down to size with that talk of friends in high places I turned to Klara Olsufyevna (it happened the day before yesterday at her father Olsufy Ivanovich's) and she'd just sung a sentimental ballad, so I told her: "The way you sang that ballad was full of feeling, but those who are listening to you are not pure of heart." And with this I dropped a clear hint, you understand, Krestyan Ivanovich, I dropped a clear hint that it was not her they were interested in but had set their sights a little higher.'

'And what did *he* say?'

'He looked as if he'd just bitten into a lemon, as the saying goes.'

'Hm . . .'

'Oh yes, Krestyan Ivanovich, I spoke to the old man too. "Olsufy Ivanovich," I said, "I know how I'm indebted to you, I fully appreciate the favours you've showered me with almost since I was a little child. But open your eyes, Olsufy Ivanovich," I said. "Take a good look around you. I myself do things fairly and squarely, Olsufy Ivanovich."'

'Well – you don't say! So, that's how things are . . .'

'Yes, Krestyan Ivanovich, that's how things are.'

'But what did he say?'

'Oh yes, what indeed, Krestyan Ivanovich! He mumbled this and that, that I know you and that His Excellency's a benevolent person – laid it on pretty thick, he did. Well, what can you expect? He's gone doddery from old age, as they say.'

'Ah! So that's how things are now!'

'Yes, Krestyan Ivanovich, that's how we all are! Poor old chap. He's got one foot in the grave – at death's door, as they say. And when they start spinning old wives' tales he's there listening. They can't do a thing without him.'

'Old wives' tales, you say?'

'Yes, Krestyan Ivanovich, they've spun some sort of tale. And our friend the Bear and his nephew – the little treasure – had a hand in it. They're in league with the old crones of course and they've cooked something up. And what do you think? They've conceived a plan to murder someone . . .'

'*Murder* someone!?'

'Yes, Krestyan Ivanovich, to murder someone, murder someone morally. They've put out a rumour . . . I'm still talking about this close acquaintance of mine . . .'

Krestyan Ivanovich nodded.

'They've spread a rumour about him. I do confess, Krestyan Ivanovich, I'm even too ashamed to talk about it.'

'Hm . . .'

'They've spread the rumour that he'd given a written under-
taking to marry someone when he was already engaged to someone else. And who do you think it was, Krestyan Ivanovich?'

'I really don't know.'

'Some brazen German slut who owns an eating-house and
cooks his dinner. Instead of paying her what he owes her in
cash he's offering her his hand.'

'Is that what they say?'

'Can you believe it, Krestyan Ivanovich? A nasty, vile, shameless German slut – Karolina Ivanovna . . . if you've heard of
her . . .'

'I must confess, for my part . . .'

'I understand you, Krestyan Ivanovich, I do understand you
and for my part I feel . . .'

'Now, please tell me where you're living now?'

'Where I'm living now, Krestyan Ivanovich?'

'Yes . . . I'd like to . . . I seem to remember you used to live
before . . .'

'Oh yes, I used to live, Krestyan Ivanovich! Yes, I did live
before – I must have done, mustn't I?' Mr Golyadkin replied,
accompanying his words with a little laugh and somewhat
taking Krestyan Ivanovich aback with his answer.

'No, you've misunderstood me. What I wanted to say was,
for my part . . .'

'For my part, Krestyan Ivanovich, I wanted to as well,' Mr
Golyadkin continued, laughing. 'I too wanted to . . . However,
I've really outstayed my welcome, Krestyan Ivanovich. I hope
you will now permit me to wish you good morning . . .'

'Hm . . .'

'Yes, Krestyan Ivanovich. I understand you, I understand you
perfectly now,' our hero said, showing off a little before the
doctor. 'So if you'll permit me to wish you good morning . . .'

At this our hero clicked his heels and walked out of the room,
leaving Krestyan Ivanovich utterly stunned. As he went down
the doctor's staircase he smiled and gleefully rubbed his hands.
Once he reached the front steps and breathed in the fresh air
and felt he was free he was even quite prepared to admit that
he was the happiest of mortals and ready to go later straight to

the office, when suddenly his carriage rumbled in through the
gate. He took one look and remembered everything. Petrushka
was already opening the carriage door. A peculiar, extremely
unpleasant sensation held Mr Golyadkin totally in its grip. For
a moment he appeared to flush; then something seemed to prick
him. As he was about to plant his foot on the carriage step he
suddenly turned round and looked up at Krestyan Ivanovich's
windows. Just as he thought! Krestyan Ivanovich was standing
at one of them, smoothing his side-whiskers with his right hand
and looking at our hero rather inquisitively. 'That doctor's
stupid,' thought Mr Golyadkin, hiding in the carriage. 'Terribly
stupid. He may be a good doctor – all the same he's as thick as
two planks!' Mr Golyadkin sat back, Petrushka shouted 'Drive
on!' and the carriage once more rolled out on to Nevsky
Prospekt.

CHAPTER III

That entire morning was spent by Mr Golyadkin in frenzied
activity. When he reached Nevsky Prospekt our hero ordered
the driver to stop at the Gostiny Dvor.[7] Leaping down from his
carriage he ran down the arcade, accompanied by Petrushka,
and made a beeline for a shop that sold gold and silver articles.
From Mr Golyadkin's appearance alone one could tell that here
was a man with a lot on his plate and a whole pile of things to
do. After haggling over a complete dinner and tea service for
1,500 roubles, striking a bargain over an elaborately fashioned
cigar case and a full silver shaving set for a similar amount, and
after asking the price of some little trifles that were useful and
pleasant in their own way, Mr Golyadkin finished by promising
to return the very next day, without fail – or even to send for
his purchases that same day, noting the shop number, listening
attentively as the shopkeeper made a fuss about a small deposit
and promising to put down a small deposit in due course. After
that, he hurriedly bade the astonished shopkeeper good day
and walked between the rows of shops, pursued by a whole

swarm of assistants, constantly looking back at Petrushka and carefully seeking out some new shop. On his way he darted into a money changer's and changed his large notes into smaller denominations, and although he lost on the transaction his wallet fattened considerably as a result, which evidently afforded him the greatest satisfaction. Finally he stopped at a shop that sold various materials for ladies. After bargaining over goods worth a significant sum, here too Mr Golyadkin promised the shopkeeper to call back without fail, noted the shop number and when he was asked for a small deposit he again confirmed that it would follow, all in good time. Then he visited a few more shops, bargained in all of them, inquired about the prices of various articles, occasionally engaged in lengthy arguments with the shopkeepers, leaving the shops only to return three times to each one of them – in brief, he was extraordinarily busy. From the Gostiny Dvor our hero headed for a well-known furniture store, where he struck a deal over enough furniture to fill six rooms, admired a highly elaborate and fashionable lady's dressing-table, in the very latest style, and after assuring the shopkeeper that he would send for everything without fail, he left the shop with his usual promise of a small deposit and then drove off somewhere to order something else. In short, there was evidently no end to his furious activity. Finally all this became tiresome in the extreme for Mr Golyadkin himself and God knows why, right out of the blue, he even began to be troubled by twinges of conscience. Not for anything would he now have agreed to meet Andrey Filippovich or Krestyan Ivanovich, for example. At last the city clocks struck three in the afternoon. When Mr Golyadkin finally took his seat in his carriage, all that his actual acquisitions of that morning amounted to was a pair of gloves and a bottle of perfume, to the value of one and a half roubles. Since it was still rather early for him, Mr Golyadkin ordered the driver to stop at a well-known restaurant on Nevsky Prospekt, which he had known of only by hearsay until then, alighted from the carriage and hurried in for a snack and a rest and to wait until the time was right.

After eating like a man who has a sumptuous banquet in prospect, that is, having a little snack to stave off the pangs as they say, after downing a glass of vodka, Mr Golyadkin seated himself in an armchair and after modestly taking a look around, quietly settled down with a certain flimsy national newspaper.[8] When he had read a line or two, he stood up, looked at himself in the mirror, spruced himself up and smoothed his clothes. Then he went over to the window to see if his carriage was there . . . then he sat down again and picked up the paper. Clearly our hero was extremely agitated. Glancing at the clock and seeing that since it was only a quarter past three and that consequently he still had quite a while to wait, and at the same time reasoning that it was indecorous to sit there just like that, Mr Golyadkin ordered some chocolate, for which he really didn't feel much inclination just then. After drinking the chocolate and noting that time had moved on a little, he went up to the counter to pay. Suddenly somebody clapped him on the shoulder.

He turned round and saw before him two of his colleagues from the office, the same ones he had met that morning in Liteynaya Street, both young lads, very junior in age and rank. Our hero's relations with them were neither one thing nor the other, neither friendly nor openly hostile. Of course, propriety was observed on both sides but there was no close intimacy, nor could there have been. An encounter at this particular time was extremely unpleasant for Mr Golyadkin. He frowned slightly and for a moment became somewhat flustered.

'Yakov Petrovich, Yakov Petrovich!' twittered the two clerks. 'You here? For what . . . ?'

'Oh, it's you, gentlemen!' Mr Golyadkin hurriedly interrupted, somewhat put out and scandalized by the clerks' surprise and at the same time by the familiarity of their approach, but playing, however, the easy-going fellow, despite himself.

'So, you've deserted, gentlemen! He he he!' And then, in order not to lower himself by behaving condescendingly towards his office juniors, with whom he always stayed within proper bounds, he tried to pat one of the young men on the shoulder. But on this occasion his attempt at camaraderie didn't succeed and instead of a seemly and friendly gesture something quite different resulted.

'Well, is that Bear of ours still in the office?' he asked.

'Who's that, Yakov Petrovich?'

'Why, the Bear. As if you didn't know who's called the Bear!' Mr Golyadkin laughed and turned to the waiter to take his change. 'I'm talking about Andrey Filippovich, gentlemen,' he continued, having finished with the waiter and this time addressing the clerks with an extremely grave air. The clerks exchanged knowing winks.

'He's still there and he was asking for you, Yakov Petrovich,' one of them replied.

'Still there, eh? In that case let him stay there, gentlemen. And he was asking for me, eh?'

'That's right, Yakov Petrovich. But what's all this – pomading and perfuming yourself like a regular fop!'

'Well, that's how things are, gentlemen! But that's enough . . .' replied Mr Golyadkin, looking away with a strained smile. Seeing Mr Golyadkin smiling, the clerks burst into loud guffaws. Mr Golyadkin started sulking a little.

'Let me tell you, gentlemen, as a friend,' our hero said after a brief pause, as if he had decided to reveal something to the clerks. 'You all know me, gentlemen, but up to now you've only known one side. For this no one can be criticized and I must confess that I myself was partly to blame.'

Mr Golyadkin pursed his lips and glanced meaningfully at the clerks. The clerks again exchanged winks.

'Up to now, gentlemen, you haven't really known me. To explain here and now wouldn't be entirely appropriate, so I'll tell you something casually, in passing. There are people, gentlemen, who don't like devious behaviour and who don masks only for masquerades. There are people who don't see as man's true purpose in life the ability to polish the parquet with their boots. There are even people, gentlemen, who don't admit they're happy and who live life to the full when, for example, their trousers are a good fit. Finally, there are people who don't like prancing and whirling around to no purpose, flirting, toadying to others – and, most important of all, poking their noses in where they're positively not asked to . . . I've told you almost everything, gentlemen. Now, please allow me to leave.'

Mr Golyadkin stopped. As the registrar clerks[9] were by now thoroughly satisfied they both suddenly started splitting their sides with laughter in the rudest manner. Mr Golyadkin flared up.

'You may laugh, gentlemen, you may laugh for the present! But just you wait and see when you're older!' he said with a feeling of wounded dignity, taking his hat and retreating to the door.

'But I shall say more, gentlemen,' he added, addressing the clerks for the last time. 'I shall tell you more, now that you're face to face with me. These are my rules, gentlemen: if things are bad I stand firm – if they go well I hold my ground. And in any event I undermine no one. I'm not an intriguer and of that I'm proud. I'd never have been any good as a diplomat. As they say, gentlemen, the bird flies to the huntsman of its own accord. That's true and I'm ready to agree. But who's the huntsman here and who's the bird? Answer that one, gentlemen!'

Mr Golyadkin lapsed into eloquent silence and with the most significant expression – that is, with his eyebrows raised and lips pursed as tightly as possible – he bowed to the gentlemen clerks and walked out, leaving them utterly stunned.

'Where to?' asked Petrushka, quite gruffly, as he was probably sick and tired of hanging around in the cold. 'Where do you want to go?' he again asked Mr Golyadkin and met with that terrifying, all-destroying look with which our hero had already twice protected himself that morning and to which he now resorted for a third time as he went down the steps.

'Izmaylovsky Bridge.'[10]

'Izmaylovsky Bridge! Let's be off!'

'They don't usually have dinner before four, perhaps not even until five,' thought Mr Golyadkin. 'Isn't it still too early? But surely I could arrive a little early? After all, it's just a family dinner. I could simply go there *sans façon*,[11] as respectable people put it. Why shouldn't I go *sans façon*? The Bear also said it would all be *sans façon*, so therefore I too . . .' – such were Mr Golyadkin's thoughts; but meanwhile his agitation was growing by the minute. One could see that he was preparing himself for something extremely troublesome, to say the least, whispering to himself, gesticulating with his right hand, constantly gazing out of the carriage windows so that nobody looking at Mr Golyadkin now would have said that he was preparing for a fine meal, informally, within his own family circle as well, *sans façon*, as respectable people say. At length, right by Izmaylovsky Bridge, Mr Golyadkin pointed out a particular house; the carriage clattered through the gates and stopped at an entrance on the right. Noticing a woman's figure at a first-floor window, Mr Golyadkin blew her a kiss. However, he himself barely knew what he was doing, for at that moment he positively felt neither dead nor alive. Pale and distraught, he emerged from the carriage, went up into the porch, removed his hat, mechanically straightened his clothes and went upstairs, feeling a slight trembling in his knees.

'Olsufy Ivanovich?' he asked the servant who opened the door to him.

'He's at home, sir – I mean, he's not. The Master's not home, sir.'

'What? What do you mean, my dear man? I've come to dinner, old chap. Surely you know me?'

'How could I not know you, sir? But my orders are not to receive you, sir.'

'You ... you ... old chap, are most likely mistaken. It's *me*. I, old chap, have been invited. I've come to dinner,' Mr Golyadkin said, throwing off his overcoat and showing every intention of entering the main reception rooms.

'Sorry, sir, but you can't. Orders are not to receive you, that's how it is.'

Mr Golyadkin turned pale. At that moment the door from one of the inner rooms opened and Gerasimych, Olsufy Ivanovich's old butler, came out.

'This gentlemen wants to come in, Emelyan Gerasimovich, but I ...'

'You're a fool, Alekseich. Now go into the rooms and send that scoundrel Semyonich here. You can't, sir,' he said politely but firmly, turning to Mr Golyadkin, 'it's out of the question, sir. The Master asks to be excused, sir, but he can't receive you.'

'So that's what he said – that he can't receive me?' Mr

Golyadkin asked uncertainly. 'Forgive me, Gerasimych, but why is it out of the question?'

'It's quite impossible, sir. I did announce you, sir, but the Master said: "Ask him to excuse me." He said he can't receive you.'

'But why not? How can this be? How . . .'

'Please, sir, please!'

'But how can this be? I'm not standing for this! Now go and announce me. How can this be? I've come to dinner.'

'Please, sir, please!'

'Well, if he's asking to be excused that's a different matter. But how can this be, Gerasimych, if you'll allow me to inquire?'

'If you don't mind, sir!' retorted Gerasimych, very determinedly shoving Mr Golyadkin to one side to allow a broad passage for two gentlemen who were entering the hall just at that moment. They were Andrey Filippovich and his nephew Vladimir Semyonovich. Both looked at Mr Golyadkin in bewilderment. Andrey Filippovich appeared about to say something, but Mr Golyadkin had already made up his mind; his eyes downcast, blushing, smiling and with a thoroughly lost expression, he was already leaving Olsufy Ivanovich's entrance hall.

'I'll call back later, Gerasimych . . . I'll have it out with him. I hope all this won't delay a proper and timely explanation,' he said, partly from the threshold and partly from the stairs.

'Yakov Petrovich! Yakov Petrovich!' resounded the voice of Andrey Filippovich, who had followed Mr Golyadkin out.

Mr Golyadkin had already reached the first landing. He turned quickly to confront Andrey Filippovich.

'What can I do for you, Andrey Filippovich?' he asked in quite a determined tone of voice.

'What's the matter with you, Yakov Petrovich? How is it that you're . . . ?'

'I'm all right, Andrey Filippovich. I'm here on my own account. This is my personal life, Andrey Filippovich.'

'What did you say, sir?'

'I said that this is my *personal* life and as far as I can see there's nothing reprehensible to be found with regard to my *official* relations.'

'What!? With regard to your official . . . What's the matter with you, sir?'

'Nothing, Andrey Filippovich, absolutely nothing. An insolent slut – that's all . . .'

'What? *What!?*' Andrey Filippovich exclaimed, lost in amazement. Mr Golyadkin, who, until then, while talking to Andrey Filippovich from the bottom of the stairs, had looked as if he were ready to jump right down his throat, seeing that the head of his department was somewhat disconcerted, took a step forward almost without realizing it. Andrey Filippovich drew back. Mr Golyadkin climbed one stair after the other. Andrey Filippovich looked around anxiously. Suddenly Mr Golyadkin rapidly bounded up the stairs. Even more rapidly Andrey Filippovich leapt into the room and slammed the door behind him. Mr Golyadkin was left alone now. Everything went dark before his eyes. He was utterly flummoxed and stood there in some kind of muddled meditative state, as if recalling some event that was also extremely stupid and that had taken place very recently. 'Oh dear! Oh dear!' he whispered, smiling from the strain. Meanwhile he could hear the sound of voices and footsteps from the stairs below – probably those of some of Olsufy Ivanovich's newly arrived guests. Mr Golyadkin partly came to his senses, hastily turned up the racoon collar of his coat to conceal himself as much as possible, and started hobbling, stumbling, scurrying down the stairs. He felt a kind of weakness and numbness. So extreme was his confusion that when he came out on to the porch he didn't wait for his carriage, but hurried straight to it across the muddy courtyard. As he approached it and prepared to get in, Mr Golyadkin mentally evinced the desire for the earth to swallow him up, or to hide away, in a mousehole, carriage and all. It struck him that every single person in Olsufy Ivanovich's house was now staring at him from every window. He knew that he was bound to drop dead on the spot if he turned round.

'What are you laughing at, you blockhead!' he rattled away at Petrushka who was preparing to help him into the carriage.

'What have *I* got to laugh about? Wasn't doing anything! Where are we going now?'

'Home . . . Let's go . . .'

'Home!' shouted Petrushka to the driver, perching himself on the footboard.

'Caws like a crow!' thought Mr Golyadkin. Meanwhile the carriage had already travelled some distance beyond Izmaylovsky Bridge. Suddenly our hero pulled the cord with all his might and shouted to the coachman to turn back immediately. The coachman turned the horses and within two minutes drove once again into Olsufy Ivanovich's courtyard. 'No, there's no need, you fool, no need! Back again!' shouted Mr Golyadkin – and it was as though the coachman were expecting these instructions, for without a word of protest or stopping at the entrance, he drove right round the courtyard and then out again into the street.

Mr Golyadkin did not go home, however, but after they passed Semyonovsky Bridge he ordered the coachman to turn down a side street and stop outside a tavern of rather modest appearance. After getting out of the carriage our hero settled up with the coachman and then, thus finally rid of his carriage, ordered Petrushka to go home and await his return, while he entered the tavern, took a private room and ordered dinner. He felt very unwell and his head was in utter turmoil and chaos. For a long time he paced the room in great agitation. Finally he sat down, propped his forehead on his hands and made a concerted effort to weigh the whole situation up and to try and come to some conclusion regarding his present situation.

CHAPTER IV

That day, the day of great festivity, the birthday of Klara Olsufyevna, only daughter of State Counsellor[12] Berendeyev, benefactor of Mr Golyadkin in bygone days – that day was celebrated with a splendid, sumptuous banquet – such a banquet as had not been seen for many a day within the walls of civil servants' apartments in the neighbourhood of Izmaylovsky Bridge and thereabouts, a banquet more like Belshazzar's

Feast,[13] redolent of something Babylonian in its brilliance, lux-
ury and good taste, a banquet with Veuve Clicquot, oysters and
the fruits of Yeliseyev and Milyutin,[14] with every kind of fatted
calf, with an official list showing the rank of every civil servant
present – that festive day, commemorated with so festive a
dinner, was concluded with a brilliant ball – a small, intimate,
family ball, yet brilliant nonetheless in its taste, elegance and
decorum. Of course, I entirely agree that such balls do take
place, only rarely. Such balls, more like joyful family occasions
than balls, can only be given in houses such as State Counsellor
Berendeyev's, for example. I shall go further: I even doubt
whether every state counsellor could give such a ball. Oh, if I
were a poet – of course, at least like a Homer or a Pushkin . . .
(with lesser talent I would not dare poke my nose in) – then I
would unfailingly portray for you, oh reader, with vivid colours
and broad brush, that day of pomp and ceremony in its entirety.
Oh yes, I would begin my poem with the banquet and pay
particular attention to that striking and at the same time solemn
moment when the first goblet was raised in honour of the Queen
of Festivities. First I would depict for you the guests, plunged
in reverential silence and expectation – more reminiscent of
Demosthenic eloquence[15] than silence. Then I would portray
Andrey Filippovich – who, as the oldest guest, even had certain
claims to precedence, adorned with silvery hair and civil orders
befitting that silvery hair, who rose from his seat and held aloft
a celebratory goblet of sparkling wine, a wine more like nectar
than wine, a wine expressly brought from some distant realm
to celebrate such moments. Then I would portray for you the
guests and the happy parents of the Birthday Queen following
the example of Andrey Filippovich in raising their glasses and
gazing at him with eyes full of expectation. Then I would
portray for you how this so frequently mentioned Andrey
Filippovich, after first shedding a tear in his glass and offering
his congratulations and good wishes, proposed a toast and
drank the health . . . But I must confess, I fully confess, that it
would be beyond my powers to depict all the solemnity of that
moment when the Birthday Queen herself, blushing like a vernal
rose with the flush of blissful modesty, sank from fullness of

emotion into her tender mother's embrace; how the tender mother dissolved in tears and how, at this, her father himself began to sob, that venerable elder and State Counsellor Olsufy Ivanovich, who had lost the use of his legs in long years of service to the State and who had been rewarded by fate for his zeal with a nice little capital, a house, some small estates and a beautiful daughter, began to sob like a child and proclaimed through his tears that His Excellency was the most benevolent of men. I could not, no, I really could not portray for you the general stirring of heartfelt emotion that immediately followed, a stirring of emotion clearly expressed even by the behaviour of a young registrar clerk (at that moment he looked more like a State Counsellor than a humble registrar) who was also shedding tears himself as he listened to Andrey Filippovich. Andrey Filippovich in turn, at that solemn moment, did not in the least resemble a collegiate counsellor[16] and head of a department – no, he appeared to be someone else . . . I do not know exactly what, but definitely not a collegiate counsellor. He was more elevated! And finally . . . oh, why don't I possess the secret of the lofty, powerful style, the solemn style, to portray all these beautiful and edifying moments of human life, which seem to be expressly devised, as it were, to demonstrate how virtue can sometimes triumph over disloyalty, free-thinking, vice and envy! I shall say nothing, but will silently point out to you – this will be better than eloquence alone – that happy youth entering his twenty-sixth spring, Vladimir Semyonovich, Andrey Filippovich's nephew, who in turn has risen to his feet and who in turn is proposing a toast and on whom are turned the tearful eyes of the parents of the Birthday Queen, the proud eyes of Andrey Filippovich, the bashful eyes of the Birthday Queen herself, the enraptured eyes of the guests and even the decorously jealous eyes of some of that brilliant young man's colleagues. I shall say nothing, although I cannot help observing that everything about that young man who (speaking in a favourable respect) was more like an old man than a young one – everything, his blooming cheeks to the very rank of Assessor invested in him – all this spoke at that solemn moment of the dizzy heights to which good conduct can raise

a man. I shall not describe how, finally, Anton Antonovich
Setochkin, head of a section in a certain department, a colleague
of Andrey Filippovich's and formerly of Olsufy Ivanovich, and
at the same time an old friend of the family and godfather to
Klara Olsufyevna, how that little old man with hair as white as
snow who, when proposing a toast, crowed like a cock and
recited some jolly verses; how, by this decorous neglect of
decorum, if I may thus express it, he reduced the whole gathering to tears of laughter and how Klara Olsufyevna herself, at
her parents' bidding, rewarded him with a kiss for such gaiety
and amiability. I shall merely say that the guests, who after
such a banquet naturally felt like brothers and kinsfolk, at last
rose from the table; how the old men and solid citizens, after a
short interval spent in friendly conversation and even in the
exchange of the most proper and needless to say polite confidences, repaired, with much decorum, to another room and,
without wasting precious time, broke up into small groups and,
conscious of their own dignity, settled themselves at tables
covered with green baize; how all the ladies, having seated
themselves in the drawing-room suddenly became unusually
amiable and started chatting about various dress materials; how
finally the highly esteemed paterfamilias himself, who had lost
the use of his legs in true and loyal service and been rewarded
for this by all that has been mentioned above, started hobbling
among his guests on his crutches, supported by Vladimir
Semyonovich and Klara Olsufyevna; and how, suddenly waxing
extraordinarily amicable too, he decided to improvise a modest
little ball, regardless of expense; how, to this end, a certain
smart youth (the very one who at dinner looked more like a
state counsellor than a youth) was dispatched to fetch
musicians; how they subsequently arrived, no fewer than eleven
of them; and how, finally, at exactly half past eight, were heard
the inviting strains of a French quadrille and various other
dances ... I need hardly say that my pen is too feeble, too
sluggish and dull to do full justice to the ball improvised with
such uncommon kindness by the hoary-haired host. And, I ask,
how can I, humble chronicler of Mr Golyadkin's adventures,
extremely interesting though they are in their own way – how

can I depict that rare and decorous blending of beauty, brilliance, gentility, gaiety, amiable sobriety and sober amiability, playfulness, all those games and jests of the high-ranking officials' wives, more like fairies than ladies – I say this in their favour – with their lilac-pink shoulders and faces, their ethereal figures and their nimble (to speak in the high style), their homeopathic feet? And finally, how can I portray for you these brilliant civil service cavaliers, so cheerful and sedate, young and elderly, gay and decorously melancholy, smoking a pipe in the intervals, between dances, in a remote small green room, or not smoking pipes; cavaliers from first to last, all of becoming rank and name, cavaliers deeply imbued with a sense of the elegant and their personal dignity, cavaliers for the most part speaking to their ladies in French, or if in Russian, with the most refined expressions, with compliments and profound phrases; cavaliers who only perhaps in the smoking-room allowed themselves the occasional courteous departure from language of the highest tone – certain phrases of genial and good-humoured familiarity, such as: 'That was a damned good polka you knocked off, Petya old man'; or: 'Vasya, you old dog, you swished your lady about with such gay abandon!' For all this, as I've already had the honour of explaining to my readers, my pen is inadequate, therefore I remain silent, oh readers! So, let's better return to Mr Golyadkin, the true and only hero of this my veracious tale.

The fact is, Mr Golyadkin was now in the most peculiar position, to say the least. He is here too, gentlemen, that is, not actually at the ball, but *almost* at the ball. He is all right, gentlemen; although he is going his own way, the road he's standing on at that moment is not exactly the most direct one. Now he is standing – strange to relate – at the entrance hall of the back stairs to Olsufy Ivanovich's apartment. But it is all right to be standing there, there is nothing wrong with it; he is quite all right. He, gentlemen, is standing huddled up in a little corner which, although not really warm is, on the other hand, comparatively dark, and he is partly hidden by a huge cupboard and some old screens, amidst all kinds of rubbish, junk and lumber, hiding until the right time and in the meantime observing the general course of events as a casual observer. He is simply observing now, gentlemen. He too might also have gone in ... So, why not go in? He only has to take one step and he will go in – and go in very niftily too. Only now, after standing, incidentally, nearly three hours in the cold, amidst all kinds of rubbish, junk and lumber, between cupboard and screens was he quoting, in self-justification, a phrase of the late-lamented French minister Villèle,[17] namely: 'All things will come in due course to him who has the gumption to be patient.' Mr Golyadkin had read this phrase at some time in a book on some completely irrelevant subject, but now recalled it extremely aptly. Firstly, the phrase suited his present situation admirably, and secondly, what doesn't enter the head of someone who has spent about three hours in a cold, dark entrance hall, awaiting a happy denouement to his tribulations! After quoting, most appropriately, as I have already said, this phrase of the former French minister Villèle, for some mysterious reason Mr Golyadkin immediately recalled the late Turkish Vizier Martsimiris, as well as the beautiful Margravine Louisa,[18] whose stories he had also read at some time or other in some book. Then he recollected that the Jesuits had even made it their rule that all means were justified as long as the end was achieved. Having somewhat reassured himself by a historical point such as this, Mr Golyadkin asked himself who the Jesuits were: they were the most dreadful idiots, to the last man, and he would put them all in the shade! – if only the refreshment room would empty just for a minute (the room whose door led directly to the back stairs and the entrance hall where Mr Golyadkin now found himself), so that despite all those Jesuits, he would pass straight through himself, first from refreshment room to tea room, then into the room where they were playing cards, then into the hall where they were now dancing the polka. He would go straight through, regardless of everything he would go through, just slip through – no one would notice and that would be that; once there he himself would know what to do. So this is the situation, gentlemen, in which we now find the hero of our perfectly veracious story, although it is difficult to explain what exactly was happening to him during that time. In fact, he had managed to reach the entrance hall and back stairs for the simple reason, as he said, that everyone had got there, so why shouldn't he? But he did not dare go further – he clearly did not dare ... not because there was something he did not dare do, but because he did not want to, because he very much preferred to do things nice and quietly. And why should he not wait? Villèle himself had waited. 'But how does Villèle come into it?' thought Mr Golyadkin. 'Why bring Villèle in? Well, what if I take the plunge and go through? ... Oh, you're such a second-rater, you!' Mr Golyadkin exclaimed, pinching his frozen cheek with frozen fingers. 'You silly fool – you old Golyadka![19] What a name you've got!' However, these self-endearments really meant nothing and were made just in passing, serving no real purpose. Now he was about to charge in and had already moved forward. The time had come: the refreshment room had emptied and not a soul was there – Mr Golyadkin could see that through the tiny window. In two strides he was at the door and had already started opening it. 'Shall I or shan't I? Shall I go in or shan't I? Yes, I will – why shouldn't I? All ways are open to the bold!' After thus reassuring himself, our hero suddenly and quite unexpectedly withdrew behind the screen. 'No,' he thought, 'what if someone came in? Yes, you see – someone *has* come in! So why did I stand there dithering when no one was around? Yes, I should have taken the plunge and barged straight in! But what's the use of barging in with a character like mine! What a vile disposition I have! I simply chickened out! That's all I'm good at, chickening out – that's right! Always making a mess of things, that's the long and the short of it. Here I am, standing around like a dummy – that's what! I wish I were at home drinking a cup of tea. Yes, a cup of tea would be so nice now! If I'm any later Petrushka will probably start grumbling. Then shouldn't I go home? Oh, to hell with it all! ... I'm going in and that's that!' Having resolved his situation this way, Mr Golyadkin whizzed forward as if someone had touched off a spring inside him. Two strides and he found himself in the refreshment room; he threw off his coat, took off his hat, hurriedly thrust everything into a corner, tidied himself and smoothed himself down, after which he proceeded to the tea-room, from the tea-room he darted into yet another room, slipping almost unnoticed between the card players lost in the excitement of their game. And then . . . and then . . . here Mr Golyadkin forgot all that was going on around him and, like a bolt from the blue, stepped straight into the ballroom.

As if it were fated, they were not dancing at that particular moment. The ladies were strolling around the room in picturesque groups. Gathered in small circles, the men were flitting about, engaging partners. Mr Golyadkin was blind to all this. He saw only Klara Olsufyevna, with Andrey Filippovich beside her, Vladimir Semyonovich, two or three officers and two or three other very interesting looking young men who, as could be seen at first glance, either showed great promise or had already fulfilled it. And he saw some other people too. Or perhaps not; he saw no one at all, nor did he look at anyone, but propelled by that same spring that had sent him whizzing uninvited into someone else's ball, he pressed on further and still further. On his way he stumbled into some counsellor, treading on his foot, at the same time he stepped on the dress of a respectable old lady and tore it slightly, bumped into a man with a tray, elbowed someone else and, without noticing any of this – rather, in fact, noticing it but at the same time not looking at anyone – he forged ahead, until suddenly he found himself right in front of Klara Olsufyevna herself. At that moment, without a shadow of doubt, without batting an eyelid, he could have sunk through the floor with the utmost pleasure. But what's done is done – in no way can it be undone . . . So what was he to do? 'If things are bad – I stand firm; if they go well I hold my ground.' Mr Golyadkin was of course not an intriguer, not adept at polishing the parquet with his boots. And this was just how it happened now . . . Besides, here the Jesuits had somehow got involved . . . however, Mr Golyadkin had no time for *them*! Then suddenly, all that walked, talked, made a noise, moved and laughed, suddenly fell quiet, as if at the wave of a magic wand, and gradually began to crowd around Mr Golyadkin. But Mr Golyadkin seemed to see nothing and hear nothing and he could not look – oh no, not for anything could he bring himself to look! He lowered his eyes and simply stood there, having incidentally vowed to blow his brains out that same night somehow or other. After making this vow, Mr Golyadkin thought to himself: 'Here goes!' – and to his own utter amazement he most unexpectedly started to speak.

Mr Golyadkin began with congratulations and appropriate good wishes. The congratulations went well, but our hero stumbled over the good wishes. He felt that once he stumbled everything would immediately go to the devil. And so it did . . . he stumbled, got stuck . . . he got stuck and he blushed; he blushed and grew flustered; he grew flustered and raised his eyes; he raised his eyes and looked around; he looked around and . . . and he froze . . . Everyone had stopped, everyone had gone silent, everyone was waiting. A little way off there was whispering; a little nearer someone burst into laughter. Mr Golyadkin cast a humble and forlorn look at Andrey Filippovich. Andrey Filippovich responded with a look that would undoubtedly have crushed our hero a second time – if that were possible – were he not crushed already. The silence continued.

'This has more to do with my domestic circumstances and my own personal life, Andrey Filippovich,' articulated the half-dead Mr Golyadkin in a barely audible voice. 'It's not an official occasion, Andrey Filippovich.'

'Shame on you, sir, shame on you!' Andrey Filippovich pronounced in a half-whisper, with a look of indescribable indignation; this said he took Klara Olsufyevna by the arm and turned his back on Mr Golyadkin.

'I've nothing to be ashamed of, Andrey Filippovich,' replied Mr Golyadkin, also in a half-whisper, utterly lost, looking around with mournful eyes, trying to find his proper milieu and social position among that bewildered crowd.

'Well, it's all right, it's all right, gentlemen! What's wrong? It could happen to anyone,' Mr Golyadkin whispered, shifting slightly and trying to extricate himself from the surrounding throng. They let him through. Our hero somehow made his way between two rows of inquisitive and nonplussed spectators. Fate was carrying him along – he himself felt that fate was carrying him along. Of course, he would have paid dearly now

to be at his former stopping-place, near the back stairs, without
any breach of etiquette. Since that was definitely out of the
question he tried to slip away into some corner where he could
simply stand, modestly, decently, on his own, without troubling
anyone, without attracting particular attention to himself, but
at the same time winning the good graces of both host and
guests. However, Mr Golyadkin felt as if something were
undermining him, as if he were tottering and about to fall.
Finally he managed to reach a corner and stood there, rather
like an outsider, a fairly indifferent observer, leaning his hands
on the backs of two chairs, thus having claimed full possession
of them and trying his utmost to look cheerfully at those guests
of Olsufy Ivanovich who had grouped themselves around him.
Nearest to him stood a certain officer, a tall, handsome youth
before whom Mr Golyadkin felt a mere insect.

'These two chairs are taken, Lieutenant: one for Klara
Olsufyevna and the other for Princess Chevchekhanova who
is dancing. I'm keeping them for them now, Lieutenant,' Mr
Golyadkin said breathlessly, looking imploringly at the lieutenant. The lieutenant gave him a murderous smile and turned
away without a word. Having misfired in this direction, our
hero decided to try his luck elsewhere and straight away
addressed a certain pompous-looking counsellor with an
important decoration around his neck. But the counsellor
measured him with such an icy stare that Mr Golyadkin felt he
had been doused with a bucketful of cold water. Mr Golyadkin
fell silent. He decided it would be best to keep quiet, not to
start a conversation, to show that he was all right, that he too
was like everyone else and that his position was, as far as he
could see at least, really quite proper. To this end he riveted his
eyes on the cuffs of his jacket, then he raised his eyes and stared
intently at a gentleman of the most respectable appearance.
'That gentleman's wearing a wig,' thought Mr Golyadkin, 'and
if it were removed there'd be a bald head – as bald as the palm
of my hand.' Having made such an important discovery, Mr
Golyadkin remembered those Arabian emirs who, if the green
turbans they wear as a mark of kinship with the prophet
Muhammed were to be removed, are also left with hairless

heads. Then, probably because of some peculiar collision of
ideas in his mind regarding the Turks, Mr Golyadkin arrived
at Turkish slippers, and now he most aptly remembered that
the boots Andrey Filippovich was wearing were more like slippers than boots. Mr Golyadkin was, to a certain extent, clearly
in command of the situation. 'If that chandelier,' he thought,
'were to come loose now and fall down on the people below,
I'd rush immediately to save Klara Olsufyevna. As I was saving
her I'd tell her: "Don't be alarmed, miss, it's nothing. I am he
who is your saviour."' And then Mr Golyadkin looked to one
side, searching for Klara Olsufyevna, and he spotted Gerasimych, Olsufy Ivanovich's old butler, heading straight for him
with the most solicitous, solemnly official expression. An unaccountable and at the same time highly disagreeable sensation
made Mr Golyadkin shudder and frown. Mechanically, he
looked around; the idea almost occurred to him to sneak off
somehow, to get out of harm's way and quietly slip and fade
into the background – that is, to act as if nothing were wrong,
as if the matter didn't concern him at all. However, before our
hero had time to come to a decision, Gerasimych was already
standing in front of him. Turning to Gerasimych, our hero
said, faintly smiling: 'Do you see that candle up there in the
chandelier, Gerasimych? It's going to fall any moment. Now,
you must go and give orders at once for someone to straighten
it. It's definitely going to fall any minute, Gerasimych.'

'The candle, sir? No, sir, it's absolutely straight . . . But someone's been asking for you, sir.'

'Who could there be asking for me, Gerasimych?'

'Can't say for sure who is it, sir. A certain gentleman from
somewhere or other. "Is Yakov Petrovich here?" he said. "Well,
call him out, he's wanted on some very urgent and vital matter."
That's what he said, sir.'

'No, you're mistaken, Gerasimych, you're quite mistaken.'

'That's doubtful, sir.'

'No, Gerasimych, that's not doubtful at all. No one's asking
for me, there's no need for anyone to ask for me . . . I'm at
home here – I mean this is where I belong, Gerasimych.'

Mr Golyadkin drew breath and looked around. It was just

as he thought! Every single person in the ballroom was straining eyes and ears at him in solemn expectation. The men had crowded closer and were listening hard. A little further off the ladies were anxiously whispering to each other. The host himself appeared not very far away at all from Mr Golyadkin and although it was impossible to tell from his look whether he in turn was taking an immediate and direct interest in Mr Golyadkin's position, as the whole thing was done on a most tactful footing, all this nonetheless gave our hero clearly to understand that the decisive moment had arrived. Mr Golyadkin clearly saw that the time had come for a bold move, the time to bring disgrace on his enemies. Mr Golyadkin was very agitated. Suddenly Mr Golyadkin felt somehow inspired and in a tremulous, solemn voice he turned to the waiting Gerasimych and began afresh:

'No, my friend, no one's asking for me . . . you're mistaken. I'll go further and say you were mistaken this morning when you assured me, when you dared to assure me (here Mr Golyadkin raised his voice) that Olsufy Ivanovich, my benefactor from time immemorial, who has, in a certain sense, taken the place of a father to me, would close his doors to me at a time of the most solemn domestic rejoicing for his paternal heart. (Smugly, but deeply moved, Mr Golyadkin looked around. Tears glittered on his eyelashes.) 'I repeat, my friend,' concluded our hero, 'you were mistaken, you were cruelly and unforgivably mistaken . . .'

It was a moment of triumph. Mr Golyadkin felt that he had achieved exactly the right effect. He stood there with eyes modestly lowered, awaiting Olsufy Ivanovich's embrace. Among the guests there were distinct signs of agitation and bewilderment. Even the unshakeable and imperturbable Gerasimych stumbled over his words: 'It's doubtful, sir!' And then suddenly, for no apparent reason, the merciless orchestra struck up a polka. All was lost, all was scattered in the wind. Mr Golyadkin shuddered. Gerasimych staggered back and all who were in the ballroom surged like the sea – and there was Vladimir Semyonovich, already whisking Klara Olsufyevna along in the leading pair, followed by the handsome lieutenant and

Princess Chevchekhanova. The spectators, curious and enraptured, crowded to watch those who were dancing the polka –
an interesting, novel and fashionable dance that had turned
everyone's head. For a time Mr Golyadkin was forgotten. But
suddenly all was commotion, confusion and bustle. The music
stopped . . . something strange had happened. Wearied by the
dance, almost breathless from her exertions, cheeks burning
and bosom deeply heaving, Klara Olsufyevna finally sank into
an armchair, utterly exhausted. All hearts went out to that
fascinating enchantress, everyone was vying with one another
to compliment her and thank her for the pleasure she had given
them – when suddenly right before her stood Mr Golyadkin. Mr
Golyadkin was pale and extremely distraught; he too seemed to
be in a state of exhaustion and he could barely move. He was
smiling for some reason and offering his hand imploringly. In
her astonishment Klara Olsufyevna had no time to withdraw
her hand and rose mechanically to Mr Golyadkin's invitation.
Mr Golyadkin lurched forward once, and then again, then he
somehow raised one foot, then he clicked his heels, stamped his
foot and then he stumbled . . . he too wanted to dance with
Klara Olsufyevna. Klara Olsufyevna screamed. Everyone
rushed to free her hand from Mr Golyadkin's and at once our
hero was pushed almost ten paces away by the crowd. A small
circle formed around him, too. The shrieks and cries of the two
old ladies whom Mr Golyadkin almost knocked over in his
retreat rang out. The commotion was terrible: everyone was
shouting, arguing, questioning. The orchestra fell silent. Our
hero was spinning around within his small circle and was mechanically, faintly smiling, muttering something to himself under
his breath, to the effect that: Why not? The polka was a novel
and most interesting dance, devised to divert the ladies . . . But
if this was how things stood now he was by all means ready to
acquiesce. But no one was asking for Mr Golyadkin's acquies-
cence, at least so it seemed to him. Our hero suddenly felt
someone's hand fall on his arm, then another pressed down
slightly against his back and he felt he was being steered with
particular solicitude in a certain direction. Finally he noticed
that he was heading straight for the doors. Mr Golyadkin

wanted to do something, to say something . . . But no, he no
longer wanted anything. He simply laughed it off mechanically.
Finally, he became aware that they were putting him into his
overcoat and pulling his hat down over his eyes; at length he
felt he was out in the passage, in the cold and dark, and then
on the stairs. He stumbled and felt he was falling into an abyss;
he wanted to cry out – and then suddenly he found himself out
in the courtyard. The fresh air wafted over him and he stood
still for a moment. At that very instant the sound of the orchestra striking up again reached his ears. Mr Golyadkin suddenly
remembered everything: he seemed to have recovered all his
lost strength. From where he had just been standing as if rooted
to the spot, he tore off and rushed headlong – anywhere, to
freedom, to fresh air, to wherever his legs would carry him . . .

CHAPTER V

Every clock tower in St Petersburg that showed and told the
hour was striking exactly midnight when Mr Golyadkin, beside
himself, ran on to the Fontanka Embankment,[20] near that same
Izmaylovsky Bridge, seeking refuge from his enemies, from
persecution, from the insults that had rained down on him,
from the shrieks of frightened old ladies, from the sobbing and
sighing of women – and from Andrey Filippovich's murderous
glances. Mr Golyadkin was crushed, absolutely crushed, in the
full sense of the word, and if he still had the ability to run at
that moment it was solely by some miracle, a miracle in which
he himself refused to believe. It was a dreadful November night
– dank, misty, raining, snowing, a night fraught with colds,
fevers, agues, quinsies and inflammations of every conceivable
variety and description – in brief, fraught with all the blessings
of a St Petersburg November. The wind howled down the
deserted streets, raising the black waters of the Fontanka above
the mooring-rings and rattling with a vengeance the feeble
lanterns along the embankment which echoed its howling with
those shrill, ear-splitting squeaks that make up the endless

concert of jarring sounds so very familiar to every inhabitant of St Petersburg. It was raining and snowing at the same time. Sheets of rain, broken up by the wind, sprayed about almost horizontally, as if from a fire hose, stabbing and stinging the face of the hapless Mr Golyadkin like a thousand pins and needles. Amidst the stillness of the night, interrupted only by the distant rumble of carriages, the howling of the wind and the squeaking lanterns, could be heard the mournful sound of water, gushing and gurgling from every roof, porch, gutter and cornice on to the granite pavement. There was not a soul to be seen, either far or near – it seemed there could not possibly be at such an hour and in such weather. And so, only Mr Golyadkin, alone in his despair, was trotting along the Fontanka at this time of night, taking his usual rapid, short steps, hurrying to reach his fourth-floor flat in Shestilavochnaya Street as soon as he possibly could.

Although the rain, the snow and everything that does not even have a name, when a blizzard rages and thick fog comes down on a St Petersburg November night, were suddenly, of one accord, attacking Mr Golyadkin, who was crushed enough by misfortune, allowing him not the least protection or respite, chilling him to the marrow, gluing up his eyes, gusting from all sides, driving him off his path and out of his mind – and although all this descended on Mr Golyadkin at once, as if deliberately conspiring with his enemies to give him a day, evening and night he would never forget – despite all this Mr Golyadkin remained almost unaffected by this final proof of a fate that was pursuing him, so thoroughly shaken and stunned was he by all that had happened to him a few minutes earlier at State Counsellor Berendeyev's! If any disinterested, outside observer had now casually glanced from the side at Mr Golyadkin in his wretched flight he would have at once fathomed the whole awful horror of his tribulations and would doubtless have said that Mr Golyadkin now looked like a man wanting to hide, wanting to run away from himself. Yes! – that really was the case. Let us say more: now Mr Golyadkin not only wanted to escape from himself, but even hide from himself, to be utterly annihilated, to exist no more and turn to dust. At that

moment he was oblivious of everything around, understood
nothing that was happening around him and he looked as if all
the nastiness of that foul night, the long walk, the rain and
wind and snow, did not in fact exist for him. One galosh,
having parted company with Mr Golyadkin's right foot, was
left behind in the slush and snow on the Fontanka pavement, but Mr Golyadkin didn't even consider going back for
it and didn't even notice he had lost it. He was so perplexed
that several times, despite all that was surrounding him, he
would suddenly stop short and stand stock-still in the middle
of the pavement, completely obsessed by the thought of his
recent appalling fall from grace. At those moments he would
die, he would vanish. Then he would suddenly tear off again
like one demented and run and run, without looking back, as
if escaping pursuit or some even more dreadful calamity. His
predicament was truly shocking. At length, his strength exhausted, Mr Golyadkin stopped, leant over the embankment railing
like a man with a sudden nosebleed and stared intently at the
dark, murky waters of the Fontanka. There is no knowing
exactly how long he spent in this occupation. All that is known
is that at that moment Mr Golyadkin plumbed such depths of
despair, was so tormented, harassed, exhausted, so bereft of
any spark of fortitude, so disheartened, that he had forgotten
everything: Izmaylovsky Bridge, Shestilavochnaya Street and
his present plight . . . But what did it matter? Really he couldn't
have cared less. Everything was all over – signed, settled and
sealed. Why should he fret over it? Suddenly . . . suddenly he
shuddered all over and instinctively leapt a couple of steps
sideways. With an indescribable feeling of uneasiness he started
looking around. But no one was there, nothing out of the
ordinary had happened and . . . meanwhile . . . meanwhile he
felt that someone had been standing right beside him just then,
his elbows similarly propped on the railings and – amazing to
relate – had even said something to him, abruptly and hurriedly,
not altogether intelligibly but about something very familiar to
him and which concerned him. 'Well now, have I imagined all
this?' Mr Golyadkin asked himself, looking round again. 'But
where am I standing? . . . Ah, ah!' he concluded, shaking his

head and meanwhile peering with an anxious, dejected feeling, even fearfully, into the wet, murky distance, straining his short-sighted eyes as hard as he could and doing his utmost to penetrate the sodden gloom that stretched before him. However, there was nothing new, nothing in particular caught Mr Golyadkin's eye. Everything appeared to be in order and as it should have been – that is, the snow was falling even harder and thicker, in larger flakes, nothing was visible at twenty paces. The lanterns squeaked even more shrilly than before and the wind seemed to be singing its melancholy song even more mournfully and plaintively than ever, like some importunate beggar pleading for a few copecks for food. 'Eh, eh! What on earth's the matter with me?' Mr Golyadkin repeated, setting off again and constantly looking round slightly. Meanwhile some new sensation took complete possession of his whole being – not really anguish, not really fear . . . a feverish tremor ran through his every sinew. It was an unbearably nasty moment! 'Well, it's nothing,' he muttered to encourage himself, 'it's nothing. Perhaps it's absolutely nothing at all and no stain on anyone's honour. Perhaps it was all meant to be,' he continued, without understanding himself what he was saying. 'Perhaps in its own good time everything will turn out for the best. There'll be nothing to complain about and everyone will be vindicated.' Talking in this way and calming himself with these words Mr Golyadkin gave himself a little shake, shook off the snowflakes that had been forming a thick crust on his hat, collar, overcoat, scarf, boots – on everything, in fact. But he still couldn't brush aside or rid himself of that strange, vague feeling of anguish. Somewhere far off the sound of a cannon rang out. 'What weather!' thought our hero. 'Just listen to that! Could it be a flood warning? Clearly the water's dangerously high.' No sooner had Mr Golyadkin said or thought this than he saw a passer-by walking towards him, most likely someone delayed for some reason himself. It was all of little consequence, it would seem, a chance encounter. But for some mysterious reason Mr Golyadkin became alarmed, afraid even, and he felt somewhat at a loss. It wasn't that he feared that it might be some nasty character . . . well, perhaps . . . 'Who knows who this belated person could be?' flashed through his mind. 'Perhaps he's part of the same thing, perhaps he's the most important person in this business and he's not here for nothing but has a purpose in coming, in crossing my path and bumping into me.' But perhaps Mr Golyadkin did not think precisely that and had only a fleeting impression of something resembling it and extremely unpleasant. Yet there was no time for thinking or even feeling; the passer-by was already within a couple of strides. As was his invariable habit, Mr Golyadkin wasted no time in assuming a very special look, a look that clearly expressed that he, Mr Golyadkin, was minding his own business, that he was all right, that the street was wide enough for everyone and that indeed he, Mr Golyadkin, was bothering no one. Suddenly he stood rooted to the spot, as if struck by lightning and then swiftly turned around after the stranger who had just passed him – turned around as if someone had tugged him from behind and turned him as the wind swings a weathercock. The passer-by was fast disappearing in the snowstorm. He too was in a hurry like Mr Golyadkin and he too was wrapped up from head to foot, he too was pattering along the Fontanka pavement with the same rapid short steps and at a slight trot. 'What, what's this?' whispered Mr Golyadkin with an incredulous smile and yet trembling in every limb. Cold shivers ran down his spine. Meanwhile the passer-by had disappeared completely and his footsteps could no longer be heard, but Mr Golyadkin still stood there, gazing after him. Gradually, though, he finally came to his senses. 'What on earth's going on?' he thought irritably. 'Have I gone mad, really gone mad?' He turned and went on his way, quickening his stride the whole time and trying his level best to avoid thinking of anything at all. To this end he even closed his eyes. Suddenly, through the howling of the wind and noise of the storm, he again heard the sound of someone's footsteps very close by. He started and opened his eyes. Ahead of him, about twenty paces away, the small dark figure of a man was rapidly approaching. This little man was in a hurry, rushing along with short rapid steps; the distance between them was rapidly diminishing. Now Mr Golyadkin could clearly make out his new, belated companion – made him out completely and he shrieked with horror and bewilderment; his legs gave way. It was that very same passer-by, already familiar to him, for whom he had made way and passed ten minutes earlier, who had now appeared before him, again quite unexpectedly. But it was not only this marvel that startled Mr Golyadkin – and Mr Golyadkin was so startled that he stopped, cried out, tried to say something – and then he raced off in pursuit of the stranger, even shouting out to him to stop as quickly as possible. The stranger did indeed stop – about ten paces from Mr Golyadkin, so that the light of a nearby street lamp fell fully on his whole figure – he stopped and turned to Mr Golyadkin and with an anxious and impertinent look waited to hear what Mr Golyadkin had to say. 'Forgive me, I seem to have been mistaken,' our hero said in a quavering voice. Without a word, the stranger turned away in a huff and swiftly went on his way, as if hurrying to make up the few seconds wasted over Mr Golyadkin. As for Mr Golyadkin, he was trembling in every fibre; his knees weakened and buckled beneath him and he squatted on a bollard, groaning. And in fact he had very good reason to feel so distressed. The fact was, this stranger now seemed somehow familiar. That in itself wouldn't have mattered. But he recognized him – he almost completely recognized that man now. He'd often seen that man at some time, quite recently even. Where could it have been? Could it have been yesterday? However, the important thing wasn't that Mr Golyadkin had often seen him; and there was hardly anything special about that man – certainly no one would have given him a second look. So, he was like anyone else, like all respectable people of course and probably even possessed some quite special qualities – in short he was an individual in his own right. Mr Golyadkin didn't feel either hatred or even open hostility, not the slightest enmity towards him: quite the opposite it would seem. And yet (and this circumstance was the essential thing), and yet, not for all the tea in China would he have wanted to meet him and particularly not to meet him as just now, for example. We shall say more: Mr Golyadkin knew that man extremely well; he even knew what he was called, his surname. But at the same time, not for all the tea in China would he have wanted to name him or agree to admit that, in a manner of speaking, that's what he was called – Christian name, patronymic and surname. Whether Mr Golyadkin's confusion was long-lasting or brief, or whether he squatted for long on that bollard I cannot say, only that, finally recovering slightly, he suddenly hared off as fast as he could without looking back, with all the strength he could muster. His lungs were bursting; twice he stumbled and nearly fell and as a result of this event Mr Golyadkin's other boot was orphaned, also abandoned by its galosh. Finally Mr Golyadkin slackened his pace a little to catch his breath, took a hurried look round and saw that he'd already run, without noticing it, the whole way along the Fontanka, had crossed Anichkov Bridge,[21] had gone down part of Nevsky Prospekt and was now standing at the junction with Liteynaya Street. Mr Golyadkin turned into Liteynaya Street. His situation at that moment was like that of a man on the brink of a terrifying precipice, when the ground is giving way beneath him; it is moving and rocking, it quakes, it sways for the last time and falls, drawing him towards the abyss, which the poor wretch has neither the strength nor the fortitude to leap back from, or to avert his eyes from the yawning chasm. The abyss is drawing him on and finally he himself leaps into it, thus hastening his own demise. Mr Golyadkin knew and felt, and was perfectly convinced, that some new evil would overtake him on his way, that more unpleasantness was bound to erupt over his head, that, for instance, he might again encounter that stranger. But – strange to relate – he positively longed for that meeting, considering it inevitable, and all he asked was that the whole thing should be over and done with, that his position should be decided quickly, one way or the other, so long as it was soon. Meanwhile on and on he ran, as if propelled by some external force, for he felt a growing weakness and a numbness in his whole being. He couldn't think of anything, although his mind clutched at everything, like blackthorn. A wretched stray dog, wet and shivering, attached itself to Mr Golyadkin and hurried along beside him, its tail between its legs and its ears laid back, looking up at him every now and then, timidly and intelligently. Some remote,

long-forgotten idea, the memory of something that had happened long ago, now entered his head, tapping away like a
small hammer in his brain, vexing him and not leaving him in
peace. 'Ugh, that nasty little cur!' Mr Golyadkin whispered,
not understanding what he was saying himself. At length he
caught sight of his stranger at the corner of Italyanskaya Street.
Only this time the stranger wasn't coming towards him but was
also running in the same direction, a few steps ahead. At last
they turned into Shestilavochnaya Street: it took Mr Golyadkin's breath away – the stranger had stopped right in front
of the block where Mr Golyadkin lodged. The sound of a bell
rang out and almost at the same time an iron bolt creaked. The
gate opened, the stranger stooped, flitted past and vanished.
Almost at the same moment Mr Golyadkin arrived too and
flew through the gates like an arrow. Ignoring the grumbling
porter he ran breathlessly into the courtyard and immediately
caught sight of his interesting companion whom he'd lost for
one moment. Then he glimpsed the stranger at the entrance of
the staircase that led to Mr Golyadkin's flat. Mr Golyadkin
hurtled after him. The staircase was dark, damp and filthy.
Every landing was heaped with all kinds of tenants' rubbish, so
that a stranger, unfamiliar with the place and have to face that
staircase after dark, was forced to spend about half an hour
climbing it, risking breaking his legs and cursing his friends
(together with the staircase) for residing in such an inconvenient
locality. But Mr Golyadkin's companion seemed to be perfectly
at home and familiar with his surroundings and he ran up
easily, without any trouble and with a complete knowledge of
the topography. Mr Golyadkin almost caught up with him;
once or twice the tail of the stranger's coat even struck his nose.
And then his heart missed a beat: the mysterious person stopped
right outside the doors to Mr Golyadkin's flat, and knocked
(at any other time this would have startled Mr Golyadkin).
Petrushka opened the door at once, as if he had been waiting
up for him and hadn't gone to bed and followed the man who
entered, candle in hand. Quite beside himself the hero of our
tale ran into his abode; without taking off hat or coat, he went
down the short passage and stopped on the threshold of his

room as if thunderstruck. All Mr Golyadkin's worst misgivings
were confirmed. All that he had dreaded and guessed at had
now taken place in reality. He gasped for breath, his head went
round. There was the stranger, sitting before him on his own
bed, also wearing a hat and coat, faintly smiling, screwing up
his eyes a little, and giving him a friendly nod. Mr Golyadkin
wanted to cry out, but he was unable to; he wanted to protest
in some way, but his strength failed him. His hair stood on end
and he squatted where he was, insensible with horror. And
besides, he had good reason. Mr Golyadkin had fully recognized his nocturnal friend: his nocturnal friend was none other
than himself, Mr Golyadkin in person – another Mr Golyadkin,
but identical to him in every way – in brief, in all respects what
is called his double . . .

CHAPTER VI

Next morning, at exactly eight o'clock, Mr Golyadkin came to
in his bed. Immediately all the extraordinary events of the
previous day, all that unbelievable night with its well-nigh
impossible events, suddenly, all at once, presented themselves
to his imagination and memory in their horrifying fullness.
Such fierce, hellish malice on the part of his enemies – and
particularly this last proof of malice – made Mr Golyadkin's
blood run cold. But at the same time it was all so strange, so
incomprehensible, so weird, so impossible even, that it was
extremely difficult to credit any of the whole business. Even Mr
Golyadkin himself was ready to admit that it was all some
fantastic raving, some momentary derangement of the imagination or darkening of the mind, had he not known – fortunately
for him, from bitter experience of life – to what length malice
can drive a man sometimes, to what extremes an embittered
enemy can sometimes go to avenge his honour and pride.
Besides, Mr Golyadkin's exhausted limbs, his befuddled head,
his aching back and his pernicious head cold were powerful
enough testimony to confirm the whole plausibility of the

previous night's walk – and in part all the other things that had
happened during the course of that walk. Finally, Mr Golyadkin
had in fact known for ages that they were cooking something
up and that someone else was mixed up in it with them. But
what then? After carefully thinking it over, Mr Golyadkin
decided to keep quiet, to submit and not make his protest before
the time was right. 'Well, perhaps they just thought they'd give
me a fright and when they see that I don't care, that I'm not
protesting, but fully resigned to it and that I'm prepared to grin
and bear it they'll just withdraw, withdraw of their own accord
– yes, they'll be the first to withdraw.'

These were the kinds of thoughts that ran through Mr Golyadkin's mind while he stretched out on his bed, relaxing his
aching limbs and waiting on this occasion for Petrushka's customary appearance in his room. He had already been waiting
nearly a quarter of an hour and could hear that lazy Petrushka
fussing with the samovar behind the partition, but at the same
time he just couldn't bring himself to summon him. We could
go further and say that Mr Golyadkin was even slightly apprehensive of a confrontation with Petrushka. 'God only knows
what that scoundrel will think about all this now,' he wondered.
'He usually keeps his mouth shut, but he's a cunning devil!'
Finally the door creaked and Petrushka appeared with a tray
in his hands. Mr Golyadkin looked at him sheepishly, with a
sidelong glance, waiting impatiently to discover what would
happen next, waiting to hear whether he would have anything
to say regarding a certain circumstance. But Petrushka didn't
say a word – on the contrary, he was even more taciturn and
truculent and angrier than usual, scowling at everything; evidently he was extremely displeased about something. Not once
did he even glance at his master and this, we can say, in passing,
rather piqued Mr Golyadkin. After putting everything he had
brought on the table he turned and vanished in silence behind
his partition. 'He knows, he knows everything, the lazy devil!'
grumbled Mr Golyadkin as he started on his tea. However, our
hero didn't question his manservant about anything, although
Petrushka subsequently entered several times, on different
errands. Mr Golyadkin was in the most agitated state of mind.

What was more, he dreaded going to the office. He had a strong presentiment that it was precisely *there* that something wasn't quite right. 'So, I'll go along,' he thought, 'and what if I run slap bang into something? Wouldn't it be best to try and be patient now? Wouldn't it be best to wait for a bit now? They can do what they like there. Really, I'd better wait here today, get my strength back, get back on my feet, have a good think about all this, then seize the right moment, turn up out of the blue and act as if nothing were wrong.' With these considerations Mr Golyadkin smoked pipe after pipe. The time flew – it was already almost half past nine. 'Ah well, it's already half past nine,' thought Mr Golyadkin, 'so it's too late now to turn up. Besides, I'm ill, of course I'm ill, no question I'm ill. Who'd deny it? What do I care? And if they send someone to check up on me, an administrative clerk, what does it matter, in effect? My back aches, I've a bad cough and a cold in the head. Finally, I couldn't, I couldn't possibly go in this weather. I might be taken seriously ill and then even die; the death rate's particularly high just now . . .' By virtue of these arguments Mr Golyadkin finally eased his conscience completely and justified himself in advance against the dressing-down he could expect from Andrey Filippovich for neglecting his work. Generally speaking, in all such cases our hero was inordinately fond of vindicating himself in his own eyes with various kinds of irrefutable arguments and thus completely salving his conscience. So, his conscience completely salved, he took up his pipe, filled it, and the moment it was drawing nicely he sprang up from the sofa, abandoned the pipe, briskly washed, shaved, smoothed his hair, put on his uniform jacket and all the rest, grabbed some papers and flew off to the office.

Mr Golyadkin entered his department timidly, trembling in expectation of something very bad – expectation which, although unconscious and vague, was nonetheless unpleasant. Sheepishly he seated himself at his customary place next to Anton Antonovich Setochkin, the chief clerk. Without looking at anything or allowing himself to be distracted he investigated the contents of the documents that were lying before him. He had resolved and had promised himself to avoid as far as possible anything that might provoke him, anything that could seriously compromise him, namely, indelicate questions, any kind of jokes and unseemly allusions regarding all the previous evening's events; he even decided to forgo the usual polite exchanges with his colleagues, such as inquiring about their health and so on. But it was also obviously clearly impossible to maintain this stance. Uneasiness and ignorance about something that intimately concerned him always tormented him more than the thing itself. So that was why, despite the promise he had made to himself not to allow himself to become involved in anything, at all costs, happen what may, to keep aloof from everything, no matter what, Mr Golyadkin, furtively and stealthily, occasionally kept raising his head very slightly, slyly looking to left and right, peering into his colleagues' faces to try and read from their expressions if anything new or special concerning him was being concealed for some improper reasons. He assumed that there was a definite link between all yesterday's events and everything around him now. Finally, in his acute distress, he began to wish that everything would be resolved quickly – God knows how – even if it had to be through some disaster, no matter what! And here fate took him at his word: no sooner had Mr Golyadkin time to wish this than his doubts were suddenly resolved, but in the strangest and most unexpected fashion.

The door from the next room suddenly opened with a timid, quiet creak, as if thus announcing the entrance of a very insignificant person, and someone's figure, incidentally very familiar to Mr Golyadkin, came in and shyly stood before the very desk at which our hero was seated. Our hero didn't raise his head – oh no! He only gave this figure the slightest, fleeting glance, but he already knew everything, he understood everything, down to the smallest detail . . . He was burning with shame and buried his wretched head in some documents for the same reason that an ostrich pursued by the hunter hides its head in the scorching sands. The newcomer bowed to Mr Golyadkin and after that he could hear an officially kind voice, the sort in which all heads of department usually address newly arrived subordinates. 'Sit here,' Andrey Filippovich said, motioning the new recruit to

Anton Antonovich's desk. 'Sit here, opposite Mr Golyadkin, and we'll give you some work right away,' Andrey Filippovich concluded by making a rapid, suitably commanding gesture to the newcomer and then he immediately absorbed himself in the contents of the various documents lying in a great pile before him.

Mr Golyadkin at last raised his eyes and if he did not faint it was only because he had a foreboding of the whole thing from the start, had been forewarned about everything from the start, and had already divined in his heart the newcomer's identity. Mr Golyadkin's first move was to take a rapid look around to see if there was any whispering, whether any office witticisms on the subject were pouring forth, whether anyone's face was contorted with surprise or, finally, whether anyone had fallen under his desk from fright. But to Mr Golyadkin's extreme amazement he could detect nothing of the kind in anyone. Mr Golyadkin was astounded by the behaviour of his colleages and comrades. It seemed beyond the bounds of common sense. Mr Golyadkin was even scared by such an unusual silence. The reality spoke for itself: it was a strange, ugly, absurd affair. There was good reason to feel disturbed. All this, of course, merely flashed through Mr Golyadkin's mind. He himself felt he was being roasted over a low flame. And he had good reason. The person now sitting opposite Mr Golyadkin was Mr Golyadkin's horror, Mr Golyadkin's shame, Mr Golyadkin's nightmare of the day before: in brief it was Mr Golyadkin himself – not the Mr Golyadkin now sitting on his chair with his mouth agape and his pen frozen in his grasp; not the one who worked as assistant to the head clerk; not the one who liked to be self-effacing and bury himself in the crowd; finally, not the one whose walk clearly announced: 'Don't touch me and I shan't touch you.' No – this was another Mr Golyadkin, a completely different one, but at the same time one who was completely identical to the first – the same height, the same build, the same clothes, the same bald patch – in brief, nothing had been omitted for a perfect likeness, so that if one were to stand them side by side, nobody, absolutely nobody would have ventured to determine who was the real Mr Golyadkin and

who the fake, who the old and who the new, who the original
and who the copy.

Our hero, if the comparison may be allowed, was now in the
situation of someone with whom some prankster was having
fun, slyly turning his burning-glass on him for a joke. 'What is
this – is it a dream or not?' he wondered. 'Is it real or simply
the continuation of yesterday's events? But how can this be? By
what right is all this happening? Who engaged such a clerk, who
authorized such a thing? Am I sleeping, am I day-dreaming?' Mr
Golyadkin tried pinching himself – he even conceived the idea
of pinching someone else . . . No, it was no dream and that was
that. Mr Golyadkin felt the sweat pouring off him, felt that
something unprecedented and hitherto unseen was happening
to him and, for that very reason, to crown his misfortune, was
improper, for Mr Golyadkin realized and sensed the disadvan-
tage of being the first example of such a scandalous business.
In the end he even began to doubt his own existence and
although he had been prepared for everything to start with and
had longed for all his doubts to be somehow resolved, the very
essence of the situation was of course its unexpectedness. His
anguish crushed and tormented him. At times he completely lost
all capacity for reasoning and remembering. Recovering after
such a moment, he noticed that he was automatically and uncon-
sciously moving pen over paper. As he did not trust himself, he
began checking all he had written but could not make head or
tail of it. At length the other Mr Golyadkin, who up to then had
been sitting decorously and demurely at his desk, got up and
disappeared through the doorway into another section on some
business. Mr Golyadkin looked around – everything was all
right, all was still. Only the scratching of pens could be heard,
the rustle of turning pages and snatches of conversation in the
corners furthest removed from Andrey Filippovich's seat. Mr
Golyadkin glanced at Anton Antonovich and since, in all probability, our hero's face fully reflected his present plight and
harmonized with all that the present business implied so that
consequently it was very remarkable in a certain respect, the
kindly Anton Antonovich put down his pen and inquired after
Mr Golyadkin's state of health with unusual solicitude.

'I – I'm all right, perfectly well, thank God, Anton Antono-
vich,' stammered Mr Golyadkin. 'I'm all right now, Anton
Antonovich,' he added irresolutely, still not fully trusting Anton
Antonovich, whom he had mentioned so often.

'Ah! I thought you were ill. But that wouldn't surprise me –
who knows what can happen! At the moment there's all sorts
of epidemics going around. Do you know . . .'

'Yes, Anton Antonovich, I know there's epidemics going
around . . . But that's not why I, Anton Antonovich . . .' continued Mr Golyadkin, staring hard at Anton Antonovich. 'You
see, I don't even know how to put it . . . that is, I mean to
say . . . from what angle should I tackle this matter, Anton
Antonovich?'

'What did you say? Well, you know . . . I must confess . . . I
don't really get your drift. You know, you must explain in more
detail in what respect you are having difficulty,' said Anton
Antonovich, who was beginning to have a little difficulty himself when he saw that tears had started to Mr Golyadkin's eyes.

'I . . . really . . . here, Anton Antonovich . . . there's a clerk
here, Anton Antonovich.'

'Well now! I still don't understand.'

'I mean to say, Anton Antonovich, there's a new clerk here.'

'Yes there is, sir, with the same surname as yours.'

'What?!' cried Mr Golyadkin.

'I'm telling you, he's got the same name. He's a Golyadkin
too. Is he your brother?'

'No, Anton Antonovich . . . I . . .'

'Hm! Then please tell me . . . I had the impression that he
must be a close relative of yours. There's a family likeness of
sorts, you know.'

Mr Golyadkin was absolutely dumbfounded and for a while
he lost the power of speech. How could he treat something so
monstrous and unprecedented so lightly, something rare
enough of its kind, something that would have astonished even
the most impartial observer, and talk of a family likeness when
it was as clear as if in a mirror!

'Do you know what I advise, Yakov Petrovich?' Anton
Antonovich continued. 'You should go to the doctor's and ask

his advice. You know, you don't look at all well. Your eyes in particular . . . you know . . . they've such a peculiar expression.'

'No, Anton Antonovich . . . of course I feel . . . I mean, I still want to ask – what do you think about this clerk?'

'Well, what exactly?'

'I mean, haven't you noticed something special about him, something very significant?'

'And what's that?'

'I mean to say, a striking resemblance to someone – to me, for example. Just now, Anton Antonovich, you remarked on a family likeness in passing . . . Do you know that twins are sometimes alike as two peas in a pod, so you can't tell the difference? That's what I meant.'

'Yes,' said Anton Antonovich, after pausing for thought and realized this was the first time he had been struck by such a circumstance. 'Yes sir, you are right! The resemblance is truly amazing and indeed you're not wrong when you say that one could be taken for the other,' he continued, opening his eyes ever wider. 'And do you know, Yakov Petrovich, it's really a miraculous resemblance, a fantastic likeness as they sometimes say . . . that is, he's you to a tee! Haven't you noticed, Yakov Petrovich? I was even intending to ask if you could explain it and I must confess I didn't pay due attention at first. It's a marvel, a sheer marvel! And you're not from these parts, are you, Yakov Petrovich?'

'No, sir.'

'He's not from here either. Perhaps he hails from the same place as you. Now, if I dare ask, where did your mother live most of her life?'

'Did you say . . . did you say, Anton Antonovich, that he's not from round here?'

'No, not from here. But really, it's an absolute miracle,' continued the loquacious Anton Antonovich, for whom it was a real pleasure to have something to gossip about, 'it could really arouse one's curiosity. And how often might you pass him, bump into him or brush against him and not notice. But don't go upsetting yourself. It happens. Do you know – I must tell you this – exactly the same thing happened to an aunt on my mother's side. Before she died she too saw herself doubly . . .'

'No . . . I . . . please forgive me for interrupting, Anton Antonovich, but I'd like to know how this clerk . . . that is, on what basis is he here?'

'Well, he's filled the position left by the late Semyon Ivanovich. The position fell vacant, so they took him on. Oh yes, that poor, good-hearted Semyon Ivanovich. He left three little children, all tiny tots, I've heard say. His widow fell at His Excellency's feet. But they do say she's hiding something: she's got a little money, but she's hidden it away.'

'No, I'm still talking about that other circumstance, Anton Antonovich.'

'What's that? Oh yes! But why are you so interested in it? I'm telling you, don't go upsetting yourself. It's only temporary. And what does it matter? It's got nothing to do with you. It's all the Lord God's work, He arranged it, it's His will and to complain about it is sinful. His wisdom is plain to see. But you, Yakov Petrovich, as far as I understand, are not to blame in any way. The world is so abundant in wonders! Mother Nature is bounteous. No one's asking you to account for this, you won't be held responsible for it. And while we're on the subject, let me give you an example. I hope you've heard of – what on earth do you call them? – oh yes, those Siamese twins,[22] born with their backs joined and they have to live, eat and sleep like that, always together. I've heard people say they're making a lot of money.'

'If you don't mind, Anton Antonovich . . .'

'I understand you, I do understand! Oh yes! Well, what of it? It's nothing! I'm telling you that as I see it there's nothing to feel upset about. So what? He's a clerk like any other and he strikes me as the efficient sort. Says his name is Golyadkin, that he's not from round here and he's a titular counsellor. He gave a good account of himself in person to His Excellency.'

'Well, what happened?'

'Oh, it went well. They say he gave a very good account of himself – provided good arguments. "Well, it's like this, Your Excellency," he said, "I've no money and I'm keen to work here and I should be especially flattered to serve under your distinguished command." – Well, he said all the right things, expressed himself well. He must be a clever chap. Of course, he came with a reference – can't get far without one of those, you know!'

'Well . . . from whom? I mean, who exactly had a hand in this shameful business?'

'Oh yes, a good reference, they say. His Excellency, so I'm told, had a good laugh over it with Andrey Filippovich.'

'Had a laugh with Andrey Filippovich?'

'Yes, he simply smiled and said it was all right, that he had no objections, as long as he served loyally.'

'Go on, you're cheering me up a bit, Anton Antonovich! Please go on, I beg you.'

'Forgive me again, there's something else I don't quite . . . Ah well, it doesn't matter, it's perfectly simple. Now don't you go upsetting yourself, I say, there's nothing at all dubious about it.'

'No . . . I . . . that is, I'd like to ask you, Anton Antonovich, if His Excellency added something else – about me, for example?'

'What do you mean? Oh yes! But no, there was nothing, so you can put your mind at rest. Of course, it goes without saying that it's something quite striking and at first . . . well, take me, for example, I almost didn't notice it at first. I really don't know why I didn't notice it, until you mentioned it. But you can relax, His Excellency said nothing special, absolutely nothing at all,' added the kindly Anton Antonovich, rising from his seat.

'So I, Anton Antonovich . . .'

'Ah, if you'll excuse me . . . Here I've been waffling away about trifles and I've important business to see to. It's urgent, I must deal with it right away.'

'Anton Antonovich!' Andrey Filippovich's politely summoning voice rang out. 'His Excellency's asking for you.'

'Right away, Andrey Filippovich, right away.' And Anton Antonovich, picking up a pile of papers, flew off first to Andrey Filippovich, then to His Excellency's study.

'So, how is this?' Mr Golyadkin thought to himself. 'So that's their little game. That's the way the wind's blowing here now . . . But it's not so bad. Things must have taken a most pleasant turn,' our hero said to himself, rubbing his hands for joy. 'So, it's quite run-of-the-mill, this business of ours. It's all ending in trivialities, just fizzling out. In fact no one's doing anything – not a squeak out of them, the scoundrels! – they're just sitting there and getting on with their work. Splendid, splendid! I like a good man, always have done, and I always have respect for him But come to think of it, it's not so good . . . I'm scared of trusting him with anything, that Anton Antonovich. He's gone terribly grey and he's on his last legs. Still, the most wonderful, stupendous thing is that His Excellency didn't say anything and simply turned a blind eye. That's good, I approve of that. Only, why does Anton Antonovich have to poke his nose into it with that chuckling of his? What's it to do with him? Cunning old fox! Always in my way, always rubbing people up the wrong way, always crossing and spiting a man, always spiting and crossing . . .'

Mr Golyadkin took another look around and again his hopes revived. For all that, a remote, nasty thought was troubling him. He even considered for the moment somehow currying favour with the clerks, somehow stealing a march on them even (as they were all leaving work, approaching them ostensibly about office matters) dropping hints during the course of a conversation to the effect: it's like this, gentlemen, there's this striking resemblance, a strange circumstance, a pure farce – so that by treating it all as a joke he could take soundings of the depth of the danger. 'Still waters run deep,' concluded our hero. But this was no more than a thought – and then he changed his mind in time. He realized that this would be going too far. 'That's you all over!' he said to himself, giving his forehead a gentle smack. 'You'll be jumping for joy in a moment, you're so pleased, you honest soul! No, we'd better be patient, you and I, Yakov Petrovich, we'll wait and be patient.' Nevertheless, as we have already mentioned, Mr Golyadkin's hopes were completely revived and he felt as if he'd risen from the dead. 'It's fine,' he thought.' It's like a ton's fallen from my chest! I mean to say – what a circumstance! "And the casket opened easily after all."23 That Krylov's right, yes, Krylov's right – he's really cunning, he's a master that Krylov – and a great fable-writer!

And as for that fellow, let him work here to his heart's content, as long as he doesn't pester anyone or get in their way. Let him work here – he has my full consent and approval!'

Meanwhile the hours were flying past and before anyone realized it four o'clock struck. The office closed. Andrey Filippovich took his hat and as usual everyone followed suit. Mr Golyadkin hung around a little, just as long as was necessary, and deliberately left later than anyone, ensuring he was last, when all had gone their various ways. Out in the street he felt as if he were in paradise, so much so that he even had the urge to go down Nevsky Prospekt, even if it meant a detour. 'Surely it's fate,' our hero said, 'the whole thing's taken an unexpected turn. And the weather's cleared up, there's a nice frost and the sledges are out. Frosts suit Russians, Russians and frosts get on splendidly. I do like Russians! And there's snow – the first powdering, as a hunter would say. How lovely it would be to go out after a hare over the newly fallen snow! Ah well, everything's fine!'

This was how Mr Golyadkin expressed his delight, yet something was still nagging away in his head, not really what you would call anguish, and at times there was such a gnawing at his heart that he didn't know how to console himself. 'Still, let's wait another day and then we can rejoice. After all, what is the problem? Let's reason it out, have a good look at it. Yes, let's reason the whole thing out, my young friend, let's reason it all out. Well, in the first place there's a man exactly like you, exactly the same. Well, what of it? If that's what he is, do I need to shed tears over it? What is it to me? I'm an outsider; I just whistle my tune and that's that! If that's what it's come to. Let him work here! They say it's a marvel, a real oddity, those Siamese twins ... But why bring those Siamese twins into it? All right, let's suppose they're twins – but even great men sometimes looked very odd. We even know from history that the famous Suvorov[24] used to crow like a cock. But then he did it for political reasons. And the same goes for the great commanders ... but why bring in commanders? I'm my own master, that's what, I don't want to know anyone and in my innocence I despise my enemy. I'm no schemer and of that

I'm proud. Pure, straightforward, neat and tidy, agreeable, inoffensive . . .'

Suddenly Mr Golyadkin fell silent, stopped short and started trembling like a leaf; he even closed his eyes for a moment. Hoping however that the object of his fear was merely an illusion, he finally opened them and timidly stole a glance to the right. No – it was no illusion! There beside him, tripping along, was his acquaintance of that morning, smiling and looking into his face and apparently waiting for the chance to start a conversation. But no conversation got underway, however. Both of them continued walking for about fifty paces like that. Mr Golyadkin's sole concern was wrapping himself up as tightly as possible, burying himself in his overcoat, and pulling down his hat over his eyes as far as it would reach. To add insult to injury, even his acquaintance's overcoat and hat were exactly the same, as if Mr Golyadkin himself had just taken them off.

'My dear sir,' our hero finally declared, trying to speak almost in a whisper and without looking at his friend, 'it seems we're going our different ways. In fact, I'm even convinced of it,' he added after a brief pause. 'Finally, I'm sure that you've completely understood me,' he added quite gruffly, in conclusion.

'I should like,' Mr Golyadkin's companion said at last, 'I should like . . . You'll probably be magnanimous enough to excuse me . . . I don't know who to turn to here . . . my circumstances . . . I hope you'll excuse my impertinence, but I thought you were so moved with compassion that you took a personal interest in me this morning. For my part I felt drawn to you at first sight . . . I . . .' Here Mr Golyadkin wished that the earth would swallow up his new colleague. 'If I dared hope that you would be indulgent enough to hear me out, Yakov Petrovich . . .'

'We – we're here . . . we'd . . . better go to my place,' replied Mr Golyadkin. 'Let's cross Nevsky now – it will be more convenient for both of us that way and then we can go down a side street . . . yes . . . it's best to take a side street.'

'Very well, sir. All right, let's take a side street,' Mr Golyadkin's meek companion timidly observed, as if hinting by the tone of his reply that in his position he had no right to pick and choose and that he was prepared to be satisfied even with a side street. As for Mr Golyadkin, he had no idea what was happening to him. He did not trust himself. He still had not got over his amazement.

CHAPTER VII

Mr Golyadkin recovered a little on the stairs, at the entrance to his flat. 'Ah! what a mutton-head I am!' he mentally cursed himself. 'So, where am I taking him? I'm putting my own head in a noose. What will Petrushka think when he sees us together? What will that rogue dare to think now? He's suspicious . . .' But it was too late for regrets. Mr Golyadkin knocked, the door opened and Petrushka started helping master and guest off with their coats. Mr Golyadkin took a brief look, just a fleeting glance at Petrushka, trying to read his expression and guess what he was thinking. But to his extreme astonishment he saw that his servant was far from being surprised and on the contrary seemed to be expecting something of the kind. Of course, he too was scowling now, squinting sideways and apparently ready to bite someone's head off. 'Has someone cast a spell over everyone today?' wondered our hero. 'Has some demon been doing the rounds? Something certainly very out of the ordinary has got into everyone today. Hell, it's real torment!' Thus reflecting and weighing everything up, Mr Golyadkin led his guest into the room and humbly invited him to sit down. The guest was evidently deeply embarrassed and terribly shy. Meekly he followed his host's every movement, caught his every glance as he apparently tried to deduce his thoughts from them, so it seemed. There was something downtrodden, cowed and abject about every gesture he made, so that at that moment he was – if I may make the comparison – rather like someone who, for lack of any clothes of his own, has put on someone else's: the sleeves ride up, the waist is around his neck and he constantly keeps tugging at his wretchedly short waistcoat, or he stands sideways, tries to hide somewhere, then peers into everyone's eyes and listens hard to discover whether people are discussing his circumstances, whether they're laughing at him or whether they are ashamed of him – and this man blushes, becomes flustered and his pride suffers ... Mr Golyadkin put his hat on the window sill; a clumsy movement sent it flying on to the floor. His guest immediately rushed to pick it up, brushed all the dust off and carefully restored it to the same spot, putting his own on the floor beside a chair, on the edge of which he meekly perched. This trivial incident opened Mr Golyadkin's eyes a little and he realized his guest was in dire straits, so that therefore he didn't bother any more as to how to start with his guest, leaving all that, as was proper, to him. But for his part his guest didn't make a start either – whether from shyness or embarrassment or simply because he was politely waiting for his host to begin was hard to determine. Just then Petrushka entered, stopped in the doorway and stared in the completely opposite direction to that where his master and guest were sitting.

'Shall I bring dinner for two?' he asked in a casual, rather husky voice.

'I, I don't know ... you – yes, bring dinner for two, old chap.' Petrushka went out. Mr Golyadkin glanced at his guest who blushed to the roots of his hair. Mr Golyadkin was a kind person and therefore out of goodness of heart he immediately formulated a theory: 'He's a poor man,' he thought, 'and he's been at his new job only one day. He's probably suffered in his time. Perhaps all he possesses is a decent suit, but has nothing left to feed himself on. Ugh, how downtrodden he looks! Well, never mind. In some ways it's better like that ...'

'Forgive me for asking,' began Mr Golyadkin, 'but please may I inquire – by what name should I call you?'

'I'm ... I'm Yakov Petrovich,' replied his guest, almost in a whisper, ashamed and embarrassed, as if he were begging forgiveness for the fact that he too was called Yakov Petrovich.

'Yakov Petrovich!' our hero repeated, unable to conceal his confusion.

'Yes, sir, exactly, sir ... Your namesake, sir,' replied Mr Golyadkin's humble guest, venturing a smile and allowing himself to say something a little more jocular. But then he immediately sank back and assumed a serious but at the same time rather embarrassed look upon seeing his host was in no mood for jokes just then.

'You, if I may inquire . . . to what circumstance do I owe the honour . . . ?'

'Knowing your goodness of heart and virtues . . .' his guest rapidly interrupted, but in a rather timid voice, half-rising from his chair, 'I made so bold as to appeal to you and ask for your . . . friendship and protection . . .' his guest concluded, evidently having difficulty expressing himself and choosing words that were neither too flattering nor obsequious so as not to compromise his pride, yet not so daring as to suggest an improper equality. In general one could say that Mr Golyadkin's guest was behaving like a noble beggar who, wearing a patched tail-coat and with a nobleman's passport in his pocket, is not yet practised in the art of duly holding out his palm.

'You're confusing me,' replied Mr Golyadkin, surveying himself, the walls of his flat and his guest, 'how can I be . . . I, that is, I'd like to say, in exactly what respect can I be of service to you?'

'I felt drawn to you at first sight, Yakov Petrovich, and – please be gracious enough to forgive me – I built my hopes on you, I dared place my hopes in you, Yakov Petrovich. I . . . I'm like someone forsaken here, I'm poor, I've suffered a great deal, Yakov Petrovich, and I'm still new here. When I found out that you, with the customary innate qualities of your beautiful soul, had the same surname as me . . .'

Mr Golyadkin frowned.

'. . . with the same surname and from the same place as me I decided to come and familiarize you with my painful position.'

'Very good, very good. But really, I don't know what to say to you,' Mr Golyadkin replied in an embarrassed voice. 'Well, let's talk after dinner.'

The guest bowed, dinner was brought. Petrushka laid the table and guest and host proceeded to satisfy their appetites. The dinner did not last long as they were both in a hurry – the host because he wasn't quite himself and felt ashamed that the dinner was poor – ashamed partly because he wanted to feed his guest well and partly because he wanted to show that he did not live like a pauper. For his part the guest was extremely embarrassed and confused. Once, having helped himself to a slice of bread and eaten it, he was afraid to stretch his hand out for another slice, was ashamed to take the best portions and constantly claimed that he wasn't at all hungry, that the dinner was excellent, that he for his part was perfectly happy and would be grateful to him to his dying day. When dinner was over Mr Golyadkin lit his pipe and offered his guest another that he kept for friends; both sat facing each other and the guest began the story of his adventures.

Mr Golyadkin Junior's tale lasted some three or four hours. The story of his adventures consisted, incidentally, of the most trifling, most inconsequential and, one might say, meagre incidents. It told of service in some provincial law-courts, of prosecutors, lawyers and court presidents, of office intrigues, of a sudden change of superiors; it told of how Mr Golyadkin Junior had suffered through no fault of his own; of his aged aunt, Pelageya Semyonovna; of how, in consequence of various intrigues initiated by his enemies, he had lost his position and had walked to St Petersburg; of his life of drudgery and misery here in St Petersburg; of his lengthy and fruitless search for a job; of how he had run through all his money, spending his last copeck to live from hand to mouth; of how he had virtually lived out on the street, eaten stale bread washed down with his tears, and had slept on bare floorboards; and finally, how some kind person had gone to a lot of trouble on his behalf, given him a letter of introduction and magnanimously fixed him up with a new job. Mr Golyadkin's guest wept as he told his tale and wiped away the tears with a blue check handkerchief that strongly resembled oilcloth. He concluded by completely unburdening himself to Mr Golyadkin and confessed that for the time being not only did he not have the wherewithal to live and settle himself in decent lodgings somewhere, but couldn't even afford to equip himself with a uniform. He added that he couldn't even scrape enough money together for a pair of rotten old boots and that his uniform coat had been borrowed from someone for a short time.

Mr Golyadkin became quite emotional and was genuinely

touched. Moreover, despite the utter triviality of his guest's story, every word of it fell on his heart like manna from heaven. The fact was, Mr Golyadkin had shed his last doubts, allowing his heart to feel joyous and free and – finally – he mentally branded himself a fool. It was all so natural! And was there any reason to distress himself so, to press panic buttons? Yes, to be sure, there was in fact that one very ticklish matter, but it wasn't too calamitous: it couldn't tarnish a man's reputation, damage his pride or ruin his career when you were innocent and where nature herself had taken a hand in matters. Besides, his guest was asking for protection, had wept and accused fate, had appeared so artless, so lacking in malice or cunning, so pitiful and insignificant, and apparently he too was perhaps ashamed now – although possibly in another respect – by the strange resemblance of his face to his host's. His conduct was proper in the highest degree, his only concern to please his host and he looked like a man tormented by pangs of conscience and conscious of his guilt before another person. If, for instance, the discussion turned on some doubtful point, the guest immediately concurred with Mr Golyadkin's opinion. If, for instance, he mistakenly advanced an opinion contrary to Mr Golyadkin's and noticed his slip, he would waste no time correcting what he'd said, would explain himself and immediately give him to understand that he held the same views as his host, that he thought like him and looked upon everything in exactly the same way. In brief, the guest made every conceivable effort to win Mr Golyadkin over, so that the latter finally decided that he must be a most amiable person in all respects. Meanwhile tea was served; it was after eight. Mr Golyadkin was in excellent spirits. He cheered up, relaxed, let himself go a little and then he finally embarked on the liveliest and most entertaining conversation with his guest. At times, when in a cheerful mood, Mr Golyadkin was fond of relating interesting items of news. And so it was now: he told his guest a great deal about the Capital, its amusements and beauties, its theatres and clubs; about Bryullov's latest painting;[25] of the two Englishmen who travelled to St Petersburg expressly to take a look at the wrought-iron railings of the Summer Gardens[26] and then went straight home again; about his work, about Olsufy Ivanovich and Andrey Filippovich; about how Russia was approaching perfection hourly, how belles-lettres were flourishing. He related an anecdote he had recently read about in the *Northern Bee*[27] concerning an extraordinarily powerful constricting snake in India; and lastly about Baron Brambeus,[28] and so on and so on. In brief, Mr Golyadkin was perfectly satisfied, firstly because his mind was completely at ease; secondly because far from fearing his enemies he was even now prepared to challenge all of them to a decisive showdown; thirdly because he himself was giving someone protection in his own right and doing a good deed. In his heart, however, he admitted that he was not entirely happy just then, that there was still a tiny worm lurking inside him which, although minute, was gnawing away at him even now. He was much tormented by the memory of the previous evening at Olsufy Ivanovich's. What would he have given for certain of yesterday's events never to have happened! 'Still, never mind!' our hero finally concluded and he firmly resolved to behave well in future and never make such awful blunders again. As Mr Golyadkin was completely relaxed and suddenly felt almost completely happy, he even had the urge to enjoy life a little. Petrushka brought rum and they made some punch. Guest and host drained a glass each, then another. The guest became even more amiable than before and for his part gave more than one proof of his forthright and easy-going, happy-go-lucky nature, sharing in Mr Golyadkin's joy to the full and apparently rejoicing in his joy alone, considering him his sole and true benefactor. Taking up pen and a small sheet of paper, he requested Mr Golyadkin not to look at what he was going to write and when he had finished showed his host all he had written. It turned out to be a rather sentimental quatrain, written in exquisite style and handwriting and evidently his amiable guest's own composition. The lines read as follows:

> If e'r you should me forget,
> I'll never forget thee;
> Whatever in life may happen yet
> Never forget me![29]

With tears in his eyes Mr Golyadkin embraced his guest and finally, overcome with deep emotion, initiated his guest into some of his most intimate secrets and confidences, laying great emphasis on Andrey Filippovich and Klara Olsufyevna. 'Well, it seems that you and I will get on famously, Yakov Petrovich,' our hero told his guest. 'You and I, Yakov Petrovich, will get on like a house on fire, live like brothers. We'll fox them, old chap, we'll be sly – we'll be sly together! We'll be the ones to do the intriguing, to spite them – yes, we'll start intrigues to spite them ... we'll start intrigues to spite them. And don't trust any of them. I know you very well, Yakov Petrovich and I understand your character. You'd go and tell them everything, you honest soul! But you must steer clear of all of them, my friend.' In complete agreement the guest thanked Mr Golyadkin and finally he too shed tears.

'Do you know, Yasha,'[30] continued Mr Golyadkin in a weak voice, trembling with emotion, 'come and live with me for a while – or for good. We'll get along so well. What do you think, old chap, eh? Now, don't you be embarrassed or complain about this strange situation between us. It's sinful to complain, old chap – it's Nature! Mother Nature is bounteous, that's what, Yasha! I'm telling you this because I love you, love you like a brother. We'll be cunning, too, Yasha, we'll lay a few traps of our own and score off them.' Finally the punch reached a third and fourth brotherly glass and Mr Golyadkin began to experience a twofold sensation: one that he was extraordinarily happy and the other that he could no longer stand on his feet. Of course, the guest was invited to stay the night. A bed was somehow made up from two rows of chairs. Mr Golyadkin Junior announced that under a friendly roof even bare boards make a soft bed, that he could in fact sleep anywhere he had to, with humility and gratitude, that now he was in paradise and that, finally, he had been through much grief and misfortune, had seen everything, suffered everything and – who knew what the future held – would perhaps have to endure much more. Mr Golyadkin Senior objected to this and argued that one must put one's whole trust in God. The guest agreed entirely, adding that there was of course no one like God. Here

Mr Golyadkin Senior observed that in a certain respect the
Turks were right in invoking the name of God even in their
sleep. And then, without concurring with the aspersions of
certain scholars directed at the Turkish prophet Muhammed
and recognizing him as a great politician in his own way, Mr
Golyadkin embarked on a very interesting description of an
Algerian barber's shop that he had read about in some miscel-
lany. Guest and host laughed a great deal at the ingenuousness
of the Turks, but they could not help being duly amazed at
their opium-induced fanaticism . . . At length the guest started
undressing and Mr Golyadkin, partly because in the goodness
of his heart he thought that his guest probably didn't have a
decent shirt, vanished behind the partition to avoid embarrass-
ing someone who had already suffered enough and partly to
reassure himself as far as possible about Petrushka, to sound
him out, to cheer him up – if he could – and be nice to the man,
so that everyone would be happy and that there should be no
ill feeling. Petrushka, it must be said, still somewhat embarrassed Mr Golyadkin.

'You go to bed now, Petrushka,' Mr Golyadkin said gently
as he went into his servant's quarters. 'You go to bed now and
wake me up tomorrow at eight. Do you understand, Petrushka?'

Mr Golyadkin spoke unusually gently and kindly, but
Petrushka remained silent. Just then he happened to be fussing
around his bed and didn't even turn to face his master, which
he ought to have done, if only out of respect.

'Did you hear, Petrushka?' continued Mr Golyadkin. 'Go to
bed now and wake me up tomorrow at eight. Got it?'

'Well, of course I'll remember – what's the problem?'
Petrushka grumbled to himself.

'All right then, Petrushka, I only mentioned it to make you
feel happy and relaxed, too. We're all happy now, so I want you
to be happy and relaxed as well. And now I wish you goodnight, Petrushka. Sleep, Petrushka, get some sleep. We all have
work to do . . . And don't start thinking things, old chap . . .'

Mr Golyadkin was about to go on, but stopped. 'Isn't that a
bit too much?' he wondered. 'Haven't I gone too far? It's always
the same with me – always overdoing things.' Highly dissatisfied

with himself our hero left Petrushka. What was more, he was
rather hurt by Petrushka's rudeness and stubbornness. 'You try
to be nice to that good-for-nothing, you go out of your way
to show that good-for-nothing some regard, but he doesn't
appreciate it,' thought Mr Golyadkin. 'But his sort all have that
same vile way with them.' A trifle unsteady on his feet he
returned to his room and when he saw that his guest had gone
to bed he sat down for a moment on the bed. 'Come on,
own up, Yasha,' he started whispering, wagging his head. 'You
scoundrel, Yasha, you're the one who's at fault, after all, you're
my namesake, you know . . .' he continued, taunting his guest
in rather familiar fashion. Finally, after wishing him a friendly
goodnight, Mr Golyadkin retired to bed. Meanwhile the guest
started snoring. In his turn Mr Golyadkin climbed into bed,
chuckling and whispering to himself: 'You're drunk tonight,
Yakov Petrovich my dear, you old rogue, you Golyadka – what
a name you've got!! Well, what are you so pleased about?
Tomorrow you'll be crying your eyes out, you great sniveller!
What am I to do with you?' Just then a rather strange sensation,
something like doubt or remorse, seemed to flood Mr Golyadkin's whole being. 'I really let myself go,' he thought, 'and
now there's ringing in my head and I'm drunk. Just couldn't
control yourself, you damned fool! And he spun me a whole
yarn and was preparing to play tricks on me, the rotter! Of
course, to forgive and forget insults is the first of virtues, but
it's still very bad, that's what it is!' Here Mr Golyadkin got up,
took a candle, and went once more on tiptoe to have another
look at his sleeping guest. For a long time he stood over him,
deep in thought. 'Not a very pretty picture. A caricature – a
pure caricature – that's all you can say about it!'

At last Mr Golyadkin really did retire for the night. His head
was splitting and filled with ringing and buzzing. Gradually
he began to doze off . . . doze off . . . he tried to think about
something, to recall something very interesting, to resolve
some very important, ticklish matter, but he could not. Sleep
descended on his miserable head and he slept the way people
usually sleep who are unused to the sudden consumption of
five glasses of punch at some friendly gathering.

CHAPTER VIII

Next day Mr Golyadkin awoke at eight o'clock as usual; once awake he immediately recalled all the events of the previous evening – he remembered them and he frowned ... 'Made a complete fool of myself yesterday,' he thought, sitting up slightly in bed and glancing at his guest's bed. But how great his astonishment on finding that not only his guest but even the bed on which he had slept had gone from the room! 'What's going on?' Mr Golyadkin almost shrieked. 'What's happened? What on earth's the meaning of this new state of affairs?' While Mr Golyadkin was gaping in open-mouthed bewilderment at the empty space, the door creaked and in came Petrushka with the tea tray. 'But where is he, where on earth is he?' our hero muttered barely audibly, pointing to the place allotted to his guest the night before. At first Petrushka did not answer or even look at his master, but peered into the right-hand corner, so that Mr Golyadkin felt obliged to look into the corner on the right. But then after a silence Petrushka replied in his gruff and husky voice: 'The Master's not home.'

'You fool, *I'm* your master, Petrushka!' exclaimed Mr Golyadkin in a faltering voice, staring wide-eyed at his servant.

Petrushka made no reply, but gave Mr Golyadkin such a look that Mr Golyadkin blushed to the roots of his hair, a look of such insulting reproachfulness that it was tantamount to nothing less than sheer abuse. Mr Golyadkin lost heart, as they say. At length Petrushka announced that the *other one* had left about an hour and a half ago, as he wouldn't wait. Of course, this reply was both probable and plausible. Petrushka was obviously not lying and his insolent look and the words the *other one* were merely the consequence of the whole beastly episode. All the same, he understood, albeit only vaguely, that something was amiss and that fate held in store for him some other present – and not in the least agreeable at that. 'Good, we'll see,' he thought, 'we'll see, we'll get to the bottom of all this, all in good time. Oh Lord!' he moaned in conclusion, already in quite a different tone of voice. 'Why did I have to invite him? What point was there in doing that? I'm well and truly putting myself into their thieves' noose and tightening it around my own neck. Oh, what a head, what a head! Just can't help blurting things out like some urchin, like some clerk, some low-ranking riff-raff, some spineless creature, some lousy dishcloth – you gossip, you old woman! . . . Saints preserve us! And the verses he wrote, the rogue, declaring his love for me! how could I . . . I mean to say . . . ? How can I show that scoundrel the door as politely as possible, should he return? It goes without saying that there's lots of different turns of phrase, there's many ways. I could say: "Well, it's like this, what with my meagre salary . . ." or I could scare him by saying: "Taking this and that into account . . . I'm obliged to express myself this way . . . you must pay half for food and lodging and give me the money in advance." Hm! No, blast it, that won't do! It would sully my reputation. It's not in the least tactful. Perhaps I could somehow do it like this: I could get Petrushka to spite him, to neglect him, to be rude to him somehow and so get rid of him – that way I could play one off against the other . . . No, damn it, no! It's dangerous And again, if you look at it from that viewpoint, it's really not good at all. Not good at all! So what if he doesn't come? Would that be a bad thing? I gave the game away to him yesterday. Oh, it's bad, it's really a very bad business. Oh, what a head I've got, what a damned head I've got! I can't seem to knock what I need to into my noddle, can't knock any sense into it. Well, what if he does come and he refuses? But God grant he will come! I'd be so terribly glad if he did come!' Such were Mr Golyadkin's reflections as he swallowed his tea, constantly glancing at the clock on the wall. 'A quarter to nine – it's really time I was off. But something's going to happen – what will it be? I'd like to know what's so particularly special that's being concealed here – I mean the aim and the objective, the various catches there? It would be good to know exactly what these people are aiming at and what their first step will be . . .' Mr Golyadkin could bear it no longer, threw down his pipe half-smoked, dressed and set off for the office, eager to nip the danger in the bud and to reassure himself by actually being there personally. And there *was* danger: that he knew himself, that there was danger. 'So, now we'll get to the bottom of this,' said Mr Golyadkin, removing his overcoat and galoshes in the vestibule. 'Now we'll fathom it all out.' Having decided on this course of action our hero tidied his clothes, assumed a formal, official air and was about to pass through into the next room when suddenly, right in the doorway, he collided with his friend and acquaintance of yesterday. Mr Golyadkin Junior appeared not to notice Mr Golyadkin Senior, although their noses nearly met. Mr Golyadkin Junior seemed terribly busy and was breathlessly dashing off somewhere. He had such an official, business-like air that anyone could see that he had been 'sent on a special mission'.

'Ah, it's you, Yakov Petrovich,' said our hero, grabbing last night's guest by the arm.

'Later, later . . . please excuse me and tell me later,' cried Mr Golyadkin Junior, pushing forward.

'If you don't mind, but it seems you wanted, Yakov Petrovich, to . . .'

'What's that? Do hurry up and explain . . .' Here Mr Golyadkin's guest of yesterday halted as if he were being forced against his will and he put one ear right up to Mr Golyadkin's nose.

'I must say, I'm most surprised at this reception, Yakov Petrovich, a reception I never could have expected.'

'For everything there is an official procedure. Report to His Excellency's secretary and then make proper application to the gentleman in charge of the office. Do you have a request?'[31]

'Well, I don't know, Yakov Petrovich! You do amaze me, Yakov Petrovich! Either you don't recognize me or you're having your little joke in keeping with your innate cheerfulness.'

'Oh, it's you!' said Mr Golyadkin Junior, as if he'd only now recognized Mr Golyadkin Senior. 'So, it's you. Well, now, did you have a good night?' Here Mr Golyadkin Junior gave a faint smile, a formal, official smile, not at all the kind he should have given (because, after all, he owed Mr Golyadkin a debt of gratitude) and after that formal, official smile he added that for his part he was absolutely delighted Mr Golyadkin had slept well. Then he bent forward slightly, shuffled his feet, looked right, then left, glanced down at the floor, headed for a side door and rapidly whispered that he was 'on a special mission', darting into the next room and disappearing in a flash.

'Well, there's a nice thing!' whispered our hero, momentarily stunned. 'There's a pretty kettle of fish! So that's how things are!' At this point, Mr Golyadkin felt shivers running up and down his spine. 'However,' he said to himself as he made his way to his department, 'I've been talking about such circumstances for ages. I had the feeling long ago that he was on a special mission – yes, only yesterday I said that man was being sent on a special mission . . .'

'Have you finished that document you were working on yesterday, Yakov Petrovich?' Anton Antonovich Setochkin asked Mr Golyadkin, as he took his seat next to him. 'Do you have it here?'

'It's here,' whispered Mr Golyadkin, looking at his head clerk with a rather lost expression.

'Right, sir. I'm saying this as Andrey Filippovich has asked for it twice already. His Excellency will be wanting it before you know it.'

'It's all right, it's finished, sir.'

'Oh, that's good, sir!'

'I, Anton Antonovich, think I have always performed my duties conscientiously and I've always taken great care over the tasks entrusted me by my superiors. I've always dealt with them most zealously.'

'Yes . . . but what are you driving at?'

'Nothing, Anton Antonovich . . . I only want to explain that I . . . that is . . . I wanted to declare that sometimes disloyalty and envy spare no one in their quest for their disgusting daily sustenance.'

'Forgive me, but I don't quite follow. I mean, to whom are you referring?'

'All I meant, Anton Antonovich, was that I keep to the straight and narrow, that I despise deviousness, that I'm not one for intrigues – if you'll permit me to express myself this way – and I can very justly be proud of this.'

'Yes, that's so, and as far as I understand it I admit the full justice of your argument . . . But allow me to point out, Yakov Petrovich, that in good society personal remarks about other people are not altogether permissible. For example, I'm prepared to tolerate them behind my back, since who isn't reviled behind his back! But, say what you like, I shall not allow anyone to be insolent to my face, my dear sir. I, dear sir, have turned grey in government service and I shall not allow anyone to be insolent to me in my twilight years . . .'

'No, Anton Antonovich, don't you see, Anton Antonovich, it appears, Anton Antonovich, you haven't quite understood. I, if you don't mind, Anton Antonovich, can only consider it an honour on my part . . .'

'Well then, I beg you to forgive me, too. I was trained in the old school. It's too late for me to learn these newfangled ways of yours. Up to now I think my grasp of things has been good enough to serve my country. As you well know, sir, I have a medal for twenty years' irreproachable service . . .'

'Yes, I appreciate that, Anton Antonovich, for my part I really do appreciate all that . . . But that wasn't what I meant . . . I was talking about a mask, Anton Antonovich . . .'

'A mask, sir?'

'I mean . . . again you . . . I'm afraid you'll misinterpret my meaning, that is, the meaning of what I've just been saying, as you yourself put it, Anton Antonovich. I'm only developing the theory, putting forward the idea, Anton Antonovich, that people who wear masks aren't at all rare now and that nowadays it's hard to recognize the man beneath the mask.'

'Well, you know, it's not so hard. Sometimes it's even fairly easy, sometimes you don't have to look very hard . . .'

'No . . . I'm talking of myself, Anton Antonovich, I'm talking of myself, for example: when I say that I wear a mask, it's only when I need to; that is, only for carnivals or festive gatherings, speaking literally. But I don't wear one every day in front of people, speaking in a different and more cryptic sense. That's what I wanted to say, Anton Antonovich.'

'Very well, but let's leave all that for the moment. Besides, I just don't have the time right now,' said Anton Antonovich, rising from his seat and collecting some papers from a report for His Excellency. 'I fancy this little business of yours will be cleared up in a very short time. You yourself will see whom you should blame, whom you should accuse, but in the meantime I humbly beg you to spare me any further private discussions and gossip that might be detrimental to work . . .'

'But no, Anton Antonovich,' Mr Golyadkin began telling the retreating Antonovich, paling slightly. 'I, Anton Antonovich, never thought that. "What *is* this? What winds are blowing here and what's the meaning of this new obstacle?" our hero, now left alone, kept thinking to himself. At that very moment when our forlorn and half-crushed hero was preparing to solve this new question, there came a noise, a surge of activity from the next room. The door opened and there appeared in the doorway a breathless Andrey Filippovich, who only a few moments before had gone to His Excellency's room on some business; he called to Mr Golyadkin. Realizing what it was all about·and reluctant to keep Andrey Filippovich waiting, Mr Golyadkin leapt from his seat and as was fitting started frantic- ally busying himself putting the required portfolio in order and prepared to follow both portfolio and Andrey Filippovich into His Excellency's study. Suddenly, virtually from under the arm of Andrey Filippovich, who was standing at that moment right in the doorway, in flew Mr Golyadkin Junior, bustling, breath- less and exhausted from his exertions, and with an important, determined air as he rolled right up to Mr Golyadkin Senior: this attack was the last thing he was expecting.

'The papers, Yakov Petrovich, the papers . . . His Excellency is pleased to inquire if you have them ready,' twittered Mr Golyadkin Senior's friend under his breath. 'Andrey Filippovich is waiting for you . . .'

'I know he's waiting, without you telling me,' retorted Mr Golyadkin Senior in a rapid whisper.

'No, Yakov Petrovich, I . . . didn't mean that. That's not what I meant at all, Yakov Petrovich. I sympathize and I'm moved by genuine concern . . .'

'From which I most humbly implore you to spare me . . . Now, if you don't mind . . .'

'Of course, you'll put them in a folder, Yakov Petrovich, and insert a marker on the third page, if you don't mind, Yakov Petrovich ...'

'If you don't mind, please let me ...'

'But there's a blot here, Yakov Petrovich. Didn't you notice that blot?'

Just then Andrey Filippovich summoned Mr Golyadkin a second time.

'I'm coming right away, Andrey Filippovich ... I'm right here ... just a little ... Do you understand plain Russian, my dear sir?'

'It's best to get it off with a penknife, Yakov Petrovich, you'd better leave it to me: don't touch it yourself, Yakov Petrovich, rely on me ... I can get most of it off with a penknife ...'

Andrey Filippovich summoned Mr Golyadkin for the third time.

'Yes, for heaven's sake – but where is there a blot? There doesn't appear to be any blot at all.'

'And it's a really huge one ... there it is! There, that's where I saw it ... allow me ... just allow me, Yakov Petrovich, I'll do it out of concern for you, Yakov Petrovich, with a penknife, from a pure heart. There, it's done!'

And then, quite unexpectedly, without rhyme or reason, Mr Golyadkin Junior, having got the better of Mr Golyadkin Senior in the momentary conflict that had arisen between them – and at any rate quite contrary to the latter's wishes – Mr Golyadkin Junior seized possession of the document requested by his superiors and instead of scraping it with a penknife from a 'pure heart' as he had treacherously assured Mr Golyadkin Senior, quickly rolled it up, stuffed it under his arm and in two bounds was at the side of Andrey Filippovich, who hadn't noticed a single one of his pranks, and shot off with him into the director's office. Mr Golyadkin Senior remained as if rooted to the spot, holding the penknife and apparently preparing to scrape something off with it ...

Our hero had not yet fully grasped his new situation. He had not come to his senses. He had felt the blow, but thought it was of no importance. In terrible, indescribable anguish he tore

himself from where he was standing and charged straight into
the Director's office, beseeching heaven on the way that everything might somehow turn out for the best and would be all
right ... In the last room before the Director's he bumped
straight into Andrey Filippovich and his namesake. They were
both already coming back; Mr Golyadkin moved to one side.
Andrey Filippovich was talking cheerfully and smiling; Mr
Golyadkin Senior's namesake was also smiling, fussing about,
tripping along at a respectful distance from Andrey Filippovich,
whispering something in his ear with a rapturous look, to which
Andrey Filippovich nodded in the most favourable fashion. Our
hero grasped the whole situation in a flash. The fact was, his
work (as he learnt later) had almost exceeded His Excellency's
expectations and had been handed in by the deadline, in good
time. His Excellency was extremely satisfied. It was even
rumoured that His Excellency had said thank you to Mr Golyadkin Junior – a very warm thank you – had said that he would
remember it when the occasion arose, and that he would not
fail to forget it ... Of course, Mr Golyadkin's first reaction was
to protest, to protest with all his might, as much as was humanly
possible. Almost beside himself and pale as death, he rushed to
Andrey Filippovich. But when Andrey Filippovich heard that
Mr Golyadkin's business was private, he refused to listen, flatly
pointing out in no uncertain terms that he didn't have a moment
to spare even for his own needs.

The brusqueness of his refusal and chilly tone stunned Mr
Golyadkin. 'Perhaps I'd better try a different approach ... I'd
better go to Anton Antonovich,' he thought. But unfortunately
for Mr Golyadkin, Anton Antonovich was not available either:
he too was busy somewhere. 'So, it wasn't without something
in mind that he asked to be spared explanations and gossip!'
our hero thought. 'So that's what the cunning old fox was
driving at! In that case I'll simply be bold and appeal to His
Excellency.'

Still pale and feeling that his head was in complete turmoil,
thoroughly perplexed as to what exactly he should decide upon,
Mr Golyadkin sat down on a chair. 'It would be much better if
all this were simply a trifling matter,' he constantly thought. 'In

fact, such a fishy business was even highly improbable. Firstly it was all nonsense and secondly it couldn't possibly happen. Most likely it was a trick of the imagination, or something different had happened from what really was the case; or perhaps I must have been walking along . . . and somehow completely mistook myself for someone else . . . in short the whole thing's absolutely impossible.'

No sooner had Mr Golyadkin decided that the whole thing was absolutely impossible than Mr Golyadkin Junior suddenly came flying into the room, with papers in both hands and under his arm. Having addressed some necessary words to Andrey Filippovich, exchanging a few more with someone else, politely greeting another, treating another with easy familiarity, Mr Golyadkin Junior, having on the face of it no time at all to waste, already seemed about to leave the room, but fortunately for Mr Golyadkin Senior he stopped right at the door to talk to two or three young clerks who happened to be standing there. Mr Golyadkin Senior rushed straight towards him. The moment Mr Golyadkin Junior spotted Mr Golyadkin Senior's manoeuvre, he immediately started looking around in panic to see where he could slip away the fastest. But our hero had already grabbed his previous evening's guest by the sleeve. The clerks surrounding the two titular counsellors fell back and awaited events with considerable curiosity. The old titular counsellor Mr Golyadkin Senior understood that favourable opinion was not on his side and he understood very well that they were all intriguing against him, which made it all the more imperative for him to make a stand. It was the moment of truth.

'Well, sir?' asked Mr Golyadkin Junior, looking rather brazenly at Mr Golyadkin Senior.

Mr Golyadkin Senior was barely breathing.

'I don't know, my dear sir,' he began, 'how to make you understand how strangely you're behaving towards me.'

'Well sir, do go on.' Here Mr Golyadkin Junior looked around and winked at the surrounding clerks, as if giving them to understand that the comedy was just about to begin.

'The insolence and shamelessness of your conduct, my dear sir, in the present circumstances, denounce you more than any words of mine could do. Don't bank on the success of the game you're playing – it's a rotten one.'

'Well, please do tell me how you slept, Yakov Petrovich,' asked Mr Golyadkin Junior, looking Mr Golyadkin Senior straight in the eye.

'You, my dear sir, are forgetting yourself,' said our titular counsellor, utterly baffled and barely feeling the floor beneath him. 'I hope you will change your tone . . .'

'My little sweetie-pie!' Mr Golyadkin Junior said, pulling a somewhat unseemly face at Mr Golyadkin Senior. And suddenly, right out of the blue, under the guise of a caress, he pinched his rather chubby right cheek between two of his fingers. Our hero reddened like fire. The moment Mr Golyadkin Senior's friend noticed that his adversary, shaking in every limb, red as a lobster and exasperated beyond all measure, might even decide on a real attack he in turn immediately forestalled him in a most shameless manner. After pinching his cheek twice more, tickling him a couple of times and toying with him in this way for a few more seconds as he stood there motionless and mad with rage, to the not inconsiderable amusement of the young clerks standing around, Mr Golyadkin Junior rounded things off with the most startling effrontery by giving Mr Golyadkin Senior's rather rotund belly a prod and saying with the most venomous leer that hinted at much: 'You're a tricky customer, Yakov Petrovich old chap, you're a tricky customer. We'll be cunning, you and I, we'll be cunning!' And then, before our hero had time to make even the slightest recovery from this latest assault, Mr Golyadkin Junior (after directing only a preliminary grin at the surrounding spectators) suddenly assumed the most business-like, formal and official air, looked down at the floor, huddled up and shrank into himself and after rapidly saying he was 'on a special mission' jerked his stumpy legs into action and darted into the next room. Our hero couldn't believe his eyes and he was still in no condition to come to his senses . . .

But at last he did come to his senses. Realizing in a flash that he was finished, that he had perished, been destroyed in a sense, that he had disgraced himself, sullied his reputation, that he

had been humiliated and made a laughing-stock in the presence
of disinterested parties, that he had been treacherously abused
by the person whom only yesterday he had considered his
greatest and most trustworthy friend, that he had finally fallen
flat on his face – and how! – Mr Golyadkin charged off in
pursuit of his enemy. At that moment he no longer wanted to
think of those who had witnessed the outrage perpetrated on
him. 'They're all hand in glove,' he told himself, 'they all stand
up for one another and each sets the other against me.' However, after about a dozen steps our hero clearly saw that any
pursuit was vain and futile and so he turned back. 'You won't
get away with it!' he thought. 'I'll trump you, all in good time,
you'll get your just deserts!' With fierce sangfroid and the most
energetic determination Mr Golyadkin returned to his chair
and sat down. 'You won't get away with it!' he repeated. No
longer was it a question of some kind of passive self-defence:
there was something decisive and aggressive in the air and
anyone who saw Mr Golyadkin just then, flushed, barely able
to contain his agitation, stabbing his pen into the inkwell, and
the fury with which he set about scribbling on the paper, might
have concluded in advance that the matter would not rest there,
nor could it fizzle out in some old-womanish way. In the depths
of his soul he had made one resolution and deep in his heart he
vowed to carry it out. If truth be told, he didn't quite know
what steps to take – rather, he had no idea at all. But it didn't
matter, it was all right! 'You will achieve nothing by imposture
and insolence in this day and age, my dear sir! Imposture and
insolence lead to no good – only to the gallows. Only Grishka
Otrepyev,[32] my dear sir, succeeded by imposture, deceiving the
blind populace, but even then not for long.' In spite of this last
circumstance Mr Golyadkin decided to wait until masks fell
from certain faces and something would come to light. To
achieve this it was first necessary for office hours to finish as
soon as possible and until that time our hero proposed to
undertake nothing. And then, when the working day was over,
he would take a certain step. Then he would know how to act
and, after taking that step, how to organize his whole campaign
in order to shatter the horn of pride and crush the serpent that

gnawed the dust in impotent scorn. To be used like a rag for people to wipe their dirty boots on – that he could not allow. To that he could not agree, particularly in the present circumstances. But for that last outrage our hero might have taken courage, perhaps he might have decided to remain silent and not protest too strongly. He might have argued a little, complained, demonstrated that he was in the right and then yielded a little and then, perhaps, a little more – and then he would have given his complete agreement, especially when the opposing party had solemnly admitted that he was within his rights; and then perhaps he would even have made peace, would even been rather touched and – who could tell? – perhaps a new friendship would have sprung up – a firm, warm friendship, on an even broader basis than yesterday evening's, a friendship that might in the end have so eclipsed all the unpleasantness of that rather unseemly likeness between two people that both titular counsellors would have been absolutely delighted and would have lived to a ripe old age, and so on. To sum up: Mr Golyadkin was even beginning slightly to regret that he had stood up for himself and his rights, and in consequence had only run into unpleasantness. 'If only he'd given in,' wondered Mr Golyadkin, 'and said it was all a joke, I'd have forgiven him, I'd even have forgiven him all the more if only he'd admitted it out loud. But no, I won't let myself be used as a rag. I've never let such people use me as a boot-cloth and even less will I allow this depraved wretch to attempt it. I'm not a rag, my dear sir, oh no, I'm not a rag!' In short our hero had made up his mind. 'You yourself are to blame, my good sir,' he thought. So, he had decided to protest – and protest to the very last, with all his strength. That's the kind of man he was! He could not possibly agree to let himself be insulted – even less to be used as a rag – and least of all by some completely depraved person. But let us not argue about it, let us not argue. Perhaps if someone had so wanted, if someone had had an irresistible urge, for example, to turn Mr Golyadkin into a rag, then he might have done so without meeting any opposition and with impunity (Mr Golyadkin himself had been aware of this on occasions) and then the result would have been a rag and not a Golyadkin – yes, a rag, a disgusting filthy rag – but not an ordinary rag, though: this rag would have had its pride, this rag would have been endowed with animation and feelings, and even though those feelings would have been mute and hidden deep within the filthy folds of that rag, they would nonetheless have been feelings . . .

The hours seemed to drag past; finally it struck four. Shortly afterwards everyone got up, followed the head of the department and headed homewards. Mr Golyadkin mingled with the crowd. He was on the alert and did not let his quarry out of his sight. Finally our hero saw his friend run up to the office porters who were handing out the coats and in his usual blackguardly way was fidgeting around everyone while waiting for his. It was a moment for decision. Mr Golyadkin somehow managed to squeeze his way through the crowd and he too started fussing about for his overcoat, not wishing to fall behind. But Mr Golyadkin's friend and acquaintance was first to get his coat, for even here he had managed in his own fashion to wheedle, to suck up to everyone, to curry favour, whisper in people's ears and behave like a cad.

After throwing on his overcoat Mr Golyadkin Junior gave Mr Golyadkin Senior an ironic look, thus spiting him openly and brazenly and then, with his characteristic insolence, minced around the other clerks – most probably to leave a favourable impression – making a witty remark to one, whispering something to another, toadying politely to a third, directing a smile at a fourth, giving his hand to a fifth – and then flitting gaily down the stairs. Mr Golyadkin went after him and to his indescribable satisfaction overtook him on the last step and grabbed his coat collar. Mr Golyadkin Junior seemed somewhat dumbfounded and looked around with a lost air.

'What do you mean by this?' he finally whispered weakly to Mr Golyadkin.

'My dear sir, if you are in any way a decent gentleman I trust you will recall our friendly relations of yesterday,' said our hero.

'Ah yes. Well, what now? Did you sleep well?'

For a moment fury deprived Mr Golyadkin Senior of the power of speech.

'Yes, I did, but please allow me to tell you ... my dear sir, that you're playing a highly complicated game.'

'Who says so? It's my enemies who say that ... !' the self-styled Mr Golyadkin brusquely replied and suddenly freed himself from the real Mr Golyadkin's feeble grasp. Once free he dashed down the stairs, looked around and, seeing a cab driver, climbed into the droshky and in a flash disappeared from Mr Golyadkin Senior's view. Despairing and deserted by all, the titular counsellor looked around, but there were no other cabs. He tried to run, but his legs gave way beneath him. With an utterly downcast face, his mouth gaping, crushed, shrunken and helpless, he leaned against a lamp-post and there he stayed for several minutes, in the middle of the pavement. All was lost for Mr Golyadkin, it seemed ...

CHAPTER IX

It seemed that everything, even Nature herself, was up in arms against Mr Golyadkin; but he was still on his feet and unvanquished: yes, he felt that he was unvanquished. He was ready to do battle. He rubbed his hands together when he recovered from the initial shock with such feeling and energy that one might conclude from Mr Golyadkin's look alone that he would not surrender. However, danger was just around the corner, that was obvious; Mr Golyadkin sensed it too. But how was it to be tackled, that danger? That was the question. For one fleeting instant the thought flashed through Mr Golyadkin's mind: 'Why not leave things as they are and simply give up, withdraw from the scene? Why not? Well, it's nothing at all. I'll stand aside, as if it isn't me, I'll let it all pass. It's not me and that's the end of it. He'll keep to himself too and perhaps he'll give up too. Yes, he'll make up to me, the scoundrel, and then the swine will turn away and withdraw. That's it! But I'll win through by my humility. And where's the danger, in fact? Well, what danger? I'd like someone to show me the danger in all this. Such a piffling matter! Such an ordinary business ... !'

Here Mr Golyadkin stopped short. The words died on his lips. He even berated himself for thinking like that; he even convicted himself of meanness and cowardice on account of that thought. However, his cause had not got under way at all. He felt that it was at that moment an absolute necessity to decide on some course of action. He even felt that he would have paid anyone handsomely who could have told him what exactly he should decide upon. So, how could he guess? But there was no time for guessing. Just in case and in order not to waste time, he took a cab and flew home.

'Well, how do you feel now?' he wondered, addressing himself. 'How are you allowing yourself to feel now, Yakov Petrovich? What will you do? What will you do now, wretch that you are, scoundrel that you are? You've driven yourself into the ground and now you're crying, now you're snivelling!'

Thus Mr Golyadkin taunted himself as he was jolted up and down in the rickety vehicle. Rubbing salt in his wounds and taunting himself at that moment gave Mr Golyadkin a kind of profound pleasure almost amounting to voluptuousness. 'Well, if some magician were to come along, or if something official were to happen, so that they said: "Give up a finger of your right hand, Golyadkin, and we'll be quits, there won't be another Golyadkin and you can be happy – only minus a finger" – then I'd surrender it, surrender it without fail, without making a face! Oh, to hell with all this,' the despairing titular counsellor finally cried out. 'Why all this? Why precisely this, why this, as if nothing else were possible? Well, why did it have to happen? Everything was fine at first, everyone was happy and contented. But no, this had to happen! Well, talking won't get me anywhere – one has to act!'

And so, having almost come to a decision, Mr Golyadkin entered his flat, grabbed his pipe without a moment's delay and sucking on it for all he was worth and scattering puffs of smoke to right and left began running up and down the room in extreme agitation. Meanwhile Petrushka started laying the table. And then, having finally come to a decision, Mr Golyadkin suddenly abandoned his pipe, threw on his overcoat,

announced he would not be dining at home and charged out of
the flat. On the stairs a breathless Petrushka caught him up,
holding his forgotten hat. Mr Golyadkin took it and felt he
should say a word or two to justify himself a little in Petrushka's
eyes, so that Petrushka should not think anything in particular
of it, to the effect that he'd gone and forgotten his hat and so
on. But as Petrushka did not even want to look and immediately
went away, Mr Golyadkin put on his hat without any further
explanations and scurried downstairs, muttering to himself that
everything was for the best, perhaps, and that this business
would be settled somehow, although he was conscious, nonetheless, of a shivery sensation even in his heels; then he went
out into the street, took a cab and hurried off to Andrey
Filippovich's. 'But wouldn't tomorrow be better . . . ?' wondered Mr Golyadkin, reaching for the bell-pull at the door of
Andrey Filippovich's flat, 'and do I have anything special to
say? Well, there's nothing special about it. It's such a wretched
business, oh yes! All said and done, it's wretched, trifling – well,
almost trifling . . . yes, that's what it is, that's what the whole
thing is.' Suddenly Mr Golyadkin pulled the bell. It rang and
some footsteps were heard from within. At this point Mr Golyadkin even cursed himself, partly for his hastiness and his aud-
acity. The recent unpleasant incidents which Mr Golyadkin had
almost forgotten while at work, and his falling-out with Andrey
Filippovich, now came to mind. But it was already too late to
escape: the door opened. Fortunately for Mr Golyadkin he was
informed that Andrey Filippovich had not returned from the
office and he wasn't dining at home. 'I know where he dines –
near Izmaylovsky Bridge, that's where,' our hero thought, and
he was absolutely delighted. To the footman who inquired as
to what message he should give he replied: 'It's all right, my
friend, I, my friend, will come back later.' And he ran downstairs, even to a certain degree in high spirits. As he went out
into the street he decided to let the cab go and settled up with
the driver. When the latter asked for something extra, claiming:
'I've been waiting a long time, sir, and I didn't spare the horse
for Your Worship,' he even willingly gave him an extra five
copecks and proceeded on foot.

'Well now,' thought Mr Golyadkin, 'it's really the sort of business that can't be left just like that. However, if you think hard about it, think sensibly, then what is there to fuss about? Well, no, I'll keep repeating it – what is there to fuss about? Why should I suffer, struggle, toil and moil, work my fingers to the bone? Firstly, the thing's done and can't be undone . . . no, it can't be undone! Let's reason like this: a man comes along – along comes a man, with fairly good references, so to speak, said to be a capable civil servant, of good conduct, only he's poor and has had some nasty experiences in one way or the other – such scrapes! Well, I mean to say, poverty's no crime. Well, that's no fault of mine. And in fact what kind of nonsense is all this? He was suitable, happened to fit the job, nature created him the spitting image of another man, so that they're as like as two peas in a pod. So, why should they refuse to take him on because of that? If it's fate, if it's fate alone, if it's blind fortune that is to blame – well, should he then be treated like a dishcloth, shouldn't he be allowed to work? What justice would there be in that? He's poor, lost, frightened – it makes your heart ache – here compassion demands that he should be taken care of. Oh yes, fine superiors they would be if they argued the same way as I do – you old reprobate! I mean to say, that noddle of mine! At times there's enough stupidity there for ten put together . . . ! No, no! They did the right thing and deserve thanks for being charitable to that poor victim of misfortune . . . So . . . let's suppose, for example, that we were born twins, born so that we're twin brothers – that's all – that's it! Well, what of it? Why, it's all right! All the clerks can be trained to accept it and no outsider coming into the department would find anything unseemly or shocking about such a state of affairs. In fact, there's something even touching here. Yes – here's a thought: Divine Providence, so to speak, created two identical beings and the benevolent authorities, recognizing the hand of Providence, took the twins under their wing. 'Of course,' continued Mr Golyadkin, catching his breath and lowering his voice a little, 'of course . . . of course it would have been better – oh yes, it would – if this touching state of affairs had never happened, if there'd have been no twins either. Oh

to hell with it all! Was it necessary? Was there any pressing
need for it that brooked no delay? My goodness! These devils
have really stirred up trouble now. And that character of his,
though, he's got such a nasty, skittish way with him – he's so
frivolous, such a lickspittle, crawler – in fact, a real Golyadkin!
On top of this I dare say he'll behave badly and blacken my
name, the swine! So now I'm supposed to keep an eye on
him and look after him, if you please! I mean to say, what
punishment! Ah well, what of it? It doesn't matter at all. So,
he's a scoundrel, so this Golyadkin's a scoundrel – let him be a
scoundrel – the other one is honest. So, he'll be the scoundrel
and I'll be the honest one and they'll say that that Golyadkin's
a scoundrel, don't take any notice of him, don't mix him up
with the other – but this one's honest, virtuous, meek and mild,
always so reliable at work and worthy of promotion. That's
how it is! Well now, that's fine . . . but what if they . . . you
know . . . go and mix us up? Anything could happen with him
around! Oh, Lord preserve us! He'd supplant someone, that
scoundrel would supplant him, as if he were a piece of rag, and
he'd never stop even to consider that a man isn't a rag. Oh
heavens above! What misfortune.'

Reasoning and lamenting in this way Mr Golyadkin ran
along blindly, almost oblivious of where he was going. He came
to his senses on Nevsky Prospekt – and then only after bumping
so violently into some passer-by that he saw stars. Without
looking up Mr Golyadkin mumbled some apology and only
when the passer-by, having growled something not very compli-
mentary, was some distance away did he raise his head to see
where he was and how things were. After looking around and
finding that he happened to be right next to the same restaurant
where he had taken a rest while getting ready for Olsufy Ivanovich's dinner party, our hero was suddenly conscious of a
tweaking and pinching in his stomach and he remembered that
he had not dined and that there was no prospect of a dinner
party anywhere and therefore without wasting precious time
he dashed up the restaurant stairs to snatch a quick snack
without hanging about any longer. And although everything in
the restaurant was on the expensive side, this minor circum-

stance did not deter Mr Golyadkin on this occasion: he had no time to linger over such trifles now. In the brightly lit room a fairly large crowd of customers were standing at a counter piled high with an assortment of the various comestibles respectable people consume by way of a light snack. The waiter was hard pressed, hardly having time to pour drinks, serve, take money and give change. Mr Golyadkin waited his turn and as soon as it came modestly reached for a fish pasty. After going away to one corner, turning his back on the crowd and eating with great appetite, he returned to the waiter, put his plate on the table and, as he knew the price, took out a ten-copeck silver piece and left it on the counter, catching the waiter's eye as if to say: here's the money for one pasty.

'That'll be one rouble ten copecks,' the waiter said through his teeth.

Mr Golyadkin was really staggered.

'Are you talking to me . . . ? I . . . I . . . had one pasty only, I think.'

'You had eleven,' the waiter retorted with great assurance.

'You, as far as I can see, are mistaken. I believe I had only one.'

'I counted them. You had eleven. If you had them you must pay for them. We don't give anything away for nothing here.'

Mr Golyadkin was dumbstruck. 'What's going on – is someone casting a magic spell over me?' he thought. Meanwhile the waiter was awaiting Mr Golyadkin's decision. A crowd surrounded Mr Golyadkin; Mr Golyadkin had already felt in his pocket to take out the silver rouble, intending to settle up at once and withdraw from the scene to avoid further trouble. 'Well, if it's eleven then eleven it is,' he thought, turning as red as a lobster. 'Well, what of it, if eleven pasties were consumed? If a man's hungry he'll eat eleven; let him eat to his heart's content, it's nothing to wonder at or laugh at . . .' Suddenly something seemed to prick Mr Golyadkin. He looked up and at once understood the whole mystery, all the witchcraft: all his difficulties were at once resolved . . . In the doorway to the next room, almost directly behind the waiter's back and facing Mr Golyadkin, there in the doorway which until then our hero

had taken for a mirror, stood a man: there he stood, there stood
Mr Golyadkin in person, not the old Mr Golyadkin, not the
hero of our story, but another Mr Golyadkin, the new Mr
Golyadkin. Clearly this other Mr Golyadkin was in excellent
spirits. He was smiling, nodding and winking at the first Mr
Golyadkin, mincing a little and looking as if at the slightest
provocation he would efface himself, slip into the next room
and sneak out by a back door, get clean away and all pursuit
would be to no avail. In his hands was a piece of a tenth pasty
which, right before Mr Golyadkin's eyes, he consigned to his
mouth, smacking his lips with pleasure. 'He's passed himself
off as me, the blackguard!' thought Mr Golyadkin, flushing
fiery red with shame, 'he's not ashamed of doing it in public.
Can they see him? I don't think anyone's noticed.' Mr Golyadkin threw down his silver rouble as if he had burnt all his
fingers on it and ignoring the waiter's significantly insolent
smile, a smile of triumph and unruffled authority, extricated
himself from the crowd and dashed off without a backward
glance. 'Thank God he didn't compromise me completely!' Mr
Golyadkin Senior reflected. 'I must thank that villain – and fate
as well – that everything was settled without any trouble. Only,
that waiter was rude. Still, the man was within his rights. One
rouble ten copecks were owing, so he was within his rights.
"We don't give anything away here for nothing," he said. But
he could have been a little more polite, the layabout!'

All this was said by Mr Golyadkin as he went downstairs to
the porch. But on the last step he stopped as if rooted to the
spot and he blushed so furiously from a paroxysm of injured
pride that his eyes even filled with tears. After standing stock-
still for half a minute he suddenly stamped one foot with determination, leapt in one bound from the porch, ran into the street
without a backward glance and rushed off home to his flat in
Shestilavochnaya Street, gasping for breath, feeling no fatigue.
Once there, without even taking off his outer clothing – quite
contrary to his usual habit of making himself comfortable when
at home and without even the preliminary picking-up of his
pipe – he at once settled himself on the sofa, drew the inkstand
closer towards him, took a pen and sheet of notepaper and

started scribbling the following epistle, his hand shaking with inner agitation.

My dear sir, Yakov Petrovich!
Never would I have put pen to paper had not my circumstances and you yourself, my dear sir, compelled me to do so. Believe me that necessity alone obliged me to enter upon this kind of explanation with you and therefore I request you, above all, to consider this measure of mine not as a deliberate attempt to insult you, but as the inevitable consequence of those circumstances that now link us together.

'That sounds good, doesn't it, polite and proper and at the same time not without firmness and strength. I don't think he could possibly take offence at that. Besides, I'm within my rights,' mused Mr Golyadkin, reading over what he had written.

Your strange and unforeseen appearance, my dear sir, on a stormy night, after that boorish and unseemly behaviour towards me on the part of my enemies, whose names I pass over in silence out of the contempt I feel for them, sowed the seeds of all those misunderstandings that at present exist between us. Your pig-headed determination, my dear sir, to have your own way and forcibly to insinuate yourself into the circle of my existence and all my relationships in everyday life, transgresses even the limits prescribed by common courtesy alone and the norms of communal life. I consider there is no need to mention your appropriation of my documents and of my own good name, my dear sir, with the intention of currying favour with your superiors – favour you have not merited. I need hardly refer here to your calculated and offensive evasiveness in proffering the explanations that this matter has necessitated. Finally, so that nothing is left unsaid, I make no reference here to your recent peculiar – one might even say incomprehensible – behaviour towards me in the coffee-house. Far be it from me to complain about the futile loss of one rouble, but I cannot help but give full vent to my indignation when I recall your blatant intrusion, prejudicial to my honour and what is more in the presence of several personages who although not actually known to me are nonetheless people of the greatest refinement . . .

'Am I going too far?' wondered Mr Golyadkin. 'Isn't it a bit on the strong side? Isn't it being rather too touchy – that allusion to great refinement, for example? Well, it doesn't matter! I must show him firmness of character! However, in mitigation, I could flatter him and butter him up a little at the end. So, let's see . . .'

But I would not have thought of wearying you, my dear sir, with my letter, were I not firmly convinced that the nobility of your sentiments and your frank and straightforward character would indicate to you yourself the means of rectifying all omissions and restoring the status quo.

In full hope I dare to remain assured that you will not consider this letter in any sense offensive to you and at the same time will not refuse to let me have an explanation on this occasion in writing through the mediation of my manservant.

In anticipation I have the honour to remain
your obedient servant
Ya. Golyadkin

'Well now, that's all very good! The thing's done! So, it's even come to writing letters! But who is to blame? He himself is to blame; he himself drives a man to demand a written reply . . . I'm within my rights . . .'

Having read the letter through a last time, Mr Golyadkin folded and sealed it and summoned Petrushka. Petrushka appeared looking sleepy-eyed as usual and extremely annoyed about something.

'I want you to take this letter, old chap . . . do you understand?'

Petrushka said nothing.

'I want you to take it to the office. There you'll find Provincial Secretary[33] Vakhrameyev – he's duty officer today. Do you understand?'

'I understand.'

' "I understand"! Can't you say "I understand, *sir*?" Ask for

Secretary Vakhrameyev and tell him: "It's like this, so to speak,
my master sends his regards and humbly requests you to have
a look in our office address book – and find out where this
Titular Counsellor Golyadkin lives."'

Petrushka remained silent and Mr Golyadkin fancied he
could detect a smile.

'So, Petrushka, you'll ask for the address first and find out
where this new clerk Golyadkin is living.'

'Yes, sir!'

'You'll ask for the address and then you'll take this letter to
that address. Do you understand?

'I understand.'

'If there . . . well, where you're taking the letter, that gentlemen to whom you're giving the letter . . . this Golyadkin . . .
What are you laughing at, you idiot?'

'Why should I be laughing? I wasn't doing anything! What
have the likes of me to laugh at?'

'All right . . . Now, if this gentleman should ask how your
master is, if he's all right, what he's doing, you know, if he
starts questioning you, just keep your mouth shut and tell him:
"My master's all right, but he requests a personal, written reply
from you." Got it?'

'Got it.'

'So, tell him: "My master's all right and is just about to go
and visit someone. But he's asking for a written reply from
you." Understand?'

'I understand.'

'Well, off with you.'

'The bother I have with that idiot, too! All he can do is laugh
to himself. What's he laughing at? I'm in real trouble now –
just see what trouble I've landed myself in! But perhaps all will
turn out for the best . . . I bet that rogue will be hanging around
for a couple of hours now and then disappear somewhere. Just
can't send him anywhere. Oh, what a dreadful mess I'm in! Oh,
what trouble I'm in . . .'

Thus fully realizing the trouble he was in, Mr Golyadkin
decided to play a passive role for about two hours while waiting
for Petrushka. One hour he spent pacing the room and smoking,

then he abandoned his pipe and sat down with a book, then he
lay down for a while on the sofa and then he took his pipe
again, after which he started chasing around the room again.
Then he would have liked to reason it all out, but he could
reason absolutely nothing out. Finally, as the agony of his
passive role had reached its climax, Mr Golyadkin decided to
take a certain step. 'Petrushka won't be back for an hour,' he
pondered, 'so I can give the key to the porter and in the meantime I myself and ... well ... I can go and investigate the
matter. I can go and investigate on my own behalf.' Without
wasting time, hurrying to investigate the matter, Mr Golyadkin
took his hat, left the room, locked the door, went to the porter
to give him the key and a ten-copeck tip – for some reason Mr
Golyadkin had become unusually generous of late – and set off
to where he needed to go. First he went on foot to Izmaylovsky
Bridge; the walk took him about half an hour. On reaching his
destination he went straight into the courtyard of the house
that was so familiar and looked up at the windows of State
Counsellor Berendeyev's apartment. Except for three windows
with their red curtains drawn, the others were in darkness.
'Olsufy Ivanovich probably doesn't have any visitors today,'
mused Mr Golyadkin, 'everyone must be sitting at home on
their own now.' Trying to come to some sort of decision, Mr
Golyadkin stood for a time in the courtyard. But the decision
was not fated to be reached, for Mr Golyadkin evidently had a
change of mind, gave it all up as a bad job and returned to the
street. 'No, I shouldn't have come here. And what can I do here
anyway? I'd better ... er ... go now ... and investigate the
matter in person.' Having reached this decision, Mr Golyadkin
headed for the office. The walk was not short and, besides, it
was terribly muddy and huge flakes of wet snow were falling
heavily. But no difficulties seemed to exist for our hero at that
moment. True, he was soaked to the skin and he was not a little
bespattered with mud – 'that's how it is, but at the same time
the objective has been attained,' he thought. And in fact Mr
Golyadkin was already approaching his objective. The great
mass of the huge government building loomed dark before him
in the distance. 'Stop!' he suddenly thought. 'Where am I going

now and what shall I do here? Supposing I do find out where
he lives – in the meantime Petrushka will most likely have
returned with the reply. I'm only wasting precious time – I've
already wasted precious time. Well, not to worry, all this can
still be sorted out. But really, shouldn't I drop in on Vakhrameyev? But no! I can do that later. Damn, there was no need to
come out at all. But that's me all over – it's a knack of mine,
always jumping the gun, whether I need to or not . . . Hm . . .
what time is it? Must be nine by now. Petrushka might get back
and not find me at home. That was an extremely stupid thing
to do, going out. Oh dear, it's all such a bother!'

Frankly admitting to himself that he had acted extremely
stupidly, our hero ran back home to Shestilavochnaya Street;
he arrived tired and weary. He learned from the porter that
Petrushka had not yet condescended to put in an appearance.
'Ah well, just as I expected!' our hero reflected, 'but meanwhile
it's nine already. Ugh! What a lazy devil he is! Always getting
drunk somewhere. Good Lord! What a wretched day has
fallen to my unhappy lot!' Thus reflecting and lamenting, Mr
Golyadkin unlocked his room, got some light, undressed completely, lit a pipe and feeling weak, worn-out, dejected and
hungry, he lay down on his sofa to await Petrushka. The candle
burned down dimly, its light flickering on the walls . . . Mr
Golyadkin gazed and gazed and thought and thought – and
then he fell asleep, dead to the world.

It was already late when he awoke. The candle had burnt
right down, was smoking and about to go out altogether. Mr
Golyadkin jumped up with a start, roused himself and remembered everything, absolutely everything. From behind the
partition resounded Petrushka's heavy snores. Mr Golyadkin
rushed to the window – not a light anywhere. He opened the
window vent – all was quiet. It was as if the city had become
deserted, was sleeping. So, it must have been two or three in
the morning – and indeed it was: the clock behind the partition
exerted itself and struck two. Mr Golyadkin rushed behind the
partition.

Somehow, and not without a lengthy struggle, he managed
to rouse Petrushka and made him sit up in bed. At that moment

the candle went out completely. It was about ten minutes before Mr Golyadkin managed to find and light another. During this time Petrushka had succeeded in dropping off again. 'You scoundrel, you damned good-for-nothing!' exclaimed Mr Golyadkin, shaking him again. 'Are you getting up now, are you awake?' After half an hour's sustained effort Mr Golyadkin succeeded however in rousing his servant completely and dragging him out from behind the partition. Only then could our hero see that Petrushka was, as they say, drunk as a lord and could barely stand up.

'Damned layabout!' shouted Mr Golyadkin. 'You ruffian! You'll be the death of me! Oh God, what on earth has he done with the letter? My God . . . where is it? And why did I write it? Was there any need to? Got carried away, you idiot – you and your pride! Went in for pride, you did – now see where pride's landed you! There's pride for you – you scoundrel! Now, you! . . . what have you done with that letter, you criminal! Who did you give it to?'

'I didn't give any letter to anyone. I never had any letter – so there!'

Mr Golyadkin wrung his hands in despair.

'Now you listen, Pyotr, you listen to me!'

'I'm listening.'

'Where did you go? Answer me!'

'Where did I go? I went to see some nice people. Where else?'

'Oh God help me! Where did you go first? Did you go to the office . . . ? Now, you listen to me, Petrushka – you're drunk, aren't you?'

'Me drunk?! May I be struck down this minute . . . n-n-not a drop . . . that's . . .'

'No, no, it's all right if you're drunk . . . I was only asking. It's quite all right if you're drunk! I don't mind, Petrushka, I don't mind at all. Perhaps it's just slipped your mind for the moment and you'll remember everything. Come on, try and remember. Did you go and see that clerk Vakhrameyev or didn't you?'

'No, I didn't. There was no clerk with that name. Strike me down . . .'

'No, no, Pyotr! No, Petrushka, you know I don't mind! You can see for yourself that I don't . . . what of it? Well, it's cold and wet outside and you had a little drink – there's no harm in that. I'm not angry, old chap. I had a drop myself today . . . Now . . . please tell me, try and remember: did you see that clerk Vakhrameyev?'

'Well, to be honest, it was like this. I did go – strike me . . .'

'Good, Petrushka, it's good that you went. You can see I'm not angry,' continued our hero, encouraging his servant even more, patting his shoulder and smiling at him. 'Well, well, so you did have a little drop, you old devil! Put away about ten copecks' worth, didn't you? You cunning rogue! Well, that's all right by me, you can see that I'm not angry, old chap . . . You can see I'm not angry, old chap, I'm not angry . . .'

'No, say what you like, sir, but I'm not a rogue. I just went to see some nice people, but I'm not a rogue . . . never have been . . .'

'Oh no, Petrushka, of course not! Now listen, Petrushka, I've nothing against it, I'm not getting at you by calling you a rogue – I only meant it nicely, I'm using the word in a noble sense. All it means is that some men consider it flattering if you call them a rogue or a crafty devil – it means they're nobody's fool and won't allow themselves to be duped by anyone. Some men like that . . . Ah well, never mind! Now, tell me, Petrushka, frankly and openly, like a friend – did you see that clerk Vakhrameyev and did he give you the address?'

'Yes, he gave me the address, too. Good at his work, that clerk! "Your master," he says, "is a good man, very good." "Go and tell your master," he says, "that I send my regards, thank him and tell him I respect your master. Your master's a good man," he said, "and you, Petrushka, are a good man too . . .", so there you are . . .'

'God help me! But the address, the address, you Judas!' Mr Golyadkin's last words were spoken almost in a whisper.

'Oh, yes, the address – he gave me the address.'

'He did? Well, where does he live, this Golyadkin, this clerk Golyadkin, this titular counsellor?'

'"You'll find Golyadkin," he says, "in Shestilavochnaya

Street. When you go down Shestilavochnaya Street," he says, "there's a flight of stairs on the right and it's on the third floor. That's where you'll find Golyadkin," he says.'

'You rogue!' cried our hero, finally losing all patience. 'You rotten crook! That's *me*! That's *me* you're talking about! But there's *another* Golyadkin, I'm talking about the other one, you scoundrel!'

'Well, as you please. What is it to me? Do what you like – so there!'

'But the letter, the letter . . .'

'What letter? There wasn't any letter. I never saw any letter.'

'What did you do with it, you scoundrel?'

'I handed it over, I did. I gave it to him. "My compliments and thanks," he says. "He's a good man, your master. Give your master my respects," he says.'

'But who said that? Did Golyadkin say it?'

Petrushka remained silent for a moment and then, grinning all over his face, he looked his master right in the eye.

'Listen to me, you criminal you!' Mr Golyadkin began, choking with rage and almost beside himself. 'What have you done to me? Tell me what you've done to me! You've finished me off, you ruffian. You've taken my head off my shoulders, you Judas!'

'Well, you can do what you like now, what do I care?' Petrushka replied in a decisive tone, retreating behind the partition.

'Come here, come here, you scoundrel!'

'No I won't come now, I just won't! I'm off to see good folk . . . Good folk live honestly. Good people live without deception and never come in twos . . .'

Mr Golyadkin's arms and legs turned to ice and he gasped for breath.

'Yes,' continued Petrushka, 'they never come in twos and they're not an insult to God and they're honest men . . .'

'You're drunk, you lazy devil! Now go and sleep it off, you ruffian. Tomorrow you'll catch it!' muttered Mr Golyadkin, barely audibly.

As for Petrushka, he muttered something else; then he could be heard lying down on his bed so that it creaked, yawned lengthily, stretched himself out and finally started to snore, sleeping the sleep of the just, as they say. Mr Golyadkin was neither dead nor alive. Petrushka's behaviour, his very strange hints, which, although vague and at which there was consequently nothing to take offence, particularly as it was a drunken man speaking, and finally the whole nasty turn of events – all this shook Mr Golyadkin to the core. 'Whatever possessed me to give him a blowing-up in the middle of the night?' our hero wondered, trembling all over from some morbid sensation. 'What the hell made me get involved with a drunk? What sense could I expect from someone drunk? Every word of his is a lie. All the same, what was he hinting at, the ruffian? Oh, my God! Why on earth did I have to go and write all those letters, like a murderer! I'm a suicide, that's what. Just can't keep my mouth shut, had to blab. And for what? I'm ruined, I'm like a rag – but no, that wasn't enough, I had to bring my pride into it. My pride's suffering, you say, so you must salvage it! I'm a suicide, that's what I am!'

Thus spoke Mr Golyadkin as he sat on his sofa, too frightened to move. Suddenly his eyes fixed on an object that aroused his attention in the highest degree. Terrified – was that which had aroused his attention an illusion or figment of his imagination? – he stretched his arm out, hopefully, timidly and with indescribable curiosity. No, it was no trick, no illusion! It was a letter, yes, a letter, no doubt about it and it was addressed to him. Mr Golyadkin picked the letter up from the table. His heart was pounding violently. 'That scoundrel must have brought it back, put it down here and forgotten all about it. Most likely that's what happened . . .' The letter was from the clerk Vakhrameyev, a young colleague and former friend of Mr Golyadkin's. 'But I anticipated all this,' thought our hero, 'I anticipated all the contents of this letter . . .' The letter read as follows:

Dear Sir, Yakov Petrovich!
Your man is drunk and it is impossible to get any sense out of him. For this reason I prefer to reply in writing. I hasten to inform you that I agree to carry out carefully and conscientiously the

task you have entrusted to me, that is, the personal transmission through my manservant of a letter to a person you know very well. That person who is familiar to you and who has now taken the place of my friend and whose name I pass over in silence on this occasion (for the reason that I do not wish to blacken unfairly the reputation of a completely innocent man) lodges with us at Karolina Ivanovna's flat, in the same room which during your residence with us was occupied by a visiting infantry officer from Tambov.[34] However, this person is everywhere to be found in the company of people who are at least honest and sincere, which cannot be said for some. I intend henceforth to sever all relations with you, as it is impossible for us to maintain the same spirit of mutual concord and harmonious comradeship as before, so therefore I request you, my dear sir, immediately on receipt of this, my frank epistle, to forward the two roubles owing to me for razors of foreign manufacture that I sold you on credit, if you will be so good as to recall, seven months ago at the time of your residence with us at Karolina Ivanovna's, for whom I have the most heartfelt respect. I am acting in this fashion since, according to reports received from judicious people, you have lost your self-respect and your reputation and become a threat to the morality of the innocent and uncontaminated, for there are certain individuals who do not live according to the truth, most of all, their words are false and their show of good intent is suspect. As for Karolina Ivanovna, who has always been a lady of exemplary conduct and, to boot, a spinster, although no longer young, but of good foreign family – people capable of defending the wronged Karolina Ivanovna can be found everywhere, which fact several persons have asked me to mention in my letter in passing and to do so speaking for myself.

In any event, you will discover everything in good time if you have not done so already, despite your giving yourself a bad name in every corner of the capital, according to the reports of judicious people and consequently you may already have received, my dear sir, such information appertaining to yourself, in many places. In conclusion, my dear sir, I must inform you that the person known to you, whose name I refrain from mentioning here for certain honourable reasons, is highly respected by right-thinking people; what is more, is of a cheerful and agreeable disposition, successful both at work and in the company of judicious people, is true to his word and his friends and does not revile behind their backs those with whom he enjoys amicable relations in person.

At all events I remain your humble servant

N. Vakhrameyev

P.S. Get rid of your man: he's a drunkard and in all probability causes you a great deal of trouble. Take on Yevstafy, who used to work here and who now finds himself unemployed. Your present servant is not only a drunkard but a thief into the bargain, since only last week he sold Karolina Ivanovna a pound of lump sugar at a reduced price which in my opinion he could not have done without craftily robbing you of it bit by bit at different times. I am writing this as I wish you well, despite the fact that some people only know how to insult and deceive everyone, particularly those who are honest and of good character. What's more, they revile them behind their backs and misrepresent them, solely out of envy and because they cannot call themselves the same.

N.V.

Having read Vakhrameyev's letter our hero remained for a long time sitting motionless on his sofa. A new kind of light was breaking through that vague and mysterious fog that had been enveloping him for the past two days. Our hero was beginning partly to understand. He attempted to get up from his sofa and take a couple of turns around the room to refresh himself, to collect his scattered thoughts somehow and focus them on a single object and then, having pulled himself together, to give the situation his mature consideration. But the moment he tried to stand up he immediately felt so weak and feeble that he fell back again in his former place. 'Of course, I had a premonition of all this. But how he writes! And what's the direct meaning of all these words? Supposing I do know their meaning – where will it all lead? If he'd told me you must do this and that and said it's like this and that, so to speak, I would have done it. Events have taken a very nasty turn! Ah, how I wish tomorrow would arrive quickly so that I can get down to business! Well, now I know what do to. I'll say: "It's like this, I agree to your arguments but I won't sell my honour." However, how does this person I know of . . . how does this disreputable character come to be mixed up in it? And why did he get mixed up precisely here? Oh, if only I could get to tomorrow quickly! Until then they'll keep dragging my name in the mud, they're scheming, they're working to spite me! The main thing is not to waste time and now I must write a letter, for example, simply to say there's this and that, that I agree to such and such. And first thing tomorrow I'll send it and then I'll move in on them from another direction and forestall them, the darlings! They'll drag my name in the mud, that's what!'

Mr Golyadkin drew some paper towards him, picked up his pen and wrote the following epistle in reply to Provincial Secretary Vakhrameyev's:

Dear Nestor Ignatyevich,
It was with heartfelt sorrow and amazement that I read your letter, so insulting to me, as I can clearly see that you are alluding to me when referring to certain unprincipled persons and others of suspect loyalty. With genuine sorrow I see how rapidly, how successfully and to what depths slander has sunk its roots, to the detriment of my welfare, my honour and my good name. And it is all the more deplorable and insulting that even honest, truly high-minded people, and, most importantly, people endowed with straightforward and open characters, should abandon the interests of noble people and should cling with the best qualities of their hearts to that pernicious putrefaction that in our troublous and immoral times has unfortunately been so widely and so insidiously propagated. In conclusion, I will say that I shall consider it my sacred duty to repay in its entirety the debt of two roubles to which you referred.

As to your references, my dear sir, to a certain person of the female sex, regarding the intentions, calculations and various projects of this same person, I must confess that I vaguely and dimly comprehend them. Allow me, dear sir, to preserve unsullied my lofty mode of thought and my good name. At all events, I am personally prepared to condescend to entering into explanations with you, preferring the trustworthiness of personal contact to the written word and, what's more, I am preparing to enter into various peacable and mutual agreements. To this end I beg you, dear sir, to convey to this person my readiness to reach a personal settlement and furthermore to ask that person to suggest a time and place to meet. Your insinuation that I insulted you, betrayed our original friendship and spoke ill of you, made bitter reading. I ascribe all of this to misunderstandings, to base calumny and to the envy and ill will of those whom I can justifiably term my deadliest enemies. But they are probably unaware that innocence is strong by virtue of its own innocence, that the shamelessness, insolence and scandalous familiarity of various people will sooner or later earn them the stigma of universal contempt and that such persons will perish from nothing but their own indecency and depravity. In conclusion, I beg you, my dear sir, to convey to these people that their strange pretensions and ignoble and fantastic desire to oust others from the positions occupied by those other people by reason of their very existence in this world and to supplant them, are deserving only of amazement, contempt and pity and – in addition – of the madhouse. Above all, such relations are strictly prohibited by the law and this, in my opinion, is perfectly just, since everyone should be content with his own place. There are limits to everything and if this is a joke then it is a most improper one – I will say more, my dear sir, that my ideas outlined above regarding *knowing one's place* are purely moral.

> At all events I have the honour to remain
> Your humble servant
> Ya. Golyadkin

CHAPTER X

All in all one could say that the events of the previous day had shaken Mr Golyadkin to the very core. Our hero passed an extremely bad night and was unable to get any proper sleep,

even five minutes. It was as if some practical joker had scattered
bristles in his bed. He spent the whole night in a half-sleeping,
half-waking state, tossing and turning from side to side, sighing
and groaning, nodding off one moment and waking a minute
later. All this was accompanied by peculiar anguish, vague
memories, horrid visions – in brief, by every conceivable nastiness. First, in the strange, mysterious half-light, he would
glimpse Andrey Filippovich, a dry, wrathful figure with a dry,
harsh gaze, uttering cruelly courteous rebukes. And the moment
Mr Golyadkin began to approach Andrey Filippovich, somehow to justify himself this way or that and claim that he wasn't
as black as his enemies had painted him, but was like this
and that and even possessed many virtues over and above his
ordinary inborn qualities, in one way or the other, then there
would appear a certain person notorious for his beastly tenden-
cies and by the most scandalous means would destroy every
initiative of Mr Golyadkin's and practically before Mr Golyadkin's very eyes thoroughly blacken his name, trample his
pride in the mire and then, without a moment's delay, usurp
his place both at work and in society. At other times Mr Golyadkin felt his head smarting from some insult recently dispensed
and humiliatingly accepted, either in the company of his fellows
or while carrying out his duties and against which insult any
form of protest would have been difficult . . . And while Mr
Golyadkin began to rack his brains as to why exactly it was so
very difficult to protest even against any kind of insult, in the
meantime the idea of the insult was imperceptibly being recast
into another form – into the form of some small or fairly
significant act of nastiness that he witnessed, heard of, or
recently carried out himself – carried out frequently even, not
on any sordid basis, not even from some vile motive, but sometimes by chance, for example, out of delicacy, at other times
because of his utter defencelessness and finally . . . in brief, Mr
Golyadkin knew very well *why*! Just then he blushed in his
sleep and as he tried to suppress his blushes he too would
mutter to himself that here, for example, he might have shown
firmness of character, could have shown considerable firmness
of character in this case . . . and then he concluded by asking

why firmness of character and why bring that up now! ...
But what incensed and exasperated Mr Golyadkin more than
anything else was, whether summoned or not, at that precise
moment a certain person notorious for his disgusting and scandalous behaviour would invariably turn up and although the
facts were sufficiently well known would mutter with a nasty
little grin: 'What's firmness of character got to do with it? What
firmness of character do you and I have, Yakov Petrovich?'
Then Mr Golyadkin would dream that he was in the company
of distinguished people, renowned for the wit and refinement
of every single member; that Mr Golyadkin in turn was distinguished for charm and wit and that everyone came to like him
– even some of his enemies who were present came to like him,
which Mr Golyadkin found extremely pleasant; all that gave
him precedence; and finally that Mr Golyadkin had the pleasure
of overhearing the host singing Mr Golyadkin's praises while
taking one of the guests aside ... Then suddenly, for no earthly
reason, there again appeared the person notorious for his perfidious ways and bestial impulses, in the shape of Mr Golyadkin
Junior and in a flash, in one fell swoop, Golyadkin Junior
destroyed Mr Golyadkin Senior's entire triumph and glory,
eclipsed Mr Golyadkin Senior, trampled Mr Golyadkin Senior
in the mire and finally demonstrated that Mr Golyadkin Senior,
who was also the real one, was not the real one at all, but a
fake and that *he* was the genuine one and that Golyadkin Senior
was not at all what he seemed but simply this and that, and
consequently ought not and in fact had no right to belong to
the company of honourable people of good taste. And all this
happened so very quickly that Mr Golyadkin Senior did not
manage to open his mouth before everyone, in body and soul,
defected to the dastardly and counterfeit Mr Golyadkin Junior,
rejected him, the authentic and innocent Mr Golyadkin, with
the profoundest contempt. Not a single person was left whose
attitude had not been altered in one flash by the repellent Mr
Golyadkin to suit his own ends. Not one person remained –
even the most insignificant out of the entire gathering – to
whom the spurious and worthless Mr Golyadkin wouldn't have
sucked up in the most unctuous manner, to whom he didn't

toady, before whom he didn't smoke something extremely pleasant and sweet as a sign of his extreme pleasure so that the person enveloped in smoke could only sniff and sneeze until the tears came. And, most important, it all happened like lightning: the speed of movement of the suspect and worthless Mr Golyadkin was amazing! For example, no sooner had he finished sucking up to someone to win his good graces, than in the blink of an eyelid he'd be with someone else. Ever so slyly he'd butter up another, extract a benevolent little smile from him, jerk his thick, round, rather dumpy legs into action and then be off and away, making up to a third, toadying to him in friendly fashion. And before you could open your mouth to show your surprise – there he'd be with a fourth, up to the same tricks with him! It was horrible, sheer sorcery and nothing less! And everyone was delighted with him, everyone liked him, everyone praised him to the skies and everyone proclaimed in unison that for amiability and satirical cast of mind he was superior to the innocent, authentic Mr Golyadkin, thus putting the real and authentic Mr Golyadkin to shame; and they rejected and drove out the genuine, truth-loving Mr Golyadkin, showering insults on Mr Golyadkin, so well known for his love for his neighbour.

Filled with anguish, terror and rage, the suffering Mr Golyadkin ran out into the street and tried to hire a cab to speed him straight to His Excellency's, or if not there then at least to Andrey Filippovich's. But – oh, the horror! The cabbies refused point-blank to take Mr Golyadkin, saying: 'We can't take two gents exactly the same, sir. A good man tries to live honestly, sir, not just anyhow and he never comes in twos.' In a paroxysm of shame the perfectly honourable Mr Golyadkin kept looking around and in fact saw for himself, with his own eyes, that the cab drivers and Petrushka, who was in league with them, were all in the right: for the depraved Mr Golyadkin was actually close by, not at all far away, and in his customary dastardly way was even here at that critical moment undoubtedly preparing to do something very improper, showing no sign of that nobility of character that is normally acquired by education, that nobility upon which the revolting Mr Golyadkin II was so pluming himself at every opportunity. Beside himself with shame and despair, the ruined and completely authentic Mr Golyadkin rushed off blindly, at the mercy of fate, wherever. But with every stride, with every thud of his foot on the granite pavement, there would spring up, as if from under the ground, a completely identical Mr Golyadkin, utterly similar in depravity. And the moment they appeared, all these perfect replicas would start running one after the other and, stretching out in a long chain like a gaggle of geese, would hobble behind Mr Golyadkin so that there was no escaping these replicas, so that the eminently pitiable Mr Golyadkin couldn't catch his breath for horror, so that in the end such a terrifying multitude of exact replicas was spawned that the whole city was finally jammed with these perfect replicas and a police officer, observing such a breach of the peace, was obliged to grab all these perfect replicas by the scruff of the neck and fling them into a lock-up that happened to be close at hand ... Our hero would wake up, rigid and frozen with horror and – rigid and frozen with horror – he felt that even his waking hours were hardly spent more cheerfully ... it was cruel, sheer agony ... The anguish was such that it seemed his heart was being gnawed out of his breast.

In the end Mr Golyadkin could endure it no longer. 'This shall not happen!' he shouted, resolutely sitting up in bed, and after this exclamation he completely came to.

It was evidently very late in the day. In the room it was somehow unusually light. The sun's rays were filtering through the frosty windowpanes and scattering themselves over the whole room, to the not inconsiderable surprise of Mr Golyadkin, for normally only at noon did the sun peer into his room as it followed its daily course. As far as Mr Golyadkin could recall no deviation from the heavenly luminary's usual course had ever occurred. Our hero barely had time to wonder at this than the wall clock behind the partition whirred preparatory to striking. 'Oh yes!' thought Mr Golyadkin as he prepared to listen with dull expectancy. But to Mr Golyadkin's complete and utter consternation the clock exerted itself and struck only once. 'What sort of nonsense is this?' our hero shouted, leaping right out of bed. Unable to believe his ears he dashed, just as he was, behind the partition. The clock really did show one. Mr Golyadkin glanced at Petrushka's bed, but there wasn't even a whiff of Petrushka in the room. His bed had evidently been made and vacated long before; his boots were nowhere to be seen either – a sure indication that Petrushka really had gone out. Mr Golyadkin rushed to the door: the door was shut. 'But where on earth's Petrushka?' he continued in a whisper, terribly agitated and feeling a quite significant trembling in every limb. Suddenly a thought flashed through his mind . . . Mr Golyadkin rushed to the table, inspected it and rummaged around – yes: that letter written yesterday to Vakhrameyev was not there; nor was there any sign of Petrushka behind the partition. The clock showed one, and several new points that had been introduced into Vahkrameyev's letter of yesterday that at first reading had struck him as utterly vague were now perfectly clear to him. Finally – Petrushka, too – obviously a bribed Petrushka! Yes, yes, that was it!

'So that's where the main knot was being tied!' Mr Golyadkin cried, striking his forehead and opening his eyes ever wider, 'so it's in that niggardly German woman's nest where all the devilry is lurking! So, it must have been only a strategic diversion when she directed me to Izmaylovsky Bridge – she was distracting me, confusing me (the old hag!) and that's how she's been undermining my position!! Yes, that's it! You only have to consider it from that angle to see exactly how the whole thing is. And it also fully accounts for that scoundrel's appearance. Yes, it all adds up now, it all makes sense. They've been keeping him in reserve for a long time, preparing him and saving him for a rainy day. And now it's all come out in the wash; that's how it's all turned out. Ah well, never mind! No time has been lost!' Here Mr Golyadkin remembered with horror that it was already after one in the afternoon. 'What if they've already managed to . . . ?' A groan broke from his chest. 'But no, they're lying, they couldn't have had time – let's see.' He somehow dressed himself, grabbed pen and paper and scribbled the following epistle:

Dear Yakov Petrovich,

It's either you or me, but there's no room for both of us! I'm telling you quite frankly that your strange, absurd and at the same time impossible desire to appear as my twin and pass yourself off as such will serve no other purpose than to bring about your complete disgrace and defeat. So therefore I must request you, for your own sake, to step to one side and make way for those who are truly noble and with honourable intentions. Failing this I am prepared to resort even to the most extreme measure. I lay down my pen and await ... However, I remain at your service – and with pistols.

Ya. Golyadkin

When he had finished this note our hero vigorously rubbed his hands together. Then, pulling on his overcoat and putting on his hat, he opened the door with a second, spare key and set off for the office. But when he arrived he could not make up his mind whether to go in. It was too late: Mr Golyadkin's watch showed half past two. Suddenly an apparently extremely trifling circumstance resolved some of Mr Golyadkin's doubts: from around the corner of the office building there suddenly appeared a small, breathless, flushed figure which stealthily, darting like a rat, scuttled up the steps and then into the lobby. It was the copy clerk Ostafyev, a man well known to Mr Golyadkin, in somewhat straitened circumstances and ready to do anything for ten copecks. Knowing Ostafyev's weak side and aware that after an absence on some very urgent, private business he was probably all the more susceptible to ten-copeck pieces, our hero decided to be generous with them and immediately tore up the steps and then into the hall after Ostafyev, called to him and with a mysterious air invited him into a secluded corner behind a huge iron stove. Having led him there our hero began cross-examining him.

'Well, my friend, how's it going, um ... er ... if you get my meaning?'

'I do, Your Honour and I wish Your Honour good health.'

'Good my friend, good. I'll make it worth your while, dear friend. Well, tell me now – how are they?'

'What are you inquiring about, sir?' Here Ostafyev for a moment gave a little support with one hand to his unexpectedly gaping mouth.

'I'm . . . well you see, my friend, I'm . . . er . . . now don't you go thinking things. Well now, is Andrey Filippovich here?'

'He's here, sir.'

'And are the clerks here?'

'Yes, sir, they're all here, as they should be, sir.'

'And His Excellency as well?'

'His Excellency too, sir.'

Here for a second time the clerk gave a little support to his mouth that had fallen open again and gave Mr Golyadkin a somewhat quizzical, peculiar look. At least so it appeared to our hero.

'And nothing special to report, old chap?'

'No, sir, nothing at all.'

'I mean, about me – is there anything going on there to do with me, my friend, anything at all . . . eh? I was just asking, you understand.'

'No, sir, haven't heard a thing up to now.' Here the clerk again supported his mouth and gave Mr Golyadkin another peculiar look. The fact was, our hero was now trying to penetrate Ostafyev's expression and read something there, to see whether he was keeping something back. And he really did seem to be keeping something or other back. Actually, Ostafyev was now becoming ruder and more off-hand and didn't show the same concern over Mr Golyadkin's interests as at the beginning of the conversation. 'He's partly within his rights,' thought Mr Golyadkin. 'After all, what am I to him? Perhaps he's already been buttered up by the other side, so that's why he was absent on urgent private business. Ah well, I'd better give . . .' Mr Golyadkin understood that the time for ten-copeck pieces had arrived.

'Here you are, dear chap.'

'I'm deeply obliged to Your Honour.'

'And there'll be more for you.'

'Yes, Your Honour.'

'I'll give you even more and when our business is finished as much again. Understand?'

The clerk said nothing, stood to attention and fixed his eyes on Mr Golyadkin, without blinking.

'Now tell me, has anything been said about me?'

'I don't think so sir . . . er . . . nothing for the time being,' Ostafyev replied in a slow drawl, also like Mr Golyadkin maintaining a mysterious air, twitching his eyebrows a little, staring at the floor and trying to strike the appropriate tone – briefly, doing his utmost to earn what had been promised, as what had been given he already considered his own and fully earned.

'So, there's nothing at all?'

'Not for the moment, sir.'

'But listen . . . um . . . er . . . perhaps there *will* be something?'

'Later, of course, sir, something might come up.'

'That's bad,' thought our hero.

'Listen, here's some more for you old chap.'

'Much obliged to Your Honour.'

'Was Vakhrameyev here yesterday?'

'That he was, sir.'

'And was there anyone else? . . . Try and remember, old fellow.'

The clerk rummaged in his memory for a moment but could find nothing to fit the bill.

'No, sir, there was nothing else.'

'Hm!' Silence followed.

'Listen, old chap, here's another ten copecks for you. Just tell me all you know, all the ins and outs.'

'Yes, sir.'

Ostafyev stood there as meek as a lamb: this was exactly what Mr Golyadkin needed.

'Tell me, old chap, what sort of footing is he on?'

'Not bad, sir – very good, sir,' the clerk replied, staring hard at Mr Golyadkin

'So, how good?'

'He's all right, sir.' Here Ostafyev twitched his eyebrows significantly. But now he was decidedly all at sea and did not know what to say. 'That's bad!' thought Mr Golyadkin.

'Is there really nothing further to report, with him and Vakhrameyev?'

'Everything's as it was before.'

'Think hard.'

'Well, they do say that . . .'

'What do they say?'

Ostafyev propped his mouth again for a moment.

'Isn't there a letter for me from there?'

'Well, Mikheyev the caretaker went to Vakhrameyev's flat today, to that German woman of theirs, so I'll go and ask if you like.'

'Please do me the favour, old chap, for God's sake! I'm only saying . . . Now don't you go thinking things, I'm only just saying. But ask a few questions, find out if they are cooking anything up that concerns me. Find out how he's acting. That's what I need to know. Now you go and find that out, dear chap, and I'll reward you for it later . . .'

'Yes, Your Honour, but Ivan Semyonych was sitting in your place today, sir.'

'Ivan Semyonych? Oh, was he now?! Really?'

'Andrey Filippovich showed him where to sit, sir.'

'Oh, really? How did that come about? Now you go and find that out, for God's sake, go and find that out. If you find everything out I'll reward you for it, dear chap. That's what I want . . . But don't go thinking things, old chap.'

'Yes, sir, I'll go up right away, sir. But aren't you coming in today, Your Honour?'

'No, my friend, um . . . er . . . I've only come to have a look. But I'll show you my gratitude later, my dear chap.'

'Very good, sir,' the clerk swiftly and zealously ran upstairs and Mr Golyadkin was left alone.

'This is bad,' he thought. 'Oh, it's bad, very bad! Oh dear! That little business of ours – how bad it seems now! What could all this mean? What exactly did some of that drunkard's hints mean, for example, and whose trickery is it? Ah! Now I know whose trickery it is! This is the kind of trickery it is: they probably got to know, then they sat him there . . . But hold on a moment . . . Did *they* put him there? It was Andrey Filippovich who put him there, that Ivan Semyonovich, but why did he make him sit there, for what precise purpose did he put him there? They probably found out ... It's all Vakhrameyev's work. No, not Vakhrameyev's, he's as thick as two planks, that Vakhrameyev. But all of them are working for him and that's precisely why they put that scoundrel up to it! And that one-eyed German slut went and complained! I always suspected that there was more to this simple intrigue, that there was something behind all those old wives' tales. I said as much to Krestyan Ivanovich: "They've vowed to murder someone," I said, "in the moral sense – and they've got Karolina Ivanovna in their clutches." No, there are clearly experts at work here, that's for sure! Yes, my dear sir, an expert's hand is at work here, not Vakhrameyev's! I've said all along that Vakhrameyev's stupid and this is ... but now I know who's working for all of them here – it's that blackguard who's working for them – that impostor! He's clinging to that one thing – and it partly helps to explain his success in the highest society. But really, I'd like to know what footing he's on now ... what's he doing there with them? But why on earth did they take on Ivan Semyono-vich? What the hell did they need him for? As if they couldn't get anyone else. Still, it would have come to the same thing whoever they put there, but what I do know is that I've had my suspicions about Ivan Semyonovich for a long time. I noticed it ages ago: what a nasty old man he is – so vile – they say he lends money and charges exorbitant interest just like a Jew. And all this is masterminded by the Bear. The Bear's mixed up in the whole proceedings. That's how it all began. It was at Izmaylovsky Bridge, that's how it all began ...' Here Mr Goly-adkin screwed up his face as if he had bitten into a lemon, most likely having remembered something very unpleasant. 'Well now, it doesn't matter,' he thought. 'All this time I've been worry-ing about my own troubles. But why doesn't that Ostafyev come? Probably sitting down somewhere or been held up for some reason. It's partly a good thing in fact that I'm doing some intriguing and undermining of my own. I only had to give Ostafyev ten copecks and he's ... well ... on my side. But that's the thing – *is* he really on my side? Perhaps for their part they've done the same from *their* side too ... and for their part they're intriguing together, they're in collusion with him. Yes

... he looks like a bandit, the ruffian, a real bandit. He's holding something back, that crook! "No, there's nothing," he says, "and I'm deeply obliged to Your Honour." Ugh, you rotten crook!' There was a noise. Mr Golyadkin shrank back and jumped behind the stove. Someone came down the stairs and went out into the street. 'Who could that be leaving at this time?' our hero wondered. A minute later someone's footsteps rang out again. Here Mr Golyadkin couldn't resist poking out the tip of his nose ever so slightly from behind the parapet – and he immediately withdrew it, as if someone had pricked it with a pin. This time someone he knew was passing by, that is, that scoundrel, that intriguer, that debauchee, tripping along as usual with those nasty little steps, pattering and jerking his legs as if he were about to kick someone. 'The scoundrel!' our hero muttered to himself. However, Mr Golyadkin could not fail to notice that under the villain's arm was a huge green portfolio belonging to His Excellency. 'He's on another special mission!' thought Mr Golyadkin, flushing and shrinking into himself still more in annoyance. No sooner had Mr Golyadkin Junior flashed past Mr Golyadkin without even noticing him than footsteps were heard for a third time and on this occasion Mr Golyadkin guessed they were the clerk's. And in fact the little figure of some greasy-haired clerk did peer from behind the stove at him. However, the figure was not that of Ostafyev but of another clerk nicknamed Scribbly. Mr Golyadkin was amazed. 'Why has he been letting others into the secret?' our hero wondered. 'What barbarians! That lot hold nothing sacred!'

'Well, what then, old chap?' he asked, turning to Scribbly. 'Who sent you, my friend?'

'Well, it's about that little business of yours. No, there's no news so far from anyone for the time being, sir. But if there is anything we'll tell you.'

'And what about Ostafyev?'

'He just couldn't get away, sir. His Excellency's already walked through the department twice and I've no time now . . .'

'Thanks, my dear chap, thank you. Only, tell me . . .'

'Honest to God, I've no time now. Every minute he keeps asking for us. But if you would care to stand here a little longer, sir, we'll let you know if there's any news regarding your business.'

'No, my friend, you tell me . . .'

'Please excuse me, but I don't have the time,' Scribbly replied, breaking away from Mr Golyadkin, who had grabbed him by the lapel. 'I really don't . . . If you'll please stand here a bit longer we'll keep you informed.'

'Just a moment, just a moment, my dear friend! Just a moment! Now, here's a letter, my friend. And there'll be something for you, dear friend.'

'Yes, sir.'

'Try and give it to Mr Golyadkin, dear chap.'

'Mr Golyadkin?'

'Yes, my friend, Mr Golyadkin.'

'Very well, sir, as soon as I've cleared up here I'll take it. And in the meantime you stand here. No one will see you.'

'No, my friend, don't go thinking that . . . I'm not simply standing here so that no one can see me. But I won't be here, my friend . . . I'll be over there, in the side street. There's a coffee-house there. I'll be waiting there and if anything crops up you must come and tell me all about it – understand?'

'Very good, sir. Only, please let me go now . . . I understand.'

'And I'll reward you, dear chap,' Mr Golyadkin shouted after Scribbly, who had at last managed to free himself. 'He's a blackguard, seems he got a bit ruder later on . . .' thought our hero, stealing out from behind the stove. 'There's another catch here, that's clear enough . . . First it was yes sir, no sir . . . But perhaps he really was in a tearing hurry. Perhaps His Excellency did walk through the department twice. And what was that in connection with? Oh well, it doesn't really matter, perhaps it's absolutely nothing . . . but now we'll see . . .'

Here Mr Golyadkin was about to open the door and already intending to go out into the street when suddenly, at that very moment, His Excellency's carriage clattered up to the entrance. Mr Golyadkin had managed to collect himself, then the carriage door opened from the inside and its occupant jumped out on to the porch. The new arrival was none other than that same Mr Golyadkin Junior, who had gone off himself only ten minutes before. Mr Golyadkin Senior remembered that the Director's apartment was just around the corner. 'He's on some special mission,' our hero thought. Meanwhile, after grabbing the fat green portfolio inside the carriage, with some other papers, and after giving orders to the coachman, Mr Golyadkin Junior flung open the door, almost hitting Mr Golyadkin Senior with it, deliberately ignoring him and therefore trying to spite him, and shot up the stairs to the department. 'This is bad!' thought Mr Golyadkin. 'See what's happening to our little business now! Good God, just look at him!' For about half a minute longer our hero stood motionless; finally he came to a decision. Without much further pause for thought and feeling moreover a violent palpitation in his heart and a trembling in every limb, he chased up the staircase after his friend. 'Well, here goes: what do I care? I'm to one side of all this,' he reflected, removing his hat, overcoat and galoshes in the ante-room.

It was already dusk when Mr Golyadkin entered his department. Neither Andrey Filippovich nor Anton Antonovich was in the room. Both were in the Director's office with their reports. The Director, as rumour had it, was in turn hurrying to report to His Supreme Excellency. As a result of these circumstances and also because dusk was infiltrating here, too, and office hours were drawing to a close, several clerks, mainly the juniors, were whiling away the time in a kind of busy inactivity just as our hero entered, having gathered in small groups, chatting, arguing and laughing, while some of the very youngest, that is, those of the very lowest rank were amidst all the noise enjoying a quiet game of pitch-and-toss in a corner over by the window. Aware of decorum and feeling just at that moment a special need to find favour and 'get in' with everyone, Mr Golyadkin immediately approached whoever he was on good terms with to wish them good day, etc. But his colleagues responded somewhat strangely to Mr Golyadkin's greetings. He was unpleasantly struck by the general chilliness, dryness and one might even say a certain steeliness in the reception he got. No one held out his hand. Some simply said 'hello' and walked away; others merely nodded, one just turned his back, pretending not to have noticed him. Finally several of them –

and this riled Mr Golyadkin most of all – several of the youngest clerks, the lowest of the low, mere whippersnappers who, as Mr Golyadkin so rightly commented, were fit only for playing pitch-and-toss given the chance and loafing around somewhere, gathered in small groups, gradually surrounding Mr Golyadkin and thus almost barring his exit. They all stared at him with a kind of insolent curiosity.

The omens were bad. Mr Golyadkin realized that and sensibly prepared, for his part, to take no notice. Suddenly a completely unexpected event finished him off, as they say, utterly annihilated Mr Golyadkin.

Among the small crowd of the young surrounding colleagues, as if deliberately, at the most distressing moment for Mr Golyadkin, there suddenly appeared Mr Golyadkin Junior, cheerful as ever, smiling and frivolous as ever: in short, mischievous, capering, toadying, guffawing, nimble of tongue and foot as ever, just as before, just as yesterday, for example. He grinned, gambolled, pranced and twisted around with a smile that seemed to say 'Good evening' to everyone. He wormed his way into the small crowd of clerks, shaking hands with one, patting another on the shoulder, hugging another, explaining to a fourth exactly the kind of mission His Excellency had employed him for, where he had gone, what he had done, what he had brought back with him. To a fifth – probably his best friend – he gave a smacking kiss, right on the lips – in brief, everything was happening exactly as in Mr Golyadkin Senior's dream. After having had his fill of dancing about, after finishing with everyone in his own unique way, manipulating them all to his own ends, whether he needed to or not, having slobbered over all and sundry to his heart's content, Mr Golyadkin Junior suddenly and most probably in error (up to that moment he had not had time to notice his oldest friend) even offered his hand to Mr Golyadkin Senior as well. Probably also in error, although he had in fact ample time to notice the dishonourable Mr Golyadkin Junior, our hero immediately eagerly grasped the so unexpectedly extended hand and shook it in the friendliest, firmest manner, shook it as if prompted by some strange, quite unexpected inner impulse, with a lachrymose feeling. Whether

our hero had been deceived by his worthless enemy's first movement or was simply at a loss, or sensed and acknowledged in
his heart of hearts the full extent of his own defencelessness, is
difficult to say. The fact is, Mr Golyadkin Senior, in full possession of his faculties, of his own free will and before witnesses,
solemnly shook hands with the person he had termed his mortal
foe. But what was the amazement, the frenzy and rage, the
horror and shame of Mr Golyadkin Senior when his foe and
his deadly enemy the ignoble Mr Golyadkin Junior, observing
the error of the persecuted and innocent man he had so perfidiously deceived, without shame, without feeling or compassion,
suddenly, with insufferable effrontery and rudeness, snatched
his hand away from Mr Golyadkin Senior's. Not only that: he
shook his hand as if he had just dirtied it on something really
nasty, spat to one side, accompanying all this with the most
obscene gesture; what is more, he took out his handkerchief
and there and then, in the most unseemly manner, used it to
wipe every one of his fingers that had momentarily been resting
in Mr Golyadkin Senior's hand. Acting in this manner, Mr
Golyadkin Junior, in his usual dastardly fashion, looked around
deliberately, made sure that everyone was witnessing his
behaviour, looked everyone in the eye, clearly trying to inspire
them with all that was most unfavourable with regard to Mr
Golyadkin Senior. The loathsome Mr Golyadkin Junior's conduct seemed to arouse the universal indignation of the surrounding clerks. Even the empty-headed, most junior clerks
showed their displeasure. All around there was murmuring
and discussion. The general stir could not fail to escape Mr
Golyadkin Senior's ears. But suddenly a well-timed little witticism that had meanwhile been simmering on Mr Golyadkin
Junior's lips shattered and destroyed our hero's last hopes,
tipping the balance once again in favour of his deadly and
worthless enemy.

'This is our Russian Faublas,[35] gentlemen. Allow me to intro-
duce the young Faublas!' squeaked Mr Golyadkin Junior, with
his own unique insolence, mincing and winding his way through
the clerks, pointing out to them the petrified and at the same
time frenzied, genuine Mr Golyadkin. 'Give us a kiss, sweetie-

pie!' he continued with intolerable familiarity, moving towards the man he had so treacherously insulted. The worthless Mr Golyadkin's witticism seemed to have found a ready response in the right quarters, all the more so as it contained a cunning allusion to a certain incident that was clearly already public knowledge. Our hero felt the heavy hand of his enemies on his shoulders. However, his mind was already made up. With eyes blazing, a fixed smile on his pallid face, he managed to extricate himself from the crowd and with uneven, hurried steps headed straight for His Excellency's office. In the penultimate room he was met by Andrey Filippovich, who had only just left His Excellency, and although there were quite a number of other people of all kinds in the room, at that moment complete strangers to Mr Golyadkin, nonetheless our hero did not choose to pay any attention to such a circumstance. Boldly, directly, decisively, almost surprised at himself and inwardly praising himself for his daring, without further ado he directly accosted Andrey Filippovich, who was considerably startled at such an unexpected assault.

'Ah, what do you . . . what do you want?!' asked the departmental chief, not listening to Mr Golyadkin, who had stumbled over some words.

'Andrey Filippovich . . . I . . . may I, Andrey Filippovich, have a talk right away, face to face with His Excellency?' our hero articulated volubly and distinctly, giving Andrey Filippovich the most determined look.

'What, sir? Of course you can't,' Andrey Filippovich replied, looking Mr Golyadkin up and down, from head to foot.

'I'm saying this, Andrey Filippovich, because I'm amazed no one here is prepared to unmask an impostor and scoundrel.'

'Wha-at, sir!?'

'A blackguard, Andrey Filippovich!'

'And to whom are you pleased to refer in such a manner?'

'A certain person, Andrey Filippovich. I, Andrey Filippovich, am referring to a certain person. I'm within my rights . . . I think, Andrey Filippovich, that the authorities should encourage such actions,' added Mr Golyadkin, clearly forgetting himself, 'you can probably see for yourself, Andrey Filippovich,

that this honourable action demonstrates my undivided loyalty
and good intentions – to accept the authorities as a father, Andrey
Filippovich, to accept the benevolent authorities as a father, and
I blindly entrust my destiny to them. That's to say, so to speak,
that's how it is . . .' Here Mr Golyadkin's voice trembled, his
face grew flushed and two tears trickled down his eyelashes.

As he listened to Mr Golyadkin, Andrey Filippovich was so
amazed that he involuntarily staggered back a couple of steps.
Then he looked around uneasily . . . It is difficult to say how
all this would have ended . . . But suddenly the door to His
Excellency's room opened and he emerged in person, accompanied by several officials. Every single person in the room
followed in his wake. His Excellency summoned Andrey
Filippovich and walked beside him, embarking on a conversation about some business matters. When they had all moved
on and left the room, Mr Golyadkin came to his senses. A little
more relaxed now, he took shelter under the wing of Anton
Antonovich Setochkin, who in turn came stumping along last
of all and as it seemed to Mr Golyadkin with a terribly stern
and apprehensive look. 'I've really let my tongue run away with
me and made a mess of things here as well,' he thought. 'Ah
well, not to worry.'

'I hope, Anton Antonovich, that you will at least agree to
hear me out and investigate my circumstances,' he said quietly,
his voice still trembling somewhat with emotion. 'Rejected by
all, I appeal to you. I am still at a loss as to the meaning of
Andrey Filippovich's words, Anton Antonovich. Please explain
if you can.'

'All will be explained in its own good time,' Anton Antonovich
replied sternly and deliberately and with a look that gave Mr
Golyadkin clearly to understand that he had no desire whatsoever to continue the conversation. 'You'll know everything
very soon. You'll be officially notified about everything today.'

'What do you mean *officially*, Anton Antonovich? Why
exactly officially, sir?' our hero inquired sheepishly.

'It's not for us to question the decisions of the authorities,
Yakov Petrovich.'

'But why the authorities, Anton Antonovich?' asked Mr

Golyadkin, even more daunted, 'why the authorities? I can see no reason why they need to be troubled on this score, Anton Antonovich . . . Perhaps you want to say something about what happened yesterday, Anton Antonovich?'

'No, it has nothing to do with yesterday. There's something else that's not up to scratch as far as you're concerned.'

'What's not up to scratch, Anton Antonovich? I don't think there's anything about me that's not up to scratch, Anton Antonovich . . .'

'Well now, with whom were you intending to get up to crafty tricks?' Anton Antonovich sharply interrupted the completely flabbergasted Mr Golyadkin, who winced and turned as white as a sheet.

'Of course, Anton Antonovich,' he said in a barely audible voice, 'if you heed the voice of slander and listen to your enemies without letting the other side justify itself, then of course . . . of course one has to suffer, Anton Antonovich – suffer innocently, for nothing.'

'Exactly. But what about your unseemly conduct prejudicial to the reputation of that noble young lady who belongs to that virtuous, highly respected and well-known family that has been so good to you?'

'What conduct do you mean, Anton Antonovich?'

'What I say. Regarding your "laudable" behaviour towards that young lady, who, although poor, is of honourable foreign extraction – are you not aware of that either?'

'Excuse me, Anton Antonovich . . . please be good enough to hear me out!'

'And your perfidious conduct, your slandering another person, accusing another person of something you yourself are guilty of – eh? What would you call that?'

'I, Anton Antonovich, didn't turn him out,' said our hero, beginning to tremble. 'And I never told Petrushka – my man-servant, that is – to do anything of the sort. He ate my bread, Anton Antonovich, he enjoyed my hospitality,' our hero added with such deep feeling and expressiveness that his chin twitched slightly and the tears were ready to well up again.

'You're only just saying that he ate your bread, Yakov

Petrovich,' pAnton Antonovich replied with a grin and with
such cunning in his voice that Mr Golyadkin felt a nagging
anxiety in his heart.

'If I may humbly be permitted to ask once more, Anton
Antonovich: is His Excellency aware of the whole affair?'

'Well, what do you think, sir? But now you must let me get
on. I've no time for you now . . . Today you'll find out all you
need to know.'

'For God's sake – please – just one more minute, Anton
Antonovich!'

'You can tell me later, sir.'

'No, Anton Antonovich. I, sir, you see, sir, please just listen a
moment, Anton Antonovich. I'm not in the least a free-thinker,
Anton Antonovich, I avoid free-thinking like the plague . . . For
my part I'm quite ready . . . and I've even advanced the idea
that . . .'

'Very well, very well . . . I've heard it all before.'

'No, you haven't heard this, Anton Antonovich. It's something different, Anton Antonovich, it's good, really good, and
makes for pleasant listening . . . I've advanced the idea, Anton
Antonovich, as I explained before, that Divine Providence has
created two people exactly alike and our benevolent superiors,
seeing Divine Providence at work, have provided sanctuary for
the two twins, sir. That's good, Anton Antonovich. You can
see that's very good and that I'm far from being a free-thinker.
I accept our benevolent authorities as a father. It's like this, so
to speak, you know, and um . . . well, a young man needs to
work. Please lend me your support, Anton Antonovich, please
intercede for me. I don't mean anything, Anton Antonovich . . .
For God's sake, Anton Antonovich, just one more tiny word
. . . Anton Antonovich . . .'

But Anton Antonovich was already some distance from
Mr Golyadkin. So shaken and confused by all that he had
heard and what was happening to him, our hero had no idea
where he was standing, what he had heard, what he had done,
what had been done to him and what else was going to be done
to him.

With an imploring look he tried to find Anton Antonovich

in the crowd of clerks with the intention of justifying himself even further in his eyes and to tell him something extremely loyal, inspiring and pleasant regarding himself ... However, a new light was gradually beginning to break through Mr Golyadkin's confusion, a new and ghastly light that suddenly, all at once, illuminated a whole vista of circumstances until then completely unknown and even totally unsuspected. Just then someone nudged our utterly devastated hero in the side. He looked around. Before him stood Scribbly.

'A letter, Your Honour.'

'Ah! So you're back already, old chap.'

'No, it was brought here this morning, as early as ten o'clock. Sergey Mikheyev the porter brought it from Provincial Secretary Vakhrameyev's flat.'

'That's good, my friend, that's good. I'll show you my gratitude for that, old chap.'

This said, Mr Golyadkin hid the letter in a side pocket of his uniform which he had buttoned all the way up. Then he looked around and to his astonishment saw that he was already in the office vestibule, among a little group of clerks who, now that office hours were over, were crowding towards the exit. Not only had Mr Golyadkin failed to notice this last circumstance up to then but he did not notice or remember how he suddenly came to be wearing his overcoat and galoshes and be hat in hand. All the clerks were standing motionless, respectfully waiting. The fact was, His Excellency had stopped at the bottom of the steps to await his carriage, which had been delayed for some reason and he was having a very interesting conversation with two counsellors and Andrey Filippovich. A little removed from these two counsellors and Andrey Filippovich stood Anton Antonovich Setochkin and some of the other clerks, all of whom broke into broad smiles when they saw that His Excellency was pleased to laugh and joke. The clerks who had congregated at the top of the stairs were smiling too and waiting for His Excellency to start laughing again. Only Fedoseich, the pot-bellied commissionaire, who stood to attention grasping the door handle, impatiently awaiting his daily ration of pleasure, which was throwing one half of the doors open with one sweep of the arm and then bending almost double and respectfully standing to one side to allow His Excellency to pass, wasn't smiling. But it was clearly Mr Golyadkin's unworthy and ignoble enemy who was experiencing the greatest pleasure and joy. At that moment he had even forgotten all the other clerks, had even stopped weaving, mincing, twisting and turning among them in his usual obnoxious way – he even missed the opportunity of sucking up to someone at that moment. He had become all eyes and ears, was strangely withdrawn, probably trying to hear better and was looking away from His Excellency. Only occasionally did his arms, legs and head twitch in barely perceptible spasms to reveal all the secret, innermost impulses of his soul. 'Just look, he's so full of himself!' our hero thought, 'everyone's favourite, it seems – the crook! I'd like to know exactly why he's so successful in high-class society. No brains, no personality, no education, no feelings. That rotter has all the luck! Heavens above! Really, if you think about it, how quickly a man can come along and "get in" with everybody! That man will go far – I swear he will, that swine . . . he'll prosper, he will – the lucky devil! I'd like to know exactly what it is he keeps whispering to everyone. What confidences does he share with these people and what secrets are they discussing? Heavens above! If only I could . . . er . . . get in with them a little as well . . . I could say: "It's this and that . . ." Or perhaps I could say: "That's how it is, I won't do it in future . . . It's my fault and a young man needs to work these days, Your Excellency. I'm not in the least embarrassed by my dubious situation." Yes – that's it! So, is that how I should act . . . ? But you can't get through to that scoundrel, you can't get through to him with words. It's impossible to hammer any sense into that desperado's head. Still, I'll have a try. If I happen to hit on a good time I'll have a shot at it . . .'

In his anxiety, agitation and confusion, feeling that he could not possibly leave things as they were, that the critical moment was now at hand, that he needed to have things out with someone, our hero was gradually moving a little nearer to where his unworthy and mysterious friend was standing, but at that moment the long-awaited carriage clattered up to the entrance. Fedoseich pulled open the door, bent double, and let His Excellency pass. All the clerks who had been waiting surged forward in one mass towards the exit and for a moment shoved Mr Golyadkin Senior away from Mr Golyadkin Junior. 'You won't get away!' our hero thought, forcing his way through the crowd without taking his eyes off his quarry. Finally, the crowd gave way. Our hero felt free now and rushed off in pursuit of his enemy.

CHAPTER XI

Mr Golyadkin gasped for breath as he flew as if on wings after his fast-retreating enemy. He felt a terrible inner energy. But for all that, Mr Golyadkin had every reason to think that at that moment even an ordinary mosquito, had it been able to exist in St Petersburg at that time of year, could very easily have broken him with one touch of its wing. What was more, he felt that he had gone downhill, grown utterly weak, and that he was being borne along by some completely strange, alien force, that he himself wasn't walking at all – on the contrary: his legs were giving way and refused to obey him. However, it all might turn out for the best. 'Whether for the best or not for the best,' thought Mr Golyadkin, barely able to catch his breath from running so fast, 'it's a lost cause – of that there's not the slightest doubt. That I'm done for, as we now know, is signed, settled and sealed.' In spite of this it was as if our hero had risen from the dead, that he'd survived a battle and snatched victory when he managed to grab his enemy's overcoat just as the latter was putting one foot on the step of the droshky he had just hired.

'My dear sir! My dear sir!' he shouted at length to the infamous Mr Golyadkin Junior whom he had finally caught up with. 'My dear sir, I trust you will . . .'

'No, please don't have any hopes on that score,' Mr Golyadkin's callous enemy replied evasively, standing with one foot on the step of the droshky, doing his utmost to get over to the other side of the carriage, vainly waving the other foot in the air as he tried to keep his balance and at the same time wrench his overcoat from Mr Golyadkin Senior, who, for his part, was holding on to it with all the strength nature had conferred on him.

'Yakov Petrovich . . . just ten minutes . . .'

'Forgive me, I haven't the time.'

'You yourself must agree, Yakov Petrovich, . . . please, Yakov Petrovich, for God's sake, Yakov Petrovich! Let's have it out, let's face up to it . . . Just one second, Yakov Petrovich!'

'My dear fellow, I haven't time,' Mr Golyadkin's falsely honourable enemy replied with ill-mannered familiarity but in the guise of goodheartedness. 'Some other time. I, believe me, with all my heart and soul . . . But now – well, really, I honestly can't.'

'Scoundrel!' thought our hero.

'Yakov Petrovich!' he exclaimed miserably. 'I have never been your enemy. Spiteful people have depicted me unfairly . . . For my part, I'm ready . . . if you like, shall we, you and I, Yakov Petrovich, pop into this coffee-house now . . . There, with pure hearts as you so rightly put it just now and in straightforward, noble language . . . here, into this coffee-house. Then everything will explain itself – that's it, Yakov Petrovich. Then everything is bound to be explained of its own accord.'

'Into this coffee-house? Very well, sir, I've no objections, let's drop in, my dear chap, only on one condition – on one condition: that everything will explain itself of its own accord. So, it's like this, so to speak, sweetie-pie,' said Mr Golyadkin Junior, getting out of the cab and shamelessly slapping our hero on the shoulder. 'You're such a good pal, you are. For you, Yakov Petrovich, I'm prepared to go down a side street (as you so rightly suggested at that time, Yakov Petrovich). You're a real rogue you are – you do just what you like with a man!' continued Mr Golyadkin's false friend with a faint smile, hovering and turning around him.

Far from the main streets, the coffee-house that the two Mr Golyadkins entered happened at that moment to be completely empty. The moment they rang the bell a rather plump German woman appeared at the counter. Mr Golyadkin Senior and his unworthy enemy went through into the second room where a puffy-faced urchin with close-cropped hair was fussing around the stove with a bundle of firewood, trying to resuscitate the fire that was about to go out. At Mr Golyadkin Junior's request chocolate was served.

'She's a scrumptious dish,' said Mr Golyadkin Junior, roguishly winking at Mr Golyadkin Senior.

Our hero blushed and said nothing.

'Oh yes, do forgive me, I quite forgot. I know your taste. You and I, dear sir, are partial to little Fräuleins, aren't we? You and I, Yakov Petrovich, my dear honest soul, fancy nice Fräuleins who are not lacking in certain other attractions, however. We rent rooms from them, lead them morally astray, dedicate our hearts to them for their *Biersuppe* and *Milchsuppe*, and promise them different things in writing – that's what we do – you Faublas, you gay deceiver!'

While he was saying all this Mr Golyadkin Junior, thus making an utterly futile but nonetheless crafty allusion to a certain person of the female sex, hovered around Mr Golyadkin, warmly smiling at him in a false show of cordiality and delight at their meeting there. But when he noticed that Mr Golyadkin Senior was by no means so stupid or by no means so completely lacking in education and refinement as immediately to trust him, the infamous man decided to change tactics and be open about everything. So after those vile remarks the spurious Mr Golyadkin concluded by slapping the respectable Mr Golyadkin on the shoulder with deeply distressing effrontery and familiarity and, not contenting himself with this, started teasing him in a manner quite improper in well-bred society. He suddenly hit upon the idea of repeating his earlier filthy trick, that is, of pinching the exasperated Mr Golyadkin Senior on the cheek, despite the distressed Mr Golyadkin Senior's resistance and faint cries of protest. At the sight of such depravity our hero flew into a rage but held his tongue . . . only for the time being, however.

'That's what my enemies say,' he finally replied in a quavering voice, sensibly restraining himself. At the same time our hero uneasily looked round at the door. Mr Golyadkin Junior was evidently in excellent spirits and ready to embark on all kinds of pranks, impermissible in a public place and generally speaking not tolerated by the rules of etiquette, especially as observed in society of the most refined tone.

'Ah well, just as you please,' gravely responded Mr Golyadkin Junior to Mr Golyadkin Senior's idea, putting his empty cup that he had drained with unseemly greed down on the table. 'Well now, there's no point in my staying long with you, but . . . Well, how are you getting on now, Yakov Petrovich?'

'There's only one thing I have to tell you, Yakov Petrovich,' our hero replied coolly and with dignity. 'I have never been your enemy.'

'Hm . . . and what about Petrushka? That's his name, isn't it? Of course it is! How is he? All right? Same as ever?'

'He's the same as ever, too, Yakov Petrovich,' replied Mr Golyadkin Senior, somewhat startled. 'I don't know, Yakov Petrovich, but for my part . . . from an honourable and frank point of view, Yakov Petrovich, you yourself will agree, Yakov Petrovich . . .'

'Yes, sir. But you yourself know, Yakov Petrovich,' replied Mr Golyadkin Junior in a soft and expressive voice, thus falsely making himself out to be a man dejected, remorseful and worthy of compassion, 'you yourself know that these are hard times . . . I refer to *you*, Yakov Petrovich. You're an intelligent man and you'll make a fair judgement,' added Mr Golyadkin Junior, basely flattering Mr Golyadkin Senior. 'Life isn't a game, you know that yourself,' concluded Mr Golyadkin Junior meaningly, thus trying to pass himself off as a learned and intelligent man capable of conversing on lofty subjects.

'For my part, Yakov Petrovich,' our hero answered with animation, 'as one who despises beating about the bush and who speaks boldly and openly, in straightforward, noble language, thus putting the whole business on a lofty basis, I can tell you, I can affirm candidly and honourably, Yakov Petrovich, that I am completely innocent and that as you yourself know, Yakov Petrovich, there can be mutual misunderstandings – anything can happen – the judgement of society, the opinion of the servile mob. I'm telling you quite frankly,

Yakov Petrovich, anything can happen. And I'll say more, Yakov Petrovich: if you judge things like that, if you consider the business from a noble and lofty point of view, then, I boldly maintain, I shall say this without any false shame, Yakov Petrovich, that it would even be a pleasure for me to discover I was mistaken – and even a pleasure to confess to it. You yourself know that, you're an intelligent man and high-minded into the bargain. Without shame, without false shame – I'm ready to confess it,' our hero concluded with nobility and dignity.

'It's fate, it's destiny, Yakov Petrovich! But let's leave it at that,' sighed Mr Golyadkin Junior. 'Let's rather spend these brief moments together in more profitable and agreeable conversation as is proper between two colleagues. Really, I don't think I've managed to say two words to you all this time. But I'm not the one to blame for it, Yakov Petrovich.'

'Nor am I,' our hero heatedly interrupted. 'Nor am I! My heart tells me I'm not the one to blame for all this. We must blame it all on fate, Yakov Petrovich,' added Mr Golyadkin Senior in a positively conciliatory tone. His voice was gradually beginning to weaken and quaver.

'So, how about your health in general?' the errant one inquired in a sugary voice.

'I've a bit of a cough,' our hero replied in an even more sugary voice.

'You must be careful. With all these infections going around you could easily catch quinsy and I admit I've already started wrapping myself in flannel.'

'Oh yes, Yakov Petrovich, you can easily catch quinsy . . . Yakov Petrovich!' our hero said after a brief silence. 'Yakov Petrovich! I can see that I was mistaken! With deep emotion I recall those happy moments we spent together beneath my humble – dare I say – hospitable roof.'

'But that's not what you wrote in your letter,' somewhat scornfully retorted the completely justified Mr Golyadkin Junior (but only in this respect was he completely justified).

'Yakov Petrovich! I was mistaken . . . Now I can clearly see that I was wrong to write that unfortunate letter of mine, Yakov Petrovich, I feel ashamed to look at you, you won't believe . . .

Now give me that letter so that I can tear it up before your eyes, Yakov Petrovich, or if that's really out of the question I beg you to read it the other way round, completely the other way round, that is, with a deliberately friendly intention, giving all the words their opposite meaning. I was in the wrong. Please forgive me Yakov Petrovich, I completely ... I was grievously wrong, Yakov Petrovich.'

'You were saying?' Mr Golyadkin Senior's perfidious friend suddenly asked, quite nonchalantly and absent-mindedly.

'I was saying that I was mistaken, Yakov Petrovich, and that for my part it was completely without false shame ...'

'Oh well – that's good! It's very good that you were mistaken,' rudely replied Mr Golyadkin Junior.

'I even had the idea, Yakov Petrovich,' nobly added our candid hero, completely failing to notice his deceitful friend's appalling perfidy, 'I even had the idea that here two identical twins have been created ...'

'Ah! So that's your idea!'

Here the notoriously worthless Mr Golyadkin Junior rose and picked up his hat. Still failing to notice the deceit, Mr Golyadkin Senior got up, too, smiling ingenuously and good-naturedly at his spurious friend and attempting in his innocence to be nice and encouraging to him, so striking up a new friendship with him.

'Farewell, Your Excellency!' Mr Golyadkin Junior suddenly shouted. Our hero shuddered, observing something almost Bacchic in his enemy's face, and simply in order to get rid of him thrust two of his fingers into the degenerate's outstretched hand. But here Mr Golyadkin Junior's shamelessness exceeded all bounds. Grabbing two fingers of Mr Golyadkin Senior's hand and first squeezing them, that worthless man decided there and then to repeat before his very eyes the shameless trick he had played on him that morning. It was more than flesh and blood could stand.

He was already stuffing the handkerchief on which he had wiped his fingers into his pocket when Mr Golyadkin Senior recovered and rushed after him into the next room where, true to his usual obnoxious habit, his uncompromising foe slipped away in a hurry. There he was, standing at the counter, as if nothing had happened, eating pies and, just like any virtuous gentleman, calmly exchanging pleasantries with the German proprietress. 'Not in front of a lady,' thought our hero and he, too, went up to the counter, beside himself with agitation.

'Really, not a bad little dish at all! What do you think?' said Mr Golyadkin Junior, embarking on those lewd sallies of his again and no doubt counting on Mr Golyadkin Senior's infinite patience. For her part, the fat German looked at both her customers with blank, pewtery eyes, smiling affably, since she evidently didn't understand a word of Russian. At these words of the utterly shameless Mr Golyadkin Junior, our hero, flushed as red as fire and losing all self-control, finally launched himself at him with the clear intention of tearing him limb from limb and thus finishing him for good. But Mr Golyadkin Junior, with his customary vileness, was far off by now – he had taken to his heels and was already outside the front door and on the top steps. It goes without saying that after the first, momentary fit of stupefaction that had naturally come over Mr Golyadkin Senior, he dashed full tilt after the offender, who was already getting into the cab that had been waiting for him and with whose driver he obviously had an agreement. But at that very moment the fat German, seeing that her two customers were fleeing, shrieked and rang her bell as hard as she could. Almost in mid-air our hero turned round, threw her some money, both for himself and for the shameless man who had not paid, and without asking for change and despite the delay this occasioned still managed – although again almost in mid-air – to catch up with his enemy. Clinging to the splashboard with all the strength bestowed on him by nature, our hero was carried some way along the street as he attempted to clamber on to the carriage, while Mr Golyadkin Junior did his level best to fend him off. Meanwhile the driver, with whip, reins, feet and exhortations, urged on his broken-down nag which, quite unexpectedly, the bit between its teeth, broke into a gallop, kicking out its hind legs – a nasty habit it had – at every third stride. Finally our hero managed to perch himself on the droshky, facing his enemy, leaning with his back to the driver, his knees pressed against his enemy's and with his right hand gripping for all he was worth the badly moth-eaten fur collar of his depraved and fiercest enemy's coat . . .

The two enemies were carried along for some time in silence. Our hero could barely catch his breath. The road was dreadful and he kept bobbing up and down at every stride, in great danger of breaking his neck. What was more, his fierce enemy still would not concede defeat and was trying to tip his opponent over into the mud. The crowning nastiness was the frightful weather; the snow was falling in large flakes, which were doing their utmost, for their part, to creep somehow under the un-buttoned coat of the genuine Mr Golyadkin. All around it was murky, difficult to see anything and to tell where they were going and along which streets. It struck Mr Golyadkin that there was something familiar about what was happening to him. For a moment he tried to remember whether he had had a kind of hunch the day before – in a dream, for example. Finally his misery turned into the most acute agony. Leaning with all his weight against his pitiless enemy, he was about to utter a cry. But his cry died upon his lips. There was a moment when Mr Golyadkin forgot everything and decided that every-thing was all right, that it was all simply happening in some inexplicable way and that in this case it would have been superfluous to protest, a complete lost cause . . . But suddenly and almost at the moment when our hero was coming to this conclusion, a careless jolt changed the whole complexion of the matter. Mr Golyadkin toppled off the droshky like a sack of flour and rolled away somewhere, admitting to himself as he fell – and quite rightly – that in fact he had let himself get excited most inopportunely. Finally, leaping up, he saw that they had arrived somewhere: the droshky was standing in the middle of a courtyard and at first glance our hero recognized it as belonging to the very same house in which Olsufy Ivanovich resided. At that very moment he noticed that his enemy was already going up on to the porch – probably he was going to visit Olsufy Ivanovich. In indescribable anguish he was about to dash off and overtake his foe but fortunately for him he prudently had second thoughts. Not forgetting to pay the driver, Mr Golyadkin tore down the street for all he was worth, wherever his legs would carry him. As before, the snow was falling heavily and it was wet, murky, dark. Our hero did not run but flew, knocking over everyone in his path – men, women, children – and he in turn rebounded from men, women and children. All around and from behind could be heard cries of distress, shrieks and screams . . . But Mr Golyadkin seemed oblivious of it all and did not deign to pay attention to any of it. But at Semyonovsky Bridge he came to his senses – and only then as a result of somehow managing to collide awkwardly with two peasant women, knocking them over together with their wares and then toppling over himself. 'It's all right,' thought Mr Golyadkin, 'all this can very easily be settled for the best.' And immediately he felt in his pocket for a silver rouble to pay for the spilt gingerbread, apples, peas and sundry items. Suddenly a new light dawned on Mr Golyadkin: in his pocket he felt the letter given him by the clerk that morning. Happening to remember that not far away was a tavern he knew, he ran into it and without wasting a moment in settling himself at a small table lit by a tallow candle and without paying attention to anything, without listening to the waiter who had come to take his order, he broke the seal and read the following, which completely stunned him:

Noble one who is suffering on my behalf and who is eternally dear to my heart!

I am suffering, I am perishing – save me! A slanderer, an intriguer, notorious for his worthless ways, has ensnared me and I am undone! I am fallen! To me he is abhorrent, while you . . . ! They have kept us apart, my letters to you have been intercepted and it is all the work of an immoral one taking advantage of his only good quality – his resemblance to you. In any event one can be ugly but still charm with intellect, powerful feelings and pleasant manners . . . I am perishing. I am to be married against my will and the one who is intriguing most is my father, my benefactor, State Counsellor Olsufy Ivanovich, doubtless wishing to usurp my place and relations in good society . . . But my mind is made up and I protest with all the powers that nature has given me. Wait for me in your carriage outside Olsufy Ivanovich's windows at exactly nine tonight. We are giving another ball and that handsome lieutenant is coming again. I shall come out – and we shall fly away. Besides, there are other places where one can still be of service to one's country. At any rate, my friend, remember that innocence is strong by virtue of its very innocence. Farewell. Wait at the entrance with the carriage. I shall throw myself into the shelter of your embrace at two o'clock in the morning.

Yours to the grave
Klara Olsufyevna

After reading this letter our hero remained for some time as if thunderstruck. In terrible distress, in terrible agitation, white as a sheet, he paced the room several times with the letter in his hand. To crown all his appalling tribulations our hero failed to notice that at that moment he was the object of the exclusive attention of everyone in the room. Probably his disordered clothes and his uncontrollable agitation, his walking – rather, his scurrying – his two-handed gesticulations and perhaps the several enigmatic words spoken down the wind in absent-mindedness – all this must have lowered Mr Golyadkin significantly in the opinion of all present. Even the waiter was beginning to look at him suspiciously. When he came to his senses our hero found he was standing in the middle of the room, staring in an almost improper, discourteous manner at one old gentleman of the most venerable appearance who, having dined and said a prayer before an icon, had returned to his seat and for his part couldn't take his eyes off Mr Golyadkin. Our hero gazed vacantly around and noticed that everyone there, every single person, was looking at him with the most ominous and suspicious expression. Suddenly a retired military man with a red collar loudly demanded the *Police Gazette*.[36] Mr Golyadkin started and blushed. Happening to look down he saw that his clothing was so unseemly that it was not fit to be worn even in his own home, let alone in a public place. His boots, trousers and the whole of his left side were completely caked with mud; his right trouser-strap was torn off and his tail-coat even torn in many places. In inexhaustible distress our

hero went over to the table where he had read the letter and saw
that the waiter was approaching with a strange and insolently
insistent expression on his face. Flustered and quite deflated,
our hero set about inspecting the table at which he was now
standing. On it lay plates yet to be cleared away from someone's
dinner, a soiled napkin and a knife, fork and spoon that had
just been used. 'Who can have been dining here?' our hero
wondered. 'Could it have been me? Anything is possible! I must
have had dinner and didn't even notice. What on earth shall I
do now?' Looking up Mr Golyadkin saw that the waiter was
again beside him and about to say something to him. 'How
much do I owe you, old chap?' our hero asked in a trembling
voice.

Loud laughter broke out all around Mr Golyadkin. Even the
waiter himself grinned. Mr Golyadkin understood that he had
blundered again, committed some awful gaffe. Realizing all this
he was so embarrassed that he felt compelled to grope in his
pocket for his handkerchief, probably for the sake of doing
something instead of simply standing there. But to his own
and everyone else's indescribable amazement, instead of his
handkerchief he pulled out the phial containing some kind of
medicine prescribed four days earlier by Krestyan Ivanovich.
'Get it at the same chemist's as before', ran through Mr Golyadkin's mind. Suddenly he gave a start and almost shrieked
with horror. A new light was dawning . . . The dark, revolting
reddish liquid shone into Mr Golyadkin's eyes with a sinister
gleam. The bottle dropped from his grasp and immediately
shattered on the floor. Our hero screamed and jumped back
from the spilt liquid . . . he was trembling in every limb and
beads of sweat broke out on his temples and forehead. 'So, my
life is in danger!' he said. Meanwhile there was uproar and
general commotion in the room. Everyone surrounded Mr
Golyadkin, everyone spoke to Mr Golyadkin, some even
grabbed hold of Mr Golyadkin. But our hero was speechless
and motionless, seeing nothing, hearing nothing, feeling
nothing . . . Finally, as if tearing off, he rushed out of the
tavern, pushing aside each and every one of those who were
endeavouring to detain him, slumped almost unconscious into

the first droshky that happened to come along and sped off to his flat.

In the entrance hall he met Mikheyev, the office porter, bearing an official envelope in his hand. 'I know, my friend, I know everything. It's official,' our exhausted hero replied in a weak, suffering voice. And in fact the envelope contained an order to Mr Golyadkin, signed by Andrey Filippovich, for him to hand over all the files in his possession to Ivan Semyonovich. After taking the envelope and giving the porter ten copecks, Mr Golyadkin entered his flat and found Petrushka getting all his things together, all his rubbish and bits and pieces and wordly possessions, with the clear intention of abandoning Mr Golyadkin and going over to Karolina Ivanovna, who had enticed him there as a replacement for Yevstafy.

CHAPTER XII

Petrushka entered the room with a rocking motion, in a peculiarly off-hand manner and with a look that combined servility and triumph. Evidently he had devised some plan, felt quite within his rights and looked like a complete stranger – that is, like someone else's servant, only nothing like Mr Golyadkin's former servant.

'Well, you see, my dear man,' our hero began breathlessly, 'what's the time?'

Without a word Petrushka withdrew behind the partition and returned to announce, in a rather independent tone, that it would soon be half past seven.

'Good, dear man, that's very good. So you see, old chap . . . let me tell you that everything appears to be over between us.'

Petrushka did not reply.

'Well, now that everything is over between us, you can tell me frankly, as a friend, where you've been, old chap.'

'Where I've been? To see good people, sir.'

'I know, my friend, I know. I've always been satisfied with

you, dear chap – I'll give you a good reference . . . Well, what
were you doing there?'

'Why, you know very well, sir! It's a fact that a good man
won't teach you bad ways, sir.'

'I know, my dear man, I know. Good people are rare nowadays, my friend. You must value them. Well, how are they?'

'What do you mean, sir? You know how they are! Only, I
can't stay in service here any more, sir. You know that for
yourself.'

'Yes, I do, dear man, I do. I know how zealous and diligent
you are . . . I've seen all that, taken note of it, my friend. I
respect you. I respect a good and honest man, even if he's only
a flunkey.'

'Why of course, sir! The likes of me, sir, as you know very
well, must go where they're best off. That's how it is. What's it
to me? You know very well that it's impossible without a good
man.'

'Oh, all right, old chap, all right! I appreciate that . . . Well,
here's your wages and your reference. Now let's kiss and let's
say farewell, old chap . . . But there's one last service I ask of
you,' said Mr Golyadkin solemnly. 'You see, my dear chap, all
sorts of things can happen. Sorrow, my friend, lurks even in
gilded palaces and you can't escape from it anywhere. I reckon,
my friend, I've always been good to you.'

Petrushka said nothing.

'I think I've always been good to you, dear fellow. Well, how
much linen do we have, dear chap?'

'All present and correct, sir. Linen shirts – six, sir; socks –
three pairs; shirt-fronts – four, sir; one flannel vest and two sets
of underwear. You know that's all, sir. I've got nothing of
yours, sir . . . I, sir, look after my master's possessions. You
know that very well, sir . . . and as for me doing anything I
shouldn't have – never, sir!'

'I believe you, my friend, I believe you. But that's not what
I meant, my friend, not that. You see, it's this, my friend . . .'

'Of course, sir. We know that very well, sir. Take when I was
still working for General Stolbnyakov – they let me go, as

they were moving to Saratov[37] – that's where the family estate was . . .'

'No, my friend, it's not about that . . . It's nothing . . . now don't start thinking things, my friend.'

'Of course, sir. You know it's easy to speak ill of the likes of us, you know that very well . . . But everywhere they've been satisfied with me. Ministers, generals, senators, counts – I've worked for them all: Prince Svinchatkin, Colonel Pereborkin, General Nedobarov – he also went off to his family estate, sir. It's a fact, sir.'

'Yes, my friend, yes. That's very good, that's very good. And now I'm going away, my friend. We all have different paths to travel, my friend, and there's no telling what path you may finally tread. Well, my friend, put my things out so I can get dressed. Lay out my uniform jacket, too . . . and my other trousers, sheets, blankets, pillows . . .'

'Shall I bundle them all up?'

'Yes, my friend, please do bundle them up. Who knows what may happen to us? And now, dear man, you can go and find a carriage.'

'A carriage, sir?'

'Yes, my friend, a carriage – a nice, spacious one, for a fixed period. And don't start thinking things, my friend.'

'Do you intend going far, sir?'

'I don't know, my friend, that's something I don't know either. You'd better pack the feather-bed, too. What do you think? I'm relying on you, my dear chap.'

'But you don't want to go right away, do you, sir?'

'Oh yes, my friend, I do! A circumstance has arisen . . . that's how it is, dear chap, that's how it is.'

'Of course, sir. It was the same with a lieutenant in my regiment, sir. Carried off a landowner's daughter he did . . .'

'Carried off? What do you mean? My dear chap, you . . .'

'Yes, he carried her off and they got married on a different estate. It was all planned in advance. There was a hue and cry. But the late prince stuck up for them and it was all patched up in the end.'

'How did you know all this about it?'

'Well, I just know! News travels fast, sir. We know everything sir . . . of course, who hasn't been guilty of sin? Only, if I may be permitted to mention it now, sir, in plain servant's talk, if this is what it's come to then I'll tell you, sir – you have an enemy – you have a rival, sir, a powerful rival, that's what, sir . . .'

'I know, my friend, I know. You know it yourself, dear chap . . . So, I'm relying on you. Well, how are we going to do it now, my friend? What do you advise me to do?'

'Well, sir, if you're going in for that kind of thing, roughly speaking, what you'll be needing to buy are sheets, pillows, another feather-bed – a double, sir – and a good quilt, from a neighbour, a tradeswoman who lives downstairs, sir. And she's got a very nice fox fur coat. You could go down there right away, sir, have a look and buy it. It's just what you'll be needing now, sir. It's a fine coat, satin – lined, with fox fur.'

'Very good, my friend, that's good. I agree. I'm relying on you entirely, my friend, but we'll have to be quick! I'll go and buy that coat – only for God's sake please be quick! It will soon be eight. Be as quick as you can, my friend, for God's sake hurry! Be quick, my friend!'

Petrushka abandoned the linen, pillows, blankets and various odds and ends he had not finished bundling up and rushed headlong from the room. Meanwhile Mr Golyadkin grabbed the letter again but he could not read it. Clutching his wretched head in both hands he leant against the wall in amazement. He was unable to think about anything, nor could he do anything. He himself didn't even know what was happening to him. Finally, seeing that time was getting on and that neither Petrushka nor the coat had appeared, he decided to go himself. Opening the door into the hall he heard voices – arguing and altercations from down below. A few women neighbours were shouting, quarrelling and passing judgement on something. Mr Golyadkin knew very well about what. He heard Petrushka's voice and then footsteps. 'Good God! They'll bring the whole world in here next!' groaned Mr Golyadkin, wringing his hands in despair and rushing back to his room. Once there he fell almost senseless on to the sofa, burying his face in the cushion.

After lying there for about a minute he leapt up and, without waiting for Petrushka, put on his galoshes, overcoat and hat, seized his wallet and charged headlong downstairs. 'I don't need anything, old chap, I don't need anything, dear chap! I'll see to everything myself. I don't need you for the moment and perhaps the whole thing will even turn out for the best in the meantime,' Mr Golyadkin muttered to Petrushka when he met him on the stairs. Then he ran out into the courtyard and away from the house. His heart stopped beating – he still hadn't decided what he should do, what steps he should take at this present critical juncture.

'Yes, I mean, what should I do, for God's sake? Why on earth did all this have to happen?' he finally cried out in despair, as he trotted blindly and aimlessly along the street. 'Why did all this have to happen? If it hadn't been for this, precisely this, then everything would have been settled once and for all, at one stroke – at one clever, energetic, powerful stroke everything would have been settled! I'd stake my finger that it would have been settled! I even know exactly how it would have been settled. It would be done like this: I'd simply say: "It's like this, my dear sir, it's this and that. If you don't mind my saying so it's neither one thing nor the other as far as I'm concerned. Things aren't done that way, so to speak," I'd have said, "and imposture, my dear sir, will get you nowhere here. An impostor, my dear sir, is . . . er . . . hm . . . someone's who's worthless, no use to his native country. Do you understand that, sir? Do you understand that, my dear sir?" That's how it would have been, you know . . . But no . . . Now why am I talking all this nonsense, you utter idiot! I'm a suicide, that's what. No . . . that's not it at all, you suicide! But this is how it's being done now, you old reprobate . . . ! Well, where shall I go now, what shall I do with myself, for example, just tell me what I'm fit for now? Well, to give an example . . . Poor old Golyadkin – you unworthy fellow! Well, what now? I need to hire a carriage, so she says, I should go and get a carriage or we'll get our feet wet, so to speak, if there isn't any carriage. And who would have thought it? Well done, my fine, well-behaved young lady, our much-praised young miss! You've really excelled yourself,

THE DOUBLE 141

young lady, no doubt about it, really excelled yourself! And it
all comes from an immoral upbringing. Now that I've looked
into this and got to the bottom of it I can see it all stems from
nothing else but an immoral upbringing. Instead of giving her,
so to speak, the occasional thrashing when she was a child, they
stuff her with all kinds of sweetmeats and bons-bons and the
old man drools over her. "You're my pretty darling," he says.
"You're my this and that and we'll marry you off to a count!"
And now she's turned out like this and shown her hand. "That's
what our game is," she says! Well, instead of keeping her at
home they send her to boarding-school, some French madame,
some émigrée lady, some Madame Falbala[38] or whatever. And
she learns all sorts of good things at that émigrée Madame
Falbala's, so that's why it always turns out like this. "Come
and rejoice!" she says, "be with the carriage under my window
at such and such a time and sing me a sentimental Spanish
serenade. I'll be waiting for you and I know you love me and
we'll run away together and we'll live in a little hut." But in the
end it simply can't be done, if this is what it's come to, young
lady, it can't be done as it's against the law to carry off an
honest and innocent girl from her parents' home without the
parents' consent. And finally, what's the point, what's the need
for it? If only she married someone she ought to marry, the one
preordained by fate, that would be the end of the matter. But
I'm a working man, I could lose my job over this! I might end
up in court, my dear young lady! That's how it is – as if you
didn't know! It's that German woman's work. It all comes from
her, the witch, she's the spark that set the house on fire. Because
a man's been slandered, because they've made up some old
woman's gossip about him, some brazen cock-and-bull story,
on Andrey Filippovich's advice – that's where it all comes from.
Otherwise why on earth should Petrushka be mixed up in it?
What's it to do with him? What need does that scoundrel have
to get involved? No, young lady, I can't, I really can't – not for
anything. On this occasion you must excuse me, it all comes
from you, young lady, it's not the German that everything
comes from, not from the old witch at all, but purely from you,
as the witch is actually a good woman, because the witch is not

to blame for anything, but it's *you*, young lady, you are to blame! That's how it is! You, young lady, are leading me into making wrongful accusations. A man's disappearing here, a man's losing sight of himself and he can't keep a grip on himself – so what kind of wedding can there be here? And how will it all end? How will it be arranged? I'd give a great deal to find that out!'

So reasoned our hero in his despair. Suddenly recovering himself he noticed that he was standing somewhere in Liteynaya Street. The weather was awful: a thaw had set in and it was snowing and raining – well, exactly as it had been on that never-to-be forgotten night, at that dread midnight hour when all Mr Golyadkin's misfortunes began. 'What kind of journey can one make in this!' thought Mr Golyadkin, looking at the weather, 'everything's dead around here . . . Good God! Where can I find a carriage, for example? Yes, I think I can see something black over there at the corner. Let's go and investigate. Oh Lord!' continued our hero, directing his feeble and faltering steps towards what looked like a carriage. 'No, this is what I'll do. I'll go there, I'll go and fall at his feet if I can, I'll humbly implore him and say: "It's like this and that, I put my fate in your hands, into the hands of my superiors . . ." I'll tell him: "Your Excellency, protect and be benevolent to a man; it's like this and that, and such and such, it's an unlawful act. Don't ruin me, I look upon you as a father, don't desert me . . . save my pride, honour, and my name . . . and save me from that scoundrel, that depraved man . . . He's a different person, Your Excellency, and I'm another, too. He's someone apart and I'm also someone in my own right. Really, someone in my own right, Your Excellency, really someone in my own right." That's how it is, I'll say. "I can't be like him," I'll say. "Please be kind, please authorize the change and put an end to that godless, wilful substitution, so that it won't serve as an example for others, Your Excellency. I look upon you as a father. Of course, benevolent and caring superiors must encourage such actions . . . There's even something chivalrous about it. I take you benevolent authorities as a father and I put my fate in your hands and I shan't contradict you. I entrust myself to you and

I myself will stand aside from the whole business ... That's
how it is!"'

'So, you're a cab driver, dear man?'

'Yes.'

'I need a carriage, old chap, for the whole evening.'

'Will you be wanting to go far, sir?'

'I want it for the evening, the evening. And to go wherever
I need to, my dear man.'

'You won't be going out of town, will you, sir?'

'Perhaps, my friend, perhaps even out of town. I myself don't
know for sure yet and I can't tell you for sure, dear chap. The
fact is, it all might turn out for the best! That's so, my friend.'

'Well of course it's so, sir. God grant that happens for
everyone.'

'Yes, my friend, yes. Thank you, dear man. Well, how much
will you charge, dear chap?'

'Will you be wanting to go right away, sir?'

'Yes ... that is ... no. You'll have to wait at a certain spot
... yes ... you won't have to wait long, dear chap.'

'Well, if you want to hire me for the whole evening I couldn't
possibly charge less than six silver roubles ... not in this
weather, sir.'

'All right, my friend, all right. And I'll show my gratitude,
dear chap. So, you can take me there right away, dear chap!'

'Get in, sir ... no, excuse me ... I'll just tidy it up a bit inside
first ... Now please get in, sir. Where to, sir?'

'To Izmaylovsky Bridge, my friend.'

The driver clambered up on to the box and was about to get
his pair of scrawny nags going – which he had difficulty in
tearing away from their trough of hay – and drive to Izmaylovsky Bridge. But suddenly Mr Golyadkin pulled the cord,
stopped the carriage and implored the driver to turn back and
go to some other street and not to Izmaylovsky Bridge. The
driver turned into another street and within ten minutes Mr
Golyadkin's newly hired carriage drew up before the house
where His Excellency lived. Mr Golyadkin alighted, entreated
the driver to wait, dashed up to the first floor and with a sinking
feeling rang the bell.

'Is His Excellency at home?' Mr Golyadkin asked, addressing the servant who opened the door to him.

'And what do you want, sir?' asked the footman, looking Mr Golyadkin up and down.

'I . . . my friend . . . er . . . um . . . I'm Golyadkin, civil servant, titular counsellor. Say it's like this and I've come to explain things . . .'

'You'll have to wait. It's impossible . . .'

'No, my friend, I can't wait. My business is important and it brooks no delay!'

'Who are you from? Have you brought some documents?'

'No, I'm here on a private matter. Please announce me. Tell him this and that, tell him I've come to explain. I'll show my gratitude, my friend.'

'But I can't. Orders are to receive no one. He has visitors just now. Please come back in the morning at ten o'clock.'

'Now do go and announce me, dear fellow. I can't wait – it's impossible! You'll answer for this, my man!'

'Oh, go on and announce him, what's the matter – saving on boot leather, eh?' said another footman who was lolling on a chest and had not said a word until then.

'To hell with boot leather! Orders are not to receive anyone, that's what. *Their* turn's in the mornings.'

'Oh, go on, announce him. Frightened your tongue'll drop off, or something?'

'Oh, all right, I'll announce him. But my tongue won't drop off. I've orders not to . . . that's what he said. Now, come through.'

Mr Golyadkin entered the first room. A clock stood on the table. He glanced at it – it was half past eight. His heart ached and he was about to turn back but at that very moment a lanky footman stationed at the threshold of the next room thunderously announced Mr Golyadkin. 'What a foghorn!' thought our hero in indescribable anguish. 'Now I should have said: "Um . . . it's like this, so to speak, I've come most humbly and dutifully to explain . . . er . . . please be good enough to receive me . . ." But my business is all ruined, my business has been blown away in the wind. Ah well, never mind!' But there was no point in reflecting, however. The footman returned and announced: 'This way please,' and led Mr Golyadkin into the study.

The moment he entered our hero felt as if he'd suddenly gone blind, as he could see absolutely nothing. However, he caught a glimpse of two or three figures and the thought, 'Yes, they must be visitors' flashed through Mr Golyadkin's mind. At length our hero could clearly distinguish a star on His Excellency's black frock-coat and then, taking a gradual approach, he progressed to the frock-coat itself, until finally he regained the faculty of full vision.

'Well, sir?' asked a familiar voice above Mr Golyadkin's head.

'Titular Counsellor Golyadkin, Your Excellency.'

'Well?'

'I've come to explain myself.'

'What's that? What did you say?'

'Yes, it's like this, so to speak, I've come to explain myself, Your Excellency.'

'And . . . who are you?'

'M-m-m-mister Golyadkin, Your Excellency, titular counsellor.'

'Well, what do you want?'

'It's like this, so to speak. I consider him my father . . . I myself am withdrawing from the whole affair . . . protection from my enemies – that's what I want!'

'What's that . . . ?'

'It's well known . . .'

'What's well known?'

Mr Golyadkin didn't reply; his chin started to twitch slightly.

'Well?'

'I thought it's chivalrous, Your Excellency . . . there's a touch of chivalry about it, I thought, and I look upon my superior as a father . . . so to speak . . . that's it . . . So please protect me . . . w-with t-t-tears in my eyes I b-b-beseech you . . . such actions should be en-en-encouraged . . .'

His Excellency turned away. For several moments our hero's

eyes could distinguish nothing. He felt a tightness in his chest; he was short of breath; he had no idea where he was standing . . . he felt somehow ashamed and sad. God knows what happened after that. When he recovered our hero saw that His Excellency was talking to his visitors, apparently engaged in a vigorous and sharp debate with them. Mr Golyadkin at once recognized one of the visitors. It was Andrey Filippovich; but the other he didn't recognize. However, his face was somehow familiar – it was a tall, thick-set elderly figure, endowed with very bushy eyebrows and whiskers and a keen, expressive look. Around this stranger's neck was a decoration and in his mouth a cigar. This stranger was smoking and without taking the cigar from his mouth he nodded significantly as he glanced occasionally at Mr Golyadkin. Mr Golyadkin began to feel somewhat awkward. He averted his eyes and at once caught sight of yet another very strange visitor. In a doorway which until then our hero had taken for a mirror, as sometimes happened with him, *he* appeared – it's obvious who – Mr Golyadkin's very intimate friend and acquaintance! Until then Mr Golyadkin Junior had been in another little room writing something in a great hurry. Now he was apparently needed and he appeared with papers under his arm, went up to His Excellency and, fully expecting everyone's exclusive attention, managed very cleverly to worm his way into the general discussion, stationing himself behind Andrey Filippovich's back and partly screening himself with the cigar-smoking stranger. Evidently Mr Golyadkin Junior was taking a great interest in the conversation, on which he was now eavesdropping in the most dignified manner, shuffling his feet, smiling and constantly glancing at His Excellency as if by his glance he was asking that he too might be allowed to get his word in. 'The scoundrel!' thought Mr Golyadkin and he involuntarily took a step forward. At that moment His Excellency turned around and he himself approached Mr Golyadkin rather hesitantly.

'Well, all right, all right. Off with you now, I'll look into your case and I'll get someone to show you out.' Here the general glanced at the stranger with the bushy side-whiskers. The latter nodded in agreement.

Mr Golyadkin felt and fully realized that he had been mistaken for someone else, not at all as he should have been. 'One
way or the other,' he thought, 'I really must explain myself.
"It's like this, so to speak, Your Excellency", I'll say.' Just then,
in his bewilderment, he looked down at the floor and to his
amazement saw a sizeable white stain on His Excellency's shoes.
'Surely they can't have split, can they?' he wondered. Soon Mr
Golyadkin discovered that in fact they hadn't split at all but
were acting as powerful reflectors, a phenomenon fully
explained by the fact that they were of extremely glossy patent
leather. 'That's called a *high-light*,' thought our hero. 'The term
is used particularly in artists' studios, but in other places these
reflections are simply called flashes of light.' Here Mr Golyadkin looked up and saw that it was time to speak, since the
whole business might easily take a turn for the worse. Our hero
stepped forward.

'It's like this and that, so to speak, Your Excellency,' he said,
'these days imposture will get you nowhere.'

The general made no reply and gave a hard tug on the bell
pull. Our hero took another step forward.

'Your Excellency,' said our hero, beside himself, almost dying
with fear, but nevertheless boldly and determinedly pointing at
his unworthy twin who at that moment was prancing about
near His Excellency. 'He's a depraved and vile man. Say what
you like, but I'm referring to a certain well-known person.'

Mr Golyadkin's words were followed by a general stir.
Andrey Filippovich and the unfamiliar figure nodded. His
Excellency impatiently tugged with all his might at the bell pull
to summon the servants. Here Mr Golyadkin Junior in turn
stepped forward.

'Your Excellency,' he said, 'I humbly beg permission to
speak.' In Mr Golyadkin Junior's voice there was an extremely
determined note; everything about him showed that he felt he
was completely within his rights.

'Allow me to ask you,'[39] he began, again anticipating His
Excellency's reply in his zeal and this time addressing Mr Golyadkin, 'allow me to ask in whose presence are you explaining
yourself, in whose presence are you standing, in whose study

are you?' Mr Golyadkin Senior was in an unusually agitated state, his face was red and burning with indignation and anger. Tears even came to his eyes.

'The Bassavryukovs!' bellowed the footman, who had appeared in the doorway, at the top of his voice.

'A good aristocratic name, of Ukrainian origin,' thought Mr Golyadkin and immediately someone laid a hand on his back in the friendliest fashion and then another hand was laid on his back. Mr Golyadkin's vile twin bustled around in front, showing the way, and our hero could clearly see that he was being steered towards the large study doors – and then he found himself out in the entrance hall. 'Just as at Olsufy Ivanovich's,' Mr Golyadkin thought. As he looked round he saw beside him two of His Excellency's footmen and one twin.

'The overcoat, the overcoat, my friend's overcoat! My best friend's overcoat!' twittered the depraved man, snatching the coat from one of the footmen and tossing it right on to Mr Golyadkin's head as a despicable and mean joke. As he struggled out from under his overcoat Mr Golyadkin Senior could clearly hear the two footmen laughing. However, listening to nothing and oblivious to all around, he left the hall and found himself on a brightly lit staircase. Mr Golyadkin Junior was following him.

'Goodbye, Your Excellency!' he shouted in Mr Golyadkin Senior's wake.

'Scoundrel!' our hero muttered, beside himself.

'So, I'm a scoundrel . . .'

'Depraved wretch!'

'So, I'm a depraved wretch,' the worthy Mr Golyadkin's unworthy foe replied, looking down at him without blinking, straight in the eye, from the top of the staircase with his characteristic vileness, as if inviting him to continue. Our hero spat in indignation and ran out on to the front steps. He was so crushed that he had absolutely no recollection of who helped him into the carriage or how. When he recovered he saw that he was being driven along the Fontanka. 'So, I must be going to Izmaylovsky Bridge,' thought Mr Golyadkin Senior. Now he wanted to think of something else, but he could not. It was all so

horrible that it defied explanation. 'Well, never mind!' concluded our hero as he drove off to Izmaylovsky Bridge.

CHAPTER XIII

It seemed that the weather was trying to change for the better.
In fact, the wet snow that had been falling up to then in great
clouds gradually began to fall more thinly and finally stopped
almost completely. The sky became visible, with a few tiny stars
twinkling here and there. It was just wet, muddy, damp and
steamy – especially for Mr Golyadkin, who already had difficulty catching his breath. His coat, which was soaked and
weighed down by the wet, made him feel a disagreeable warmth
and dampness all over and its weight made his already terribly
weak legs buckle. A feverish trembling spread all over his
body, producing a sharp, tingling sensation. Sheer exhaustion
squeezed a cold, sickly sweat out of him, so that at this suitable
moment Mr Golyadkin forgot to repeat his favourite phrase,
with his characteristic determination and resolve, that somehow it might possibly, surely, undoubtedly, certainly, turn out
for the best. 'Still, none of this matters for the moment,' added
our plucky and undaunted hero, wiping from his face the drops
of cold water streaming in all directions from the brim of his
hat that was too sodden to hold any more water. Adding that
everything was still all right, our hero tried to take a seat on a
large log lying near a stack of firewood in Olsufy Ivanovich's
courtyard. Of course, there was no question now of thinking
of Spanish serenades or silken ladders. But what he did need to
think about was finding a quiet little corner which, if not actually warm, would at least be comfortable and secluded. He
was strongly tempted, let it be mentioned in passing, by that
particular little corner on Olsufy Ivanovich's landing, where
our hero had once before, almost at the beginning of this
veracious story, waited for a whole two hours between the
cupboard and some old screens, among all kinds of domestic
rubbish and unwanted junk. The fact was that even now he had

been standing waiting two solid hours in Olsufy Ivanovich's courtyard. But now there were certain inconveniences that had not existed before concerning his former quiet and cosy little corner. The first was that the place had probably now been noted since that scandal at Olsufy Ivanovich's last ball and precautionary measures taken. Secondly, he must now await the agreed signal from Klara Olsufyevna, since there must be some kind of agreed signal. That was the way these things were always done and 'We're not the first and we shan't be the last', as he put it. Just then, most opportunely, Mr Golyadkin remembered in passing a novel he had read a long time before, where the heroine had given a prearranged signal to Alfred in exactly similar circumstances, by tying a pink ribbon to her window. But now, at night, and with the St Petersburg climate, so notorious for its dampness and unreliability, a pink ribbon was out of the question – in brief, it was quite impossible. 'No, this isn't the time for silken ladders,' thought our hero. 'I'd better stay where I am, on my own – stand here, for example, nice and quietly where no one can see me.' And he selected a spot in the courtyard directly opposite the windows, near the stack of wood. Of course, many postilions, coachmen and visitors were constantly passing through the courtyard, and in addition there were wheels clattering and horses snorting and so on. But for all that it was a convenient spot: whether he was noticed or not, there was now at least the advantage that everything, in a manner of speaking, was to some extent in shadow, so that he could see absolutely everything and no one could see Mr Golyadkin. The windows were brightly lit; some kind of ceremonial gathering was in progress at Olsufy Ivanovich's. As yet no music could be heard. 'So, it can't be a ball, they must have gathered for another reason,' our hero thought, his heart sinking. 'But is it today?' flashed through his mind. 'Was there a mistake about the date? Well, it's possible, anything is possible. Oh yes, anything is possible . . . It's possible it was yesterday that the letter was written but it didn't reach me – it didn't reach me because Petrushka got involved in it – the scoundrel! Or perhaps "tomorrow" was written there, that is . . . I . . . that everything had to be done tomorrow, that is, to be waiting with a carriage . . .' Here our hero went cold all over and fumbled in his pocket for the letter, so that he could check. But to his amazement the letter was not in his pocket. 'How is this?' the half-dead Mr Golyadkin whispered. 'Where could I have left it? Does this mean I've lost it? Well, that's the last straw!' he groaned at length. 'What if it falls into evil hands now? (Perhaps it already has!) Good heavens! What will be the upshot of all this! The upshot will be that . . . Oh, my wretched fate!' Here Mr Golyadkin trembled like a leaf at the thought that his shameless twin, when he had got wind of it from Mr Golyadkin's enemies, had perhaps hurled his coat over his head with the express purpose of stealing that letter! 'What's more, he's intercepting it as evidence . . . but why evidence?' After the initial shock and stupor of horror the blood rushed to Mr Golyadkin's head. Groaning, gnashing his teeth and clutching his burning head, he sank down on his log and started thinking about something . . . But somehow his thoughts wouldn't connect with anything. There were glimpses and memories of faces, at times vividly and vaguely of others and of long forgotten events; silly song-tunes filled his head. The anguish, the anguish was really unnatural! 'Oh God!' he thought, slightly recovering and suppressing the dull sobs in his breast, 'Oh God! Grant me fortitude in the bottomless depths of my tribulations! But there's no doubt whatsoever that I'm done for, I've disappeared, gone from this world completely and all this is in the natural order of things and just couldn't be otherwise. To start with I've lost my job, I must have lost my job, in no way could I not have lost it. Well, supposing it will all be sorted out there. Supposing the little bit of money I've got will be enough to begin with. I'll need a different little flat, a few bits of furniture . . . But for a start I shan't even have Petrushka with me. I can cope without that scoundrel . . . and I'll have lodgers as well, that's good! And I can come and go as I please and Petrushka won't be there to grumble if I'm late. That's good, that's why it would be a good thing to have lodgers. Well, supposing that's all very good, only why do I always talk about the wrong thing, always the wrong thing completely?' Here the thought of his present predicament again lit up his memory. He looked around. 'Oh God! Oh God! What am I talking about now?' he wondered, clutching his burning head in utter confusion . . .

'Will you be wanting to go soon, sir?' said a voice above Mr Golyadkin. Mr Golyadkin gave a start. But it was only his cab driver, also soaked to the skin, chilled to the marrow, having taken it into his head, in his impatience and from having nothing to do, to come and have a look at Mr Golyadkin behind the woodpile.

'I'm all right, my friend . . . I . . . my friend soon, very soon . . . so please wait.'

The cab driver went away, grumbling to himself. 'What's he grumbling about?' thought Mr Golyadkin through his tears. 'After all, I hired him for the evening so . . . really . . . er . . . I'm within my rights now – that's it! I hired him for the evening and that's the end of it, it makes no difference even if one has to stay here like this. I can please myself. I'm at liberty to go or not to go. And the fact that I'm standing here behind the woodpile . . . well, there's nothing at all wrong with that . . . and don't you dare contradict me! I say, the gentleman chooses to stand behind firewood . . . so he stands behind firewood . . . and he won't blacken anyone's name by so doing – that's right! That's how it is, my dear young lady, if you really want to know. In our day and age just no one, so to speak, lives in a hut. And in this industrial age, young lady, you'll get nowhere without good behaviour, of which you provide such proof. One has to be a magistrate's clerk and live in a hut by the sea.[40] Firstly, young lady, there are no magistrate's clerks on the seashore and secondly you and I couldn't even get a job as one of those magistrate's clerks. Let's suppose, for example, I apply for the job and present myself and say: "It's like this and that . . . and to be a magistrate's clerk and . . . you know . . . and protect me from my enemy" – they'll tell you, young lady, such and such, that there's lots of magistrate's clerks and here you're not at Madame Falbala's where you learned good behaviour, of which you provided such a baneful example. Good behaviour, young lady, means staying at home, respecting your father, and not hankering after nice suitors before the time is ripe, young lady. Suitors, young lady, will come along all in good time –

that's how it is! Of course, there's no doubt that you need to have acquired various talents, such as playing the piano now and then, speaking French, knowing history, geography, divinity and arithmetic – that's how it is! But you don't need more than that. And cookery in addition. A knowledge of cookery should definitely be within the sphere of knowledge of every well-behaved young lady! Otherwise what is there? Firstly, my beauty, my dear young lady, they won't let you go but they'll raise a hue and cry and you'll be trumped – and then it's into a convent. So what then, young lady? What would you have me do then? Would you have me go to a nearby hill and dissolve in tears, after the fashion of certain novels,[41] as I contemplate the cold walls of your confinement and finally expire after the example of certain bad German poets and novelists – isn't that so, young lady? But first allow me to tell you as a friend that things aren't done that way; and secondly I'd give you and your parents a good thrashing for letting you read French books, for French books will teach you no good. There's poison in them, pernicious poison, my dear young lady! Or do you think, if I may ask, do you think this and that, so to speak, that we'll run away unpunished and there's . . . um . . . so to speak . . . a hut for you by the seashore and we'll start billing and cooing and talk about different feelings and live happily ever after? And then along comes a nestling, so we'll . . . well, it's like this, it's this and that, so to speak. We'll tell our father and State Counsellor Olsufy Ivanovich that a nestling's come along, so on this auspicious occasion will you withdraw your curse and bless the couple? No, young lady, once again things aren't done like that and the first thing is that there won't be any billing and cooing, so please don't pin your hopes on that. Nowadays the husband, young lady, is master and a good well-brought-up wife must try and please him in everything. Displays of affection aren't in fashion in this industrial age. The days of Jean-Jacques Rousseau are past, so to speak. For example, these days a husband comes home hungry from work and asks if he could have a little snack before dinner, darling, perhaps a glass of vodka to drink and a bit of herring? Well, young lady, you must have vodka and herring all ready for him. The husband will eat heartily and won't so much as give you a look – all he'll say is: "Just pop into the kitchen, my little kitten, and see to dinner." And perhaps, just once a week, if you're lucky, he'll give you a kiss and a pretty casual one at that! That's the way we do it, so to speak – and even then indifferently! That's how it will be if we think about it like that, if that's what things have come to, if that's the way we've started looking at things . . . But what's it all to do with me? And why, young lady, have you mixed me up in your idle fancies? "A benevolent man who is suffering for my sake," you say, "in so many ways dear to my heart, and so on." Well, firstly, young lady, I'm not suited to you – you know that yourself, I'm no expert at paying compliments, I don't like uttering all that sweetly scented non-sense to the ladies, I've no time for womanizers and I must confess my looks have never got me anywhere. You won't find any false bragging or false modesty in me and now I confess it in all sincerity. That's how it is, so to speak. All I possess is a straightforward, open character and good sense. I don't get mixed up in intrigues. I'm not an intriguer, so to speak, and I'm proud of it – so there you are! I don't wear a mask when I'm with decent people and to tell all . . .'

Suddenly Mr Golyadkin gave a start. The drenched ginger beard of his cab driver again appeared around the woodpile.

'Coming right away, my friend,' Mr Golyadkin replied in a trembling, languishing voice. 'I'm coming right away.'

The driver scratched the back of his head, then stroked his beard, then took one step forward . . . he stopped and eyed Mr Golyadkin mistrustfully.

'I'm coming right away, my friend . . . you see, my friend . . . I'll only be here a few seconds . . . you see . . . my friend . . .'

'Aren't you going anywhere at all?' the driver finally said, going up to Mr Golyadkin, resolutely and decisively.

'Oh yes, my friend, I'm coming right now. You see, my friend, I'm waiting . . .'

'Yes, sir.'

'I, you see, my friend . . . what village are you from, my dear man?'

'I'm a serf.'

'Do you have a good master?'

'He's all right.'

'Well, my friend, you just wait here, my friend. You see, my friend – have you been long in St Petersburg?'

'Been driving a cab for a year.'

'Are you doing well, my friend?'

'All right.'

'Yes, my friend, yes. Thank Providence, my friend. You, my friend, should try and find a good man. These days a good man is rare, my friend; he'll bathe you, give you food and drink, my dear chap. But sometimes you see that even money doesn't bring happiness – you see a lamentable example of that, my friend. That's how it is, dear chap.' The cab driver suddenly appeared to feel sorry for Mr Golyadkin.

'All right, as you like, I'll wait, sir. Will you be waiting much longer, sir?'

'No, my friend . . . I . . , er . . . well, you know how it is . . . I shan't wait any longer, dear man. What do you think, dear chap? I'm relying on you. I shan't be waiting here any longer . . .'

'So do you want to be going anywhere?'

'No, my friend, no. But I'll show my gratitude, dear man . . . that's it. Well, how much do I owe you, dear chap?'

'What we agreed on, sir – that's what you should give me. I've been waiting a long time, sir. Please don't be hard on me, sir.'

'Well, here you are, my friend, here you are.' Mr Golyadkin paid the cab driver the full six silver roubles and having decided in earnest not to waste any more time – that is, to leave while the going was good, particularly now that the matter had finally been settled and the driver sent away there was no point in waiting any longer – he walked out of the courtyard, out through the gates, turned left and without a backward glance, panting and rejoicing, broke into a run. 'Perhaps it will all be settled for the best,' he thought, 'and this way I've avoided trouble.' In actual fact Mr Golyadkin had suddenly grown unusually light at heart. 'Ah, if only it could be settled for the best,' our hero wondered, but he did not put very much trust in his own words. 'Now I can . . .' he thought. 'No, I'd better try a different approach, but on the other hand ... wouldn't it be better to do ... ?' With these doubts and seeking a key and a solution to all his doubts our hero ran as far as Semyonovsky Bridge and having run as far as Semyonovsky Bridge he prudently and finally decided to turn back. 'That's best,' he thought. 'I'd better take a different approach, I mean, like this. I'll simply be an outside observer and that's the end of the matter. I'll say I'm an observer, someone not involved – that's all, and whatever happens there I'm not to blame. That's it! That's how it will be now!'

Having decided to return our hero did in fact turn back, particularly in view of the fact that, thanks to his happy idea, he had now set himself up as a complete outsider. 'That's best: you're not responsible for anything and you'll just see what comes of it ... that's the way!' Therefore his calculations were absolutely correct and the matter would be closed. Having set his mind at rest he withdrew into the tranquil haven of his comforting and protective woodpile and began to concentrate his attention on the windows. This time he did not have to watch and wait for long. Suddenly there was a strange kind of movement at the windows, all at once, figures were glimpsed, curtains drawn back and Olsufy Ivanovich's windows became crowded with whole groups of people, all of them searching for something in the courtyard. Secure behind his woodpile our hero in turn watched the general commotion with curiosity, stretching his head to right and left, at least as far as the short shadow the woodpile that was concealing him allowed. Suddenly he was struck dumb, shuddered and sat cowering on the spot in horror. He realized – in brief he had guessed correctly – that they were not looking for anyone or anything: they were simply looking for *him*, Mr Golyadkin. Everyone was looking in his direction, everyone was pointing in his direction. To run away was impossible ... they would see him! The dumbstruck Mr Golyadkin huddled as closely as he could to the woodpile and only then did he notice that the treacherous shadow had betrayed him by failing to conceal all of him. With the greatest pleasure our hero would have agreed to creep into a mousehole in the woodpile and sit there quietly – if only that were possible!

But it was absolutely impossible. In his agony he finally began to stare directly and boldly at all the windows at once; that was best ... Suddenly he blushed furiously with shame. He had quite clearly been spotted, everyone had seen him at the same time, everyone was beckoning to him, everyone was nodding, everyone was calling out to him; several windows clicked open, several voices started shouting something to him simultaneously. 'I'm amazed those sluts aren't thrashed when they're still little girls,' he muttered to himself, utterly flustered. Suddenly *he* (we know who) came running down the steps, wearing only his uniform, hatless, breathless, prancing and frisking, perfidiously giving expression to his overwhelming joy at seeing Mr Golyadkin at last.

'Yakov Petrovich!' twittered that man, so notorious for his worthlessness. 'Are you here? You'll catch cold, Yakov Petrovich, it's cold here. Please come in.'

'Yakov Petrovich! No, I'm all right, Yakov Petrovich,' our hero muttered submissively.

'But you can't, you can't, Yakov Petrovich. They're begging you most humbly, they're all waiting. "Do make us happy," they say, "and bring Yakov Petrovich here!" That's what they're saying.'

'No, Yakov Petrovich, I'd better ... you see ... I'd better be going home now,' our hero said, so mortified and horrified that he felt as if he were being roasted over a slow fire and at the same time freezing with shame and horror.

'No-no-no-no!' twittered the loathsome man. 'No-no-no. Not for anything! Let's go!' he said with determination, dragging Mr Golyadkin towards the porch. Mr Golyadkin Senior had no desire whatsoever to go; but since everyone was watching it would have been silly to struggle and dig his heels in. So in went our hero – however, it couldn't be said that he went, because he had positively no idea what was happening to him. But then, at the same time, it was all right!

Before our hero had time to somehow recover and come to his senses he found himself in the reception hall. He was pale, harassed and dishevelled; he glanced at the whole crowd with lacklustre eyes – and, horror!: the reception hall, all the rooms

were filled to overflowing. There were masses of people, a whole
hothouse of ladies; all were milling around Mr Golyadkin, all
were surging towards Mr Golyadkin, and he could see very
well that they were pushing him in a certain direction. 'Surely
not to the doors!' flashed through his mind. Indeed, they were
not pushing him towards the doors, but straight towards Olsufy
Ivanovich's comfortable armchair. On one side of the chair
stood Klara Olsufyevna, pale, languid and melancholy, but
sumptuously attired. Mr Golyadkin was particularly struck by
the little white flowers in her black hair that created such a
wonderful effect. On the other side of the chair, in black tail-
coat and with his new decoration in his buttonhole, stood
Vladimir Semyonovich. Mr Golyadkin, as we have already said,
was taken by the arms and escorted straight towards Olsufy
Ivanovich – on one side by Mr Golyadkin Junior, who had
now assumed an extraordinarily decorous and loyal air, which
gladdened our hero no end, and on the other by Andrey
Filippovich, wearing the most solemn expression. 'What could
it be?' wondered Mr Golyadkin. But when he saw that they
were leading him to Olsufy Ivanovich it all dawned on him in
a flash. The thought of that intercepted letter darted through
his brain. In unbounded agony our hero stood before Olsufy
Ivanovich's chair. 'What shall I do now?' he thought. 'Of course
it should all be on a bold footing, that is, with candour not
lacking in nobility. I'll say this and I'll say that, and so on.' But
what our hero had evidently been fearing did not come to pass.
Olsufy Ivanovich seemed to give Mr Golyadkin a very warm
reception and although he did not offer his hand he at least,
when looking at him, shook his hoary head that inspired great
respect – shook it with a sad yet at the same time well-disposed
air. At least, so it seemed to Mr Golyadkin. He even thought
he could detect glistening tears in Olsufy Ivanovich's lacklustre
eyes. He looked up and it seemed to him that there was also
a tiny tear gleaming on an eyelash of Klara Olsufyevna, who
was standing close by, and that something of the kind was
also visible in Vladimir Semyonovich's eyes; and that, finally,
Andrey Filippovich's calm, imperturbable dignity was no less
appropriate amidst all that general lachrymose sympathy and

that even the young man who had once so strongly resembled
an important counsellor was sobbing bitterly, taking advantage
of the moment. Or perhaps it was all in Mr Golyadkin's imagination, since he himself had burst into tears and was acutely
conscious of his hot tears coursing down his cold cheeks . . . In
a voice filled with sobs, reconciled with mankind and destiny,
at that moment overflowing with affection not only for Olsufy
Ivanovich and all the guests taken together but even for his
pernicious twin who was evidently not in the least pernicious
now and not even Mr Golyadkin's twin but a somehow
extraneous and extremely amiable person in himself, our hero
attempted to address Olsufy Ivanovich with a touching effusion
and soulful outpouring. But in the fullness of all that had been
accumulating within him, he could not express anything at all
but could only point with an eloquent gesture at his heart . . .
At length, Andrey Filippovich, probably wishing to spare the
hoary-headed old man's sensibilities, drew Mr Golyadkin a
little to one side and left him completely to his own devices.
Smiling and muttering to himself, somewhat bewildered, but in
any event almost entirely reconciled with mankind and destiny,
our hero began to make his way somewhere through the solid
crowd of guests. Everyone made way for him, everyone looked
at him with a kind of strange curiosity and a mysterious,
unaccountable sympathy. Our hero passed into the next room
and was accorded the same attention everywhere. He was
vaguely aware of the entire crowd following hard on his heels,
noting his every step, furtively discussing among themselves
something extremely interesting, shaking their heads, talking,
arguing, passing judgement and whispering. Mr Golyadkin
longed to know what they were passing judgement on, arguing
and whispering about. Looking around our hero saw Mr Golyadkin Junior at his side. Feeling the urge to grab his arm and
take him aside, Mr Golyadkin earnestly implored the other
Yakov Petrovich to cooperate with him in all his future under-
takings and not to abandon him at a critical juncture. Mr
Golyadkin Junior nodded gravely and firmly squeezed Mr Golyadkin Senior's hand. Our hero's heart started palpitating
from an excess of emotion. At the same time he felt he was

suffocating, being hemmed in, terribly hemmed in; that all those
eyes fixed on him were somehow oppressing and crushing him.
Mr Golyadkin happened to catch a glimpse of the bewigged
counsellor who was giving him a severe, searching look, quite
unmoved by the general mood of sympathy . . . Our hero almost
decided to go right up to him in order to smile at him and to
have things out with him there and then but for some reason
this came to nought. For a moment Mr Golyadkin almost
completely lost consciousness, lost his memory and all feeling.
When he recovered he noticed that he was rotating in a wide
circle of guests who had gathered around him. Suddenly someone shouted Mr Golyadkin's name from the next room and this
shout was immediately taken up by the entire crowd. Everything
became agitated, noisy, everyone in the rooms rushed to the
doors of the reception hall. Our hero was almost carried aloft
with them; just then the stony-hearted, bewigged counsellor
turned up right beside Mr Golyadkin. Finally he took the latter
by the arm and sat him on a chair next to him, opposite Olsufy
Ivanovich's chair but at a quite considerable distance from
him. Every single person became hushed and quietened down;
everyone observed a solemn silence, everyone kept looking at
Olsufy Ivanovich, evidently expecting something not quite in
the normal run of things. Mr Golyadkin noticed that the other
Mr Golyadkin, together with Andrey Filippovich, had taken
their places next to Olsufy Ivanovich's chair and also exactly
opposite the counsellor. The silence continued; they really were
expecting something. 'Yes, exactly like in a family when someone's going away on a long journey. All we need to do now is
stand up and say a prayer,' reflected our hero. Suddenly there
was a great stir which cut short all Mr Golyadkin's reflections.
That long-expected something had come to pass. 'He's coming,
he's coming!' ran through the crowd. 'Who's coming?' ran
through Mr Golyadkin's head and some strange sensation made
him shudder. 'It's time!' said the counsellor, looking attentively
at Andrey Filippovich, who in turn glanced at Olsufy Ivanovich.
Olsufy Ivanovich nodded solemnly and gravely. 'Let us all be
upstanding' said the counsellor, helping Mr Golyadkin to his
feet. Everyone stood up. Then the counsellor took Mr Goly-

adkin by the arm, while Andrey Filippovich took Mr Golyadkin
Junior's and both solemnly led the two absolutely identical men
through to the middle of the crowd that had gathered around
and whose eyes were straining in expectation. Our hero looked
around in bewilderment, but he was immediately stopped and
his attention directed to Mr Golyadkin Junior, who offered his
hand. 'They want us to make peace,' our hero thought and,
deeply moved, stretched out his hand to Mr Golyadkin Junior;
and then he leant his head towards him. The other Mr Golyadkin followed suit. At this point Mr Golyadkin Senior had the
impression that his treacherous friend was smiling, that he had
given a fleeting, roguish wink at the entire surrounding crowd,
that there was something sinister in the improper Mr Golyadkin
Junior's expression, that he had even grimaced at the moment
of his Judas-kiss ... There were ringing noises in Mr Golyadkin's head, there was darkness before his eyes; it seemed that
a great multitude, a whole file of absolutely identical Golyadkins was noisily forcing open every door in the room. But it
was too late. A resounding kiss of betrayal had rung out and ...

And then something totally unexpected happened. The doors
of the reception hall opened with a crash and on the threshold
appeared a man whose look alone made Mr Golyadkin's blood
run cold. His legs became rooted to the spot. A cry of terror
died away in his tightened chest. However, Mr Golyadkin had
known this all along and had long been expecting something
like it. The stranger solemnly and gravely approached Mr Golyadkin ... Mr Golyadkin knew that figure very well. He had
often seen it, had even seen it that very same day ... The
stranger was a tall, thickset man, wearing a black tail-coat and
with an important-looking decoration in the form of a cross
around his neck and he was endowed with thick, jet-black
side-whiskers; only a cigar was needed to complete the likeness.
But the stranger's stare, as we have said already, made Mr
Golyadkin go cold with horror. With solemn and grave countenance, this terrifying person approached the sorry hero of our
tale ... Our hero stretched out his hand to him; the stranger
took it and hauled him along after him. With a lost, crushed
expression our hero glanced around.

'This is Krestyan Ivanovich Rutenspitz, Doctor of Medicine and Surgery, an old acquaintance of yours, Yakov Petrovich!' someone's loathsome voice twittered right into Mr Golyadkin's ear. He looked around: it was Mr Golyadkin's twin, so repulsive for the vile qualities of his soul. An unseemly, malicious glee shone in his face. He was rubbing his hands in delight, rolling his head in delight, pattering around everyone in delight; he seemed ready to dance for delight right away; finally he leapt forward, grabbed a candle from one of the servants and walked ahead to light the way for Mr Golyadkin and Krestyan Ivanovich. Mr Golyadkin could clearly hear everyone in the hall surge after him, crowding and jostling one another and all of them repeating with one accord: 'It's all right, don't be afraid, Yakov Petrovich, after all it's your old friend and acquaintance Krestyan Ivanovich Rutenspitz.' Finally they came out on to the main, brightly lit staircase; the staircase too was packed with people. The doors on to the porch were flung open with a crash and Mr Golyadkin found himself on the steps together with Krestyan Ivanovich. A carriage harnessed with four impatiently snorting horses was drawn up at the bottom. In three bounds the gloating Mr Golyadkin Junior reached the bottom of the steps and opened the carriage door himself. With an imperious gesture Krestyan Ivanovich invited Mr Golyadkin to take a seat. However, there was no need at all for such a gesture, as there were sufficient people there to help him in. Numb with horror, Mr Golyadkin looked back: the entire brightly lit staircase was swarming with people; inquisitive eyes were looking at him from all sides. On the uppermost landing, in his armchair, presided Olsufy Ivanovich himself, watching attentively and with profound interest all that was taking place below. They were all waiting. A murmur of impatience ran through the crowd when Mr Golyadkin looked back.

'I hope there's nothing here . . . reprehensible . . . nothing that might provoke disciplinary measures and draw everyone's attention to my official relationships,' our hero said in bewilderment. There was a clamour all around; everyone shook their heads negatively. Tears streamed from Mr Golyadkin's eyes.

'In that case I'm ready . . . I fully entrust myself . . . I put my fate in Krestyan Ivanovich's hands . . .' The moment Mr Golyadkin spoke of fully entrusting his fate to Krestyan Ivanovich a terrible, deafening, joyous cry rolled in the most sinister echo among the whole expectant throng. Then Krestyan Ivanovich from one side and Andrey Filippovich from the other took Mr Golyadkin by the arm and began putting him in the carriage. As for his double, he was helping him in from behind in his usual dastardly way. The hapless Mr Golyadkin Senior took a last look at everyone and everything, and shivering like a kitten drenched with cold water – if the comparison may be permitted – climbed into the carriage. Krestyan Ivanovich followed him immediately. The carriage doors slammed; the crack of a whip was heard and the horses jerked the carriage into motion . . . everyone rushed after Mr Golyadkin. The piercing, frenzied cries of all his enemies rolled after him like a valediction. For a while a few figures could still be seen running around the carriage that was bearing Mr Golyadkin away; but gradually they fell further and further back until they were finally completely lost to sight. Mr Golyadkin's unseemly twin kept up longer than all the others. With hands in the trouser pockets of his green uniform he ran along with a contented look, leaping up first on one side on the carriage and then the other; at times he grabbed the window frame and hung from it, poking his head in and blowing farewell kisses at Mr Golyadkin; but even he too began to tire, his appearances grew fewer and fewer until he finally vanished altogether. Mr Golyadkin's heart was filled with a dull ache. The hot blood rushed into his head and throbbed; he was suffocating and wanted to unbutton his coat, to bare his chest and sprinkle it with snow and pour cold water over it. Finally he lapsed into unconciousness . . . When he came to he saw that the horses were bearing him along some unfamiliar road. To right and left loomed dark forests; all around it was bleak and deserted. Suddenly his heart stood still: two fiery eyes were peering at him out of the darkness and those two eyes were burning with malevolent, hellish glee. But it was not Krestyan Ivanovich! Who was it? Or *was* it him? It was! It was Krestyan Ivanovich – not the earlier one but a different, fearful Krestyan Ivanovich!

'Krestyan Ivanovich . . . I . . . I think I'm all right,' our hero tried to begin, timidly and trembling, wishing at least somehow to mollify the fearful Krestyan Ivanovich with his meekness and submission.

'You vil haf kvarters, mit vood, licht und serfants of vich you do not diserf,' Krestyan Ivanovich's reply rang out, stern and dreadful as a judge's sentence.

Our hero shrieked and clutched his head. Alas! He had long been expecting this!

NOTES

1. *Titular Counsellor*: Grade 9 in the fourteen ranks established by Peter the Great in 1722.
2. *Shestilavochnaya Street*: Lit. Street of the Six Shops, now Mayakovsky Street, in Liteynaya district of central St Petersburg.
3. *... bundle of nice green, grey ... banknotes*: The value of banknotes according to colour was: green – 3 roubles; grey – 50 roubles; blue – 5 roubles; red – 10 roubles. The notes were known by these colours in everyday speech.
4. *Nevsky Prospekt*: Famous avenue in St Petersburg, about two and a half miles long, running from the Admiralty to the Aleksandr Nevsky Monastery. The main focus of St Petersburg life.
5. *'It's a Russian proverb'*: The basic meaning is a present, a delicacy. In the metaphorical sense it signifies an unexpected 'treat' – or unpleasantness.
6. *'... promotion to assessor's rank'*: This is collegiate assessor, grade 8 – one grade higher than titular counsellor in the Table of Ranks.
7. *Gostiny Dvor*: Or Trading Rows, the commercial centre of St Petersburg at the beginning of the eighteenth century and still a centre of business activity. The original wooden stalls were destroyed by fire in 1736 and rebuilt (1761–85) by Vallin de la Mothe. About half a mile long, it is bounded on one side by Nevsky Prospekt. With its columned arcades, it was a fashionable promenade in the nineteenth century.
8. *flimsy national newspaper*: Most probably the *Northern Bee*, arch-reactionary journal published 1825–64 by the 'reptile journalists' F. V. Bulgarin and N. I. Grech.
9. *registrar clerks*: Collegiate registrars, the lowest grade (14) in the Table of Ranks.
10. *'Izmaylovsky Bridge'*: Spans the Fontanka River (see also note 20, below).
11. *'... sans façon'*: Simply, without ceremony.
12. *State Counsellor*: Fifth in the Table of Ranks.
13. *Belshazzar's Feast*: After Belshazzar, son of the last Babylonian emperor who saw the 'writing on the wall' at a great feast which foretold his own fate and that of Babylon.
14. *Yeliseyev and Milyutin*: Purveyors of high-quality foods and drinks. Yeliseyev's was founded by Pyotr Yeliseyev, a peasant, in 1813, and is still trading today.

15. *Demosthenic eloquence*: A reference to Demosthenes (384–22 BC), the famous Athenian orator.
16. *collegiate counsellor*: Sixth in the Table of Ranks.
17. *... French minister Villèle*: Jean Baptiste, Joseph, Comte de Villèle (1773–1854), reactionary President of the Council under Louis XVIII. The quoted phrase was Villèle's political slogan.
18. *... Turkish Vizier Martsimiris as well as the beautiful Margravine Louisa ...*: Reference to the highly popular cheap novel by M. Komarov (c. 1730–1812), *The Tale of the Adventures of the English Milord George and the Margravine Fredericka Louisa of Brandenburg, with the Appended History of the Former Turkish Vizier Martsimiris and Queen Terezia of Sardinia* (1782). It went into an eighth edition in 1840.
19. *'... you old Golyadka'*: *golyadka* means 'beggar'.
20. *Fontanka Embankment*: The Fontanka is the widest of St Petersburg's waterways, about four miles long and once the city border.
21. *Anichkov Bridge*: A three-span bridge that carried Nevsky Prospekt across the Fontanka. Built in 1839–41, it is famous for Pyotr Klodt's sculptures of wild horses at each corner.
22. *'Siamese twins ...'*: Conjoined twin brothers Chang and Eng (1811–74) left Siam (Thailand) and earned considerable amounts by giving lectures in Europe and the United States, becoming 'celebrities' of the time. They married two sisters in North Carolina and between them produced twenty-one offspring. All conjoined twins were subsequently called 'Siamese'.
23. *'And the casket opened easily after all'*: Reference to 'The Casket', a fable by I. A. Krylov (1769–1844), in which every possible way of opening the casket is attempted except the obvious.
24. *'the famous Suvorov'*: From *Anecdotes of the Prince of Italy, Count Suvorov-Rymniksky*, published by Ye. Fuchs in St Petersburg, 1827. Count A. V. Suvorov (1730–1800) was one of Russian's greatest military commanders.
25. *about Bryullov's latest painting ...*: Reference to K. P. Bryullov's famous painting, *The Last Days of Pompeii*, finished in Italy and shown in St Petersburg at the Academy of Arts.
26. *... wrought iron railings of the Summer Gardens*: Created in 1771–84, in the reign of Catherine the Great, the fine filigree iron grille, or railings, extend along the Neva Embankment and are the work of Yury Velten and Pyotr Yegorov. The railings referred to in Pushkin's *The Bronze Horseman* (1833).
27. *Northern Bee*: See note 8, above.

28. *Baron Brambeus*: *Nom de plume* of Osip Senkovsky (1800–1858), editor of *Library for Reading*, Russia's most widely read journal, catering for provincials, low-grade civil servants and those with a taste for cheap sensationalism.

29. *'If e'er you should me forget . . .'*: Album verses very popular among girls at boarding-school, etc.

30. *'. . . Yasha'*: Affectionate diminutive of Yakov.

31. *'Report to His Excellency's . . .'*: These lines are strongly reminiscent of those spoken by the Very Important Person to Akaky Akakicvich in Gogol's 'The Overcoat': 'It's high time you knew that first of all your application must be handed in at the main office, then taken to the chief clerk, then to the departmental directory, then to my secretary, who *then* submits it to me for consideration . . .'

32. *'. . . Grishka Otrepyev'*: Or False Dmitry. Also known as 'First Pretender'. He opposed the rule of Boris Godunov, claiming to be Dmitry, a son of Ivan the Terrible. He was recognized as Tsar after Godunov's death in 1605, but was deposed and put to death in 1606.

33. *'. . . Provincial Secretary'*: Grade 13 in the Table of Ranks.

34. *Tambov*: Large town about 300 miles south of Moscow.

35. *'. . . our Russian Faublas'*: Faublas, cunning deceiver and hero of the French libertine novel *Amorous Adventures of Ch. de Faublas*, 1787–90, by J. B. Louvet de Couvry (1760–97). (French title *Les Amours du Chevalier de Faublas par Louvet de Couvry*.) The novel appeared in Russian translation, 1792–96; 1805.

36. *Police Gazette*: Full title *St Petersburg City Police Gazette*, published 1839–1917. It gave details of daily events in the capital.

37. *Saratov*: A city on the Volga, once capital of the Lower Volga region.

38. *Madame Falbala*: Derives from the French for a frill or flounce. In Pushkin's poem *Count Nulin* (1825), a Madame Falbala is the owner of a pension for young ladies:

> . . . she was not educated
> According to her father's rule,
> But in a noble boarding-school,
> At émigrée Madame Falbala's.

39. *'Allow me to ask you . . .'*: These lines recall those spoken by the Very Important Person in Gogol's 'The Overcoat': 'Do you realize

who you're talking to? Do you know who is standing before you?' etc. (See also note 31, above)

40. '... *a hut by the sea*...': This theme appears in Friedrich Schiller's poem, *The Youth by the Stream* (1803; Russian translation 1838). Dostoyevsky was passionately fond of the German poet, particularly in his younger days.

41. '... *after the fashion of certain novels*...': Reference to similar situations in Schiller's ballad 'The Knight Toggenburg' (1797), which appeared in a Russian translation by the poet Zhukovsky in 1818; also to the sentimental, highly popular novel *Siegwart* (1776) by I.-M. Miller (1750–1814).

THE STORY OF PENGUIN CLASSICS

Before 1946 ... 'Classics' are mainly the domain of academics and students; readable editions for everyone else are almost unheard of. This all changes when a little-known classicist, E. V. Rieu, presents Penguin founder Allen Lane with the translation of Homer's *Odyssey* that he has been working on in his spare time.

1946 Penguin Classics debuts with *The Odyssey*, which promptly sells three million copies. Suddenly, classics are no longer for the privileged few.

1950s Rieu, now series editor, turns to professional writers for the best modern, readable translations, including Dorothy L. Sayers's *Inferno* and Robert Graves's unexpurgated *Twelve Caesars*.

1960s The Classics are given the distinctive black covers that have remained a constant throughout the life of the series. Rieu retires in 1964, hailing the Penguin Classics list as 'the greatest educative force of the twentieth century.'

1970s A new generation of translators swells the Penguin Classics ranks, introducing readers of English to classics of world literature from more than twenty languages. The list grows to encompass more history, philosophy, science, religion and politics.

1980s The Penguin American Library launches with titles such as *Uncle Tom's Cabin*, and joins forces with Penguin Classics to provide the most comprehensive library of world literature available from any paperback publisher.

1990s The launch of Penguin Audiobooks brings the classics to a listening audience for the first time, and in 1999 the worldwide launch of the Penguin Classics website extends their reach to the global online community.

The 21st Century Penguin Classics are completely redesigned for the first time in nearly twenty years. This world-famous series now consists of more than 1300 titles, making the widest range of the best books ever written available to millions – and constantly redefining what makes a 'classic'.

The Odyssey continues ...

The best books ever written

PENGUIN (🐧) CLASSICS

SINCE 1946

Find out more at www.penguinclassics.com